WHEN THE MOON OVER KUALINA MOUNTAIN COMES

LEAH R. CUTTER

KNOTTED ROAD PRESS

When the Moon Over Kuala Mountain Comes
Copyright © 2015 Leah Cutter
All rights reserved
Published by Knotted Road Press
www.KnottedRoadPress.com

Cover Art:
© Fil101 | Dreamstime.com - Reflected Moon

Cover and interior design copyright © 2015 Knotted Road Press
http://www.KnottedRoadPress.com

Come someplace new…
Are you a traveler? Do you enjoy exploring strange new worlds, new cultures, new people?

Journey into the various lands envisioned by Leah Cutter.

Sign up for my newsletter and I'll start you on your travels with a free copy of my book, *The Island Sampler.*

I will never spam you or use your email for nefarious purposes. You can also unsubscribe at any time.

http://www.LeahCutter.com/newsletter/

 Created with Vellum

The Chronicles of Franklin

The Popcorn Thief

The Soul Thief

The Child Thief

Contemporary Fantasy

Siren's Call

The Immortals' War

PROLOGUE

THE DOOM OF ALOKAI TEMPLE

Storm stirred the sand with her driftwood cane, smearing the runes and sigils. She didn't deny the future they foretold—she couldn't—but she didn't have the strength to face it just then.

Instead, she picked up the long trails of seaweed and flung them into the encroaching waves. The water would purify them, scour them with sand and salt before casting them back onto the land to proclaim another future for those who dared read it.

Painfully, Storm hitched up her skirt to more easily bend down and collect the handful of bright *serat* shells, purple and luminescent in the fading light, still warm against her palm. The *serat* lived for centuries. To kill them when they were so young was cruel. However, the goddess Brikal had demanded an extravagant sacrifice that night.

Storm now knew why.

Finally satisfied that she'd covered her tracks and that no one could divine her work or easily spot the trails of blood, Storm allowed herself a few moments to stare across the water. The two moons had yet to rise and clouds blocked the rivers of stars, ominously hiding the sea—if Storm believed in omens, which she did not. Fortunes drawn out of the deaths of small beings, bespelled chalk lines, and weeds coaxed from the depths? Yes. Mere physical phenomenon, without the *geas* of augury? No.

Still, Storm pulled her shawl closer and tighter over her rough blouse as the night blanked out the ocean, until all she knew of it was the soft splashing of the waves. Even when Ty—the smaller moon—rose, its red light barely reflected off the water.

However, Storm didn't have all night to wait for the second moon, Gulik, to rise as well. Instead, she turned and slowly made her way up the sand, past the logs and ocean debris scattered, to the small path between the scraggly thorns that encrusted the dunes. She'd walked the path so often over the decades that she could do it blindfolded, counting her footsteps as she padded softly to the end of the sand, then beyond the rough rocks and into the next open bay protected by coral shoals so the waves merely lapped at the sands.

Only a short distance along the circle of the cove sat Storm's house, its logs encrusted with salt and sand. Inside, the fire was banked, warm red coals that just needed a sprinkling of firedust to spring back to life.

Storm stored her supplies in the nets above her head, hiding the jars of colored chalk beside the long buoy-like gourds and stringy lures. She ignored the way her back ached from stooping too long, forcing her fingers to move nimbly as if they hadn't been working in wet sand and cold all afternoon. Only with the fire blazing, sea- and dew-misted clothing changed for a clean skirt and blouse, and a pot of fish and other bounty reheating over the flames, did Storm allow herself to ponder the fortune laid out that night.

She hadn't had a choice about doing the divination, and had resisted the goddess' call as long as she could.

The price of this reading had shocked her—so many lives.

Closing her eyes, Storm could still see the quicksilver light that had sprung up after the last rune had been drawn, as she'd closed the circle with the living vines from the sea. The pictures exploded in her mind as they had across the bloodstained sand.

Alokai Temple, drowned.

The temple sat well inland. No river ran nearby. However, Storm couldn't deny the towering wave of water that crashed over the grounds. She couldn't tell the direction it came from, if the day had been sunny or storm-filled. All she knew was that the day was coming soon.

Storm had to warn the priestesses at the temple without revealing her own foresight or showing herself to be a witch.

The temple burned witches.

Pillars of their remains stretched behind the main grounds, stark black smudges beside the pure white stone walkways. Storm shivered. The taint of burned flesh never left the compound, no matter how the winter winds blew.

The cost of disrespecting the goddess Brikal by not spreading her word was as just as high. Storm would never be able to cast another fortune. What little luck she had would vanish. Brikal did not like to be ignored.

Could Storm claim she'd had a dream when she told the temple priestesses? Maybe she could declare it as some sort of omen.

Possibly that would work, but then her warnings would be ignored, and she herself would be put under more scrutiny than she already was. The townspeople didn't trust her, living alone and so close to the sea. They were suspicious of her goods, though she had pure salt to trade, as well as fish, well-seasoned and smoked. But few enough bought her wares.

More scrutiny could bring the temple guards. It had happened before. She'd seen the guards form a line in front of poor Willow's table so none could get through to her.

A loud knock startled Storm out of her thoughts.

No one came to her hut.

Anyone who came so late probably meant no good.

With a sigh, she swung the pot out of the flames—it might be a while before she got to it, and no sense in wasting good food. She picked up her driftwood cane (though it was more for show) and made her slow way across the room.

"Who is it?" she called out as she neared the door.

A fervent pounding came in response.

Storm threw open the door before it had slacked off.

A soldier stood just outside, tall and proud, one of the king's men. He peered at her with dark eyes, his face partially covered by his plumed helmet. His bare arms bulged with muscles, his chest made broader by the heavy rings sewn to his leather shirt. A sword, a cudgel, and a knife all protruded from his wide leather belt. Though the night was cool, his legs were bare, and his boots only came up midcalf.

"What do you want?" Storm asked crossly. If he'd come to rob her, well, she wasn't as helpless as she appeared.

The soldier looked her up and down, glanced over her shoulder into her room, then over his own shoulder briefly, as if determining that they were alone.

"I know what you did," he announced with the finality of a body falling from a cliff. "And I know the prophesy you saw."

CRAEG, THE KING'S GUARD, REFUSED TO SAY ANYTHING UNTIL after they were settled next to the fire. When he cast a longing look at the stew bubbling there, Storm offered him a bowl. Though the goddess Brikal was strict regarding fortunes, the god Kireg was even more of a stickler regarding the customs of hospitality.

As Craeg sat down on Storm's footstool, stiffer than dried leather, he drawled, "Now, if anyone comes, this can be seen as a social visit."

Storm couldn't contain her snort. No matter how friendly the pair of them seemed, no one would believe such a fiction, not if they knew her past troubles with the guards.

Craeg just drew himself up tighter, though he gratefully took a sip of the stew.

The quiet of the night stretched between them. Without his plumed helmet, Craeg stood not much taller than Storm, though her bulk was made up of layers of cloth, whereas his was all muscles. The sword and cudgel lay beside him on the floor within easy reach, while his knife stayed in his belt.

Finally Craeg put the empty bowl of soup to the side.

Storm followed suit. Though she'd been starving earlier, she'd managed only a few bites.

"I know what you did," he repeated, softer this time, more like sharing a secret. "And I know what you saw." He paused, then added, "I've seen it, too."

Startled, Storm grew very still. Why would Craeg admit to the gift of foresight? The priestesses would draw and quarter him if they found out. Or was it a trick, designed to get her to admit her own prescience?

"I don't know what you're talking about," Storm finally said.

"Anyone who has even an inkling of the gift has foreseen the fate of Alokai Temple," Craeg said dismissively. He took a deep breath and stared hard at Storm. "But only a few have dreamed of the one who might stop it."

Storm had been careful not to confess to her ability to divine the future, but she had to say something now.

"Go on," she said, nodding yes, finally, *yes*, telling the truth of her talent.

"You can't do it," Craeg said. "You can't stop it. The temple has to go, be washed from the face of this world."

"How could I stop it?" Storm asked, incredulous. "No one has the power to stop such a force."

"You do," Craeg insisted. "I've seen it."

Storm shook her head, denying the stirring she felt in her soul, the rising in her gut, as if the goddess Brikal demanded yet another sacrifice and prophesy.

"You can," Craeg said again, softer now. "Shoal, the high priestess, will beg for your help. You won't be able to refuse. But you must. You must not stop the cleansing."

"Why do you bargain with me? Why not just kill me if I'm the only one with the power?" Storm asked, not caring about the death she was courting.

It was Craeg's turn to snort. "Fate cannot be denied that way, as you well know. All but the priestesses of Alokai Temple know that. If you were unavailable, another would take your place, maybe one not so amenable to persuasion."

"So, what exactly are you trying to persuade me to do?" Storm asked, raising one eyebrow. "To stand aside as thousands are killed?"

"In the hope of saving ten thousand more souls? Yes."

"It's never that easy," Storm said. "Without the temple, the people will be lost. The kingdom will be ripe for attack."

Everyone knew the western king envied their lands, and would maybe even offer help after such a disaster, sending soldiers with healers, if only to get a foothold here.

"Yes," Craeg said. "The king may get washed away as well."

Ripples of possibilities echoed around Storm. Was Craeg already working for the western king? Was the army planning a coup?

"What would you have me do? I can't deny this foretelling, any more than you could deny coming to see me," Storm asked, too buffeted by waves to see clearly.

"Go to the temple. Tell them what you've seen," Craeg urged.

"What?" Storm had been so cautious all her life. For someone to ask her to be bold, to proudly proclaim her heritage—she'd never expected that.

"You must go. We both know why," Craeg said dryly.

"I know that," Storm hissed. The price of hiding such a prophesy was too high.

"Then, when the high priestess asks for your help, refuse."

Storm shook her head. "The temple can also be very persuasive," she pointed out. Though their persuasion was more likely to involve broken bones and the threat of burning.

"So let yourself be persuaded. Pretend to cooperate. But you must break at the last minute and let the wave fall."

"It will drown me as well." Storm swallowed around the sudden dryness of her throat. She pulled her shawl closer over her shoulders, the realization making her cold.

"You were dead the moment you walked out to the beach and called the seaweed from the waves." Craeg gave a laugh, brittle and harsh. "It's your time to go, grandmother."

Storm looked at Craeg sharply. She'd whelped a son many eons ago, left him behind as her visions had dictated. She didn't feel any kinship to this man, and *grandmother* was a common enough term. She still had to ask. "Are you?"

Craeg shrugged. "Orphaned from birth, raised by the army and the king. I am no one and everyone's grandson. And I'm begging you, for the sake of my own unborn son, let this cup pass you by."

Storm shivered. "I'll try," she promised.

It was the best she'd ever be able to do, the most honest she could be. Death was a powerful motivator, and it appeared that no matter what path she chose, it was bound to encase her soon.

~

Storm stretched her leg out against the packed dirt floor of her cell, seeing if she could straighten it. The temple guards hadn't been kind after her declaration and they'd given her a beating fit for a younger person.

Still, she thought only her ribs were broken. She took another cautious breath, the pain sharp at her side. When they'd thrown her into the cell they'd done her a favor, shoving her left arm back into its socket with the force of her fall. All her fingers worked, as well as her toes.

It was just her knee that worried her. It had swelled to the size of a baby's head. Her cane would never again just be for show.

What had she been thinking, announcing the doom of the temple that way, at the high priestess' morning court? Craeg's words had made her stupidly brave, thinking the priestesses would recognize the savior of the temple in her unveiling. She should have found another way to deal with the *geas* of augury—a way without sacrificing so much of her own flesh.

Storm had also believed Craeg—too much, perhaps—that she now faced her own doom. The puzzles the gods had laid before her were too complex, the games they played far beyond her ken. Maybe she should have accepted their wrath instead and just gone to the southern islands. It was a one-way trip. She'd never make it back to the mainland. But it was rumored that the southerners welcomed any and all people who washed up on their shores.

However, Storm had never merely accepted anything, let alone never being able to walk again.

She pushed at her leg, trying to shift her knee around. The sliding disc of the kneecap wouldn't set right. She pushed again. The pain made her whimper and her vision darkened. It wouldn't budge.

Storm took a deep breath, then two more, before she begged any gods who were listening to help and *slammed* her palm against the side of her knee. She screamed as the agony washed through her.

When she woke from passing out, the throbbing ache made her want to vomit, but she could finally straighten her leg.

"I could help with that," came a slithering whisper. "Help ease your pain."

Storm squinted and peered into the dark corners of her cell. She didn't see anyone or anything, just straw and the latrine ditch that flowed into open sewers below. There was no cot of course, but someone had thrown a moldy, lice-infested blanket into the other corner. Storm had already vowed not to go near it.

"Who are you?" Storm whispered after the voice had grown still. "Where are you?"

"By the door," the voice promised.

Storm didn't hold back her groan. Walking that far was out of the question, though it was only a few feet away. "Why would you help me?"

"You're the temple's only hope." The voice changed timbre now, losing its smoky edge and becoming more human. "And the temple is the last hope for the kingdom."

"From the western kingdom?" Storm asked.

"Yes. They've already bought the guard."

Storm couldn't help the full-body shiver. So Craeg might have been corrupted.

"And the western kingdom treats its witches much worse," the voice assured her.

"Worse than burning them at the stake?" Storm asked, incredulous.

"We only burn a few," the voice said dismissively. "We let all who would leave go south, to the islands."

"How noble of you, high priestess Shoal," Storm said, finally identifying the speaker.

The priestess continued, as if she hadn't heard Storm. "The greatest witches, of course, hide in plain view—priestesses, all of them. They carry the word of god to the people, that they receive through wholesome prayer, not archaic blood rites."

Storm sat shocked into stillness. She'd never heard of such a thing, not even a hint. The priestesses stood above all but the king—some might even say the high priestess stood level with the king.

And they were witches?

Witches were despised more than undertakers, more feared than the guard. "How can you do this to your own kind?" Storm hissed.

"Our ancestors made this choice, long ago, based on augury that would turn your stomach," Shoal said through gritted teeth. "An entire army of soldiers, tricked, trapped, and slaughtered for their entrails. It was the only way we could save ourselves."

"So all witches could disappear into the temples without being persecuted," Storm said, still reeling.

"It's the will of the people," Shoal recited, as if by rote. "The strongest of us are given the chance to recant publicly, coming into the temple."

Storm had seen that—at least two women she'd known had recanted, shaved their heads, and become nuns in the temple, their eyes always lowered, never accepted by anyone after that.

"So that's what you offer me? A barely tolerated place beside you?"

The temple might take care of Storm, but no one would smile at her ever again. Not that many did now, but at least a few of the merchants didn't give her a cold shoulder.

"No, not merely that. Stand by us as we defy the wave with the will of god. You will be celebrated to the end of your days and beyond."

A cool breeze fluttered through the cell. This time, Storm didn't shudder, but stretched as her muscles suddenly relaxed. She saw nothing. However, cool tendrils massaged her knee, chasing away the pain. A second breeze licked her side, soothing her ribs. Her bruised eyes and split cheek stopped aching, and the swelling across her lips receded.

Storm had never known such a powerful healing. No witch she knew could have done this work without sight or touch.

"A small token of how you will be repaid," promised Shoal. A will-o'-the-wisp light appeared in the corner, brightening Storm's heart. A soft blanket, warm and clean, lay beside it.

"I will think on what you've said," Storm promised.

If she saved the temple, could she also save herself?

WHEN STORM AWOKE, ALL HER ACHES HAD PASSED, SLIDING AWAY with her dreams. If it hadn't been for the stark cell, the dark stains she knew were blood, and the vile odor of the trench, she might have thought everything that had happened the day before just a dream as well.

The crusts of bread thrown into her cell by the jailor were augmented by a jug of clean water that magically appeared in the corner. Storm used it sparingly, drinking a few teeth-chilling mouthfuls, then wetting the corner of her blanket to scrub the dried blood off her itching skin. She almost felt refreshed by the time she'd finished.

As Storm settled into the boredom of her empty cell, the sibilant voice came again.

"Put it on," it whispered.

Storm glanced at the door, then back around her cell.

There, in the corner, now lay a bundle of clothes. It contained n priestess' habit, bright blue and gold, with its high wimple that covered her hair and a half-veil that revealed only her eyes.

"Put it on," the voice repeated. "Then come see."

A loud *click* echoed through the still morning. The lock of her cell unlatching.

An unknown nun stood in the dim corridor, dressed in similar robes, though hers were the gray of a teacher, leaving her face uncovered. "You can call me Janus," she said with a sly grin.

"Janus—the two-faced?" Storm asked, falling into place beside her, walking more strongly than she had in ages.

"I know you have questions about our program, about divided

loyalties. Today is a day of truths, so why not give you a name more true than my given one?"

Janus' honesty startled Storm, but she kept walking. The air was getting more clear, the stench of the jail falling away.

"And I will call you Hope," Janus continued. "Because there should be more truth in your name as well."

Storm shook her head. She wasn't convinced the new name was right, though it pleased her that this youngster thought so. Storm hadn't had hope in many decades.

The pair of them stayed inside the temple complex, never reaching the common parts of the town. Storm both regretted and was grateful for their path. If she'd found the opportunity to slip away, she might not have been able to stop herself.

The first place Janus took Storm was to an outdoor classroom. The priestess sat on a carved stone bench while the children sprawled gracelessly before her, absorbing every word of the half-lies she told them.

Storm had always sacrificed to Brikal for foretelling, prayed to Kireg for hospitality and everything regarding her home, given blessings to Zeka for the storms and the sea, and even whispered to Hyn for good fortune, sometimes.

Yet, here was this priestess, proclaiming that the god of the Alokai Temple, Myat, was superior to all.

Storm didn't even know how to counter such a lie. It was laughable.

However, the children didn't know any better.

Then Janus and Storm stepped into a darkened cubby, far from the sun. A little girl lay on a bench, shivering yet sweating at the same time. A healer in bright red passed her hands over her while prayers were muttered, useless words masking powerful deeds.

They stopped a third time where the children were being asked to pray for miracles, not knowing they were being tested for power, the priestess looking for any glimmer to nurture. The priestess wasn't seeking a witch, no, she sought the *holy*.

By the time Storm stripped off the habit she felt as though her world and everything she'd known had been turned upside down.

Witches had been persecuted for generations. It was all Storm had ever known.

Yet, here was a community where witches worked together to raise water in a well, held hands and directed their power, and were sought after for their help and advice.

If Storm saved the temple, she could join them. She would just have to rename herself. Instead of *witch*, she would go by *priestess* instead.

Storm awoke with a start, the darkness of her sleep carried into her waking. No lights shone in her cell. The stench of the open latrine told her where she was.

A woman moaned in the night. She was nearby, and in pain. "No, no, not me, no."

"What happened?" Storm called out. She knew better than to ask what was wrong. Though Shoal had healed most of Storm's wounds, the memory of her beating still ached.

"I don't want to die," the woman whimpered.

"What was your crime?" Storm asked, though she thought she already knew. Little other than witchcraft put a woman in a place like this.

"Being too good at healing," the woman declared. "I don't know why they wouldn't cherish me. I wouldn't hurt a person, I couldn't."

"What about becoming a priestess?" Storm asked.

"Never," the woman declared.

"They're witches, too," Storm told her.

The woman's laughter was dryer than a winter wind. "They'd never ask me to join," she declared. "I'm nobody, with no connections. Plus I'm only a little good at healing, not like *them*."

Storm had no words to comfort her. With the noon bells came the sweet scent of roasted flesh.

When Janus came later that afternoon, Storm confronted her. "Is it true? Do you only save the stronger witches? Those with both power and connections?"

"That's true everywhere," Janus said quietly. "The strong survive."

"We're burning our own people!"

"But *we* will survive." Janus gave Storm her sly grin. "If you help us—join with us and stand with us—maybe you can save more of the weaker ones yourself."

Though Storm had never been nurturing, she did take comfort in that.

~

EVEN FROM THE GLOOM OF HER CELL, STORM COULD TELL THE day dawned brightly. She'd hoped for yet more days of reprieve from her terrible decision, but a thrumming in the floor under her hands told her it was time.

Janus threw her cell door open, blasting it off its hinges.

Storm scrambled after her. She knew she couldn't run far enough now to escape the fate of the temple, so instead she followed Janus.

Storm heard the roaring of the wave before she saw it, the mad howling of a timeless beast, no relation to the gently lapping waves at her cove. Storm's knee ached as she ran. Despite Shoal's efforts, it hadn't quite healed.

Finally, they came around a corner and halted.

A long line of priestesses, all holding hands, stood in front of Alokai Temple. All the different colors of their habits would have made the gathering seem festive if their faces hadn't been grim.

Janus dragged Storm to the center, where the witches made room.

Storm clasped hands with a humming novice on one side, her clear blue eyes shining with faith, and with the cynical Janus on the other side, scared but determined to make a stand.

The power of these women coursed through Storm, binding her talent up with theirs. As sisters, they stood ready to defeat the coming maelstrom, humming and surging with incredible energy. Storm tasted the current in her mouth, dark and coppery, her very bones creaking with power. She felt more alive than ever before.

However, Storm also no longer felt single, solitary, and complete. She was part of something, and she wasn't sure she could be alone again. And she didn't know if she liked that. Witches had always worked alone in her experience.

Storm wrenched open her eyes, away from the seductive net of power, and looked outward. She wanted to see the enemy they faced, as well as collect her singular thoughts.

What Storm saw were the people. No matter the explanation the priestesses had given their current ritual, the people knew.

It wasn't their god, but their magic the priestesses called on.

The man before Storm sneered even as he prayed to Myat for survival. The mother to the side hid her children's eyes from the sin the priestesses committed.

Even as the people of the city begged for enough power for them to be saved, they'd been taught for too long to shun that very power.

The scattered bodies in front of Storm formed long lines, shifting one into the other. She recognized the *geas* of augury. The strings of people were like the ropes of seaweed, living bands of divination. It didn't take Storm but a moment to read their future and the future of all the witches.

Even if the temple survived the storm, the priestesses were doomed. The people would never forgive them for their deception. The decimation of the witches would be systematic and complete, worse than what the western kingdom could do.

Storm turned her sight back inward. Shoal, Craeg, and the others had been wrong. Storm wasn't necessary to defeat the wave. She was quite certain of this given the power that flowed through her.

However, Storm was the only one capable of destroying them.

With a strength Storm didn't know she possessed, she wielded the black knife of foresight, demanding all the lives surrounding her as sacrifice for her foretelling, cutting through the lines of power generated by the witches, breaking their shield apart as the water crashed down.

Seaweed caught Storm's legs, or maybe it was her sisters turned against her as she had them, holding her under the water.

Storm didn't care, despite how her body struggled to breathe.

She'd saved them. All of them. All of the future generations of witches.

Storm's prophecy would come true. She'd made a horrible sacrifice of the entire city to ensure the survival of the witches.

Many witches—like Storm, herself—had been in hiding, denying the blood of their birthright.

Now, the survivors of the temple would drive the witches out. They'd all go to the southern islands where they'd start anew, in a territory they could defend against the western kingdom, a home they could call their own.

There would be more dooms for the witches to face, Storm was certain, more sacrifices to make.

She wished her future sisters well as she let go, letting her soul float away on the sea.

CHAPTER 1

Ephanie blows the petals down
   And marks the end of spring
   —*Northern children's song, teaching the names of the winds*

EPHANIE SCOWLED AT THE TINY *MAMAPO'O* PLANT IN ITS WOVEN cup. She squirmed on the hard bench in front of the work table, sweating in her apprentice robe. The bright blue material showed every wet patch—under her arms, across her shoulders, in the middle of her back—even though it was sleeveless and cut short, above her knees.

At least Ephanie was alone in the workroom, no one telling her to stop looking so angry. All the other apprentice growers had left for the heat of the afternoon, either sleeping in hammocks or swimming in the nearby lagoon.

Today, the *mamapo'o* plant wasn't much bigger than Ephanie's small palm. It would grow into a large bush in a few summers' time, with broad flat leaves the color of deep ocean water and bright red berries that fed songbirds all year round.

If Ephanie could make her magic work, she could grow the plant to full size in just a few days' time, just like all the other growers. Even the newest student among the growers—who was only eight and a whole year younger than Ephanie—could coax an easy plant like the *mamapo'o* to bloom. It just wasn't fair.

However, nothing Ephanie tried worked. She stroked the smooth brown stem, tracing a path around the leaves, encouraging the stem to go *up*, but it still didn't spring up. She tugged (*gently, gently*) on the each of the eleven leaves, but they didn't suddenly follow her fingers, lengthen, and grow. She prayed to Caduk, the traditional goddess of all the growers, using both formal prayers as well as sometimes begging for her help.

When Mama and the other teachers couldn't hear, Ephanie even tried praying to Kalluka, Ailani Island's goddess of the jungle.

But the *mamapo'o* plant stubbornly stayed the exact size it had always been, taking its own time to reach full height.

"Growers always take time to grow into their powers," Mama said frequently when Ephanie walked out of the workroom disappointed and upset.

Ephanie had only asked once, "But Mama, what if I'm not a grower?"

Maybe Ephanie didn't have any powers. If that was so, she'd have to change into the purple robes of a powerless girl. Maybe she wasn't a grower, a healer, or even a witch who received prophesies. Fortunetellers usually had their first vision by the time they were four, and Ephanie was well past that age. Healing powers generally came when a girl was six, but Ephanie couldn't understand how to close a cut at all, while growing powers came at eight. Now, at nine, Ephanie couldn't get any plants to grow.

Mama had turned her clear gray eyes on Ephanie and drawn herself up so she towered above her daughter. "You will not say such a thing. You are a witch of the north. Though some of the other witches, after two centuries living here on the southern islands, don't breed true, *I* have. Your power *will* come. Or else."

Ephanie hadn't dared asked what *or else* meant, but she suspected it wasn't good. She might get sent away to the head temple on the main island, like Nyandar had when she turned eleven and still hadn't found her powers.

Nyandar had never been allowed to come back home.

Or maybe Ephanie would be forced to live in the jungle all by herself, like Bircha the healer, who in the stories didn't find her powers until she was old and gray, and then been challenged by a river demon.

So Ephanie sat, hours after all the others had left, begging and pleading with the little plant, sometimes even cursing it, trying to make it grow.

It never did.

THE FIRST VISION POUNCED ON EPHANIE ONE YEAR LATER, WHEN she was ten. It came at night with heart-pounding surety, its need overwhelming her. She stumbled off her straw-stuffed mattress laying on the floor, the room dark and swaying like a boat staked to the shore when the waves came in.

Ephanie couldn't think, couldn't call out—could barely breathe.

All she craved was the life of something, *anything*, to satisfy the vision clawing to come out.

But what? The sheets at Ephanie's feet were long dead, though they'd once had been living plants. Pounded dirt made up the floor and wouldn't grow a thing, no matter how hard she'd tried. The thick woven rush mats that covered the dirt were also dead.

Ephanie felt her head turn. There. To the left.

A long, low table stood under the window, covered with Ephanie's plants. The ones she was supposed to grow. The ones that had defied her. Those green things she'd never been able to shape to her will.

Ephanie gasped. She wasn't a grower! Mama had been wrong. That wasn't Ephanie's power. She was a fortuneteller instead—a teller of prophesies that always came true. Why had her powers come so late?

It didn't matter.

What mattered was that Ephanie finally knew what she was, what she was supposed to do. She had found her destiny. She would have important visions. She just knew it.

For now, though, Ephanie had to feed this first vision. Gleefully, she marched over and yanked out the first seedling—another stupid *mamapo'o* plant.

With suddenly clever fingers, Ephanie twisted the stem and tore off the leaves. She threw the bare stem to the ground and stomped on it, pounding the stick into the dirt, squishing out what little life remained. Then, she tore the leaves into small pieces and left the pile on the table.

Teeth bared in joy, Ephanie attacked the next plant. And the next. *Jaikulai. Poihu.* Even the fragile ivy from the mainland, sickly in heat of the southern islands.

When the pile of leaf bits had grown to the size of a small melon, Ephanie stopped. She whined low in her throat, the sound loud in the quiet, moonlit room. She wanted to destroy all the plants, but this was enough. More would be too much, unnecessary. The goddess didn't need them.

Slowly, Ephanie gathered the leaf bits in both of her hands, then turned back toward the room. A prayer that she'd learned when she'd been younger sprang unbidden to her lips.

> *O goddess Brikalla*
> *I delicate these lives to thee.*
> *Let my telling be true.*
> *Let my sight be clear.*
> *Let my victim accept her fate easily.*
> *So shall it be.*

Ephanie cast the leaf bits into the air. A sudden wind flew from her hands as well, carrying the small pieces out across the room, causing them to fall into a specific pattern on the floor.

The leaves created easy, rolling lines that obviously made up waves. Another line, curved like half a melon rind, sat on top of them—a small boat.

Though the leaves showed just a straight stick resting in the boat, Ephanie knew who it was. She could see his face in her mind, brown and warm, particularly compared with her mother's pale white skin.

Nawai, her mother's lover, was coming home. He'd be arriving in the morning. He had left more than two weeks ago, going to the closest island to the east of Ailani Island to gather more of the beautiful white feathers of the *imuaki* bird, that he used making his cloaks.

Ephanie collapsed onto the floor. Exhaustion slammed into her, as if she'd been hoeing in the garden all day, working in the hot sun.

However, Ephanie couldn't rest. First one arm rose, then another, as if she were a puppet on stings. Slowly, Ephanie dragged herself to her feet.

She had to tell the owner of the fortune their fate. But who? Nawai knew he was coming. The fortune insisted that she tell Mama, though. Because Mama would care.

Ephanie lurched from her room, staggering the three steps to her mother's room.

Standing in the doorway, using a booming voice that didn't sound like her own, Ephanie announced, "Nawai is arriving in the morning."

Now, Ephanie could collapse. The strings holding her up snapped and she sank down where she was, the soft night taking her into dreamless sleep.

THE NEXT MORNING, THOUGH STILL TIRED, EPHANIE PROUDLY marched into the fortuneteller's classroom. It was so different than the grower's workroom. Instead of wooden shelves overflowing with plants and growing things, the room felt empty, with bare woven walls, a single wooden table, and four plain reed chairs. No windows opened up to the jungle on one side, or the temple courtyard on the other, making the room feel stuffy. A small altar dedicated to Brikalla sat in the far corner, with a bowl holding a large, purple sea-fig flower in the very center of it.

The two other students—Zakiel and Reyeni—already sat at the work table, studiously mixing purple, red, and yellow powders in small bowls, then adding them to the traditional fortuneteller chalk bags.

Ephanie knew the chalk would be worked with a spell after it was mixed. When an augury came, a witch could use the special chalk to draw out the vision. Ephanie had never seen the chalk made, though, and so went to look. A grower didn't use chalk—she may carve lines to channel power into the dirt, or away from greedy plants, but that wasn't the same.

Reyeni hunched over the table, blocking Ephanie's view.

Ephanie gave a huffed sigh.

Stupid Reyeni. She always thought she knew better than everyone at the temple, though she was only fifteen.

Zakiel wasn't much better. She was the same age as Reyeni, and the pair of them always were together. Aside from their matching black robes, though, they looked nothing alike. Reyeni had pure white skin —whiter than Ephanie's, which had a touch of brown in it—with a long nose topped by small gray eyes and rounded out with a small pink mouth. While Zakiel wasn't as brown as the southern island natives, she was darker than most of the witches. Her eyes were brown too, though with specks of green in them. Rumor was that Zakiel was a strong witch—stronger than even Seprhya, the head fortuneteller at their temple.

Before Ephanie could say anything to Reyeni about being able to see, Seprhya walked into the classroom. She was old, much older than Mama, and would probably retire soon, giving up the gray robes of a teacher for clear white. Her white hair hung down low, braided to her waist. Brown age spots covered her hands as well as her much of her face. Her eyes had once been gray, like the robes she wore, but were now so washed out they almost had no color. She always appeared to be looking down her nose at people, though maybe that was also because she was so very tall.

"I'd heard you'd been moved here," Seprhya said, glancing over Ephanie.

"Yes, ma'am," Ephanie said. She took two steps forward. "I had a vision last night," she said proudly. Finally, she knew where she belonged.

"Your mother's lover coming home. Yes, we've all heard," Seprhya said dismissively. "I certainly hope it wasn't a fluke."

"It wasn't," Ephanie replied hotly. She shivered, remembering how the goddess had *moved* through her, demanding the life be taken, insisting that she go and tell Mama of her future. This was Ephanie's destiny.

"Well, maybe another will come to you quickly," Seprhya said, almost kindly. "Where's your proper robe? To mark your new status?"

"Mama said it would be a few days," Ephanie said, looking down at her bright blue apprentice robe. At least she wore a black sash, to show that she'd transitioned to being a fortuneteller. She needed new sandals as well: instead of the thin flats that growers used to feel the earth better, that were similar to what the southern natives wore, she needed proper footwear that tied around her ankles, like all the other witches wore.

"Your new robe is important, to mark you as different than the others," Seprhya told her. "If—when another vision comes, it's better for those around you to know why you're staggering around like you're drunk, instead of having to guess."

Reyeni sniggered.

Ephanie's cheeks grew warm. "I'll see if Mama can dye my old robes today," she offered.

"That would be good." Seprhya stalked over to the table and examined the chalk jars. "Too much red," she told Reyeni. "It won't hold a spell if it's too colored. Here," she said, gesturing for Ephanie to come closer. "It's better for you to learn this as well, even if you never end up using them."

Ephanie hurried over to stand next to Seprhya, watching her carefully measure out powdered colors using the ornately carved wooden spoons, listening to her instructions on where the colors came from, how they were made, the amounts that should be used. Ephanie was determined to learn everything she could, because she *would* be using the chalks and everything else they could teach her about having visions. She had a destiny. She just knew it.

"DID YOU HEAR, IPO?" EPHANIE ASKED, DANCING INTO THE BACK kitchen area. "Did you hear?" Only one of the seven cooking fires was lit that afternoon: all the flat bread for the temple had been baked early in the morning, before the heat of the day.

The large southern island native slowly turned away from the low cooking hearth. "And what news might that be, *uuka?*" Ipo asked with a sly grin.

Ephanie shook her head. *Uuka* meant "little one" in the southerner's tongue, one of the few words Ephanie knew. Yet, Ephanie, even at ten, was as tall as Ipo.

Today, Ipo wore a traditional *sulluu*, a single piece of colorful cloth many yards long, wrapped around her waist and then draped over her chest. The cloth was batik, dyed dark red with cracked yellow and green patterns. Her short hair flared over her head like a sea-urchin's halo. Ipo was one of the darker southern natives, though she claimed it was the fires that turned her so brown.

"I found my powers! I'm a fortuneteller!" Ephanie announced proudly.

"Really now? I'd heard you'd just told of a journey already known," Ipo teased.

"I know, I know," Ephanie grumbled. "The other fortunetellers said the same thing. But it really truly had been a vision." Why did she have to prove this to everyone?

"I'm sure it was," Ipo said. She brought out one hand that she'd been holding behind her back. "We give necklaces when a woman comes to power," she added, handing over simple black string with a lavender *serat* shell tied to the center of it.

"*Serat* live for centuries," Ephanie said, taking the necklace reverently. "This must have cost you a lot."

Ipo shook her head. "No, I just saw the shell. Thought it was pretty."

Ephanie saw the knot around the shell was crude, and the string was common, not even braided. "Thank you," she said anyway, holding the necklace in her hand. She'd never wear it—she'd be teased mercilessly by the other students if they ever saw her wearing something so plain.

Ipo seemed to have realized there was something wrong. "Eh," she said, shrugging with one shoulder and turning back to the stove.

"Do you often see witches come to power?" Ephanie asked.

Ipo looked over her shoulder. "What you going on about?"

Ephanie held up the necklace. "You said you give these when women come to power."

Ipo shook her head. "Don't know what you mean."

Ephanie rolled her eyes and sighed. She was never certain what was wrong with Ipo, who lost her train of thought frequently, denying that she'd done or said things, though Ephanie had just seen her or heard her.

This was just one more strange thing. Ephanie was glad that Ipo wouldn't remember the shell. Ephanie would never wear it, and would probably exchange it for something useful at the market.

EPHANIE TUGGED AT HER OLD ROBE AND SQUIRMED IN HER SEAT, trying to make herself comfortable out on the wooden patio behind the house. Her latest growing spurt had put her eye-to-eye with her mother, though she had just turned seventeen. Nothing fit right—not her clothes, her sandals, her bed, her calling, her life.

"Do you have to do that here?" Ephanie snapped at her mother as she walked up, carrying a basket of reeds for weaving. Then Ephanie realized what she'd said and put both her hands over her mouth, as if to hide where the words had come from. "I'm sorry," she said.

It was beautiful that afternoon on the lanai behind the house. The garden bloomed profusely around the wooden patio, as did everything Mama touched, the pink orchards and white-and-orange lilies releasing a heady scent, while the *mamapo'o* plants burst with dark green leaves and brilliant red berries. The thick bush hid them from their neighbors, making the space feel sacred and isolated. Birds sang happily from the nearby trees, their bright plumage adding stripes of color as they flew from one branch to the next.

Unlike the healers or the growers, there wasn't that much for a fortuneteller to learn or do between visions. Once Ephanie had memorized her prayers, chants, and songs, and made her chalk, all she could do was wait until the next time the goddess spoke to her.

Most fortunetellers had a second career, though nothing Ephanie had tried had worked. She couldn't weave without breaking the threads, the nets she'd tried knotting had all fallen apart, she shredded any bird feathers she touched for making cloaks, and she had no sense of style, so her beaded necklaces looked ungraceful next to even a child's.

The only time Ephanie's hands turned clever was when she had a vision and had to kill something.

Fortunately, Ephanie had had regular visions, one every two to three months. No one denied her power, though she still hadn't had what she would have called an important vision.

Her destiny would call on her soon. It had to. She just knew she had a special destiny. One more important than her artful, useless name in these islands that had no spring, not like the mainland had, or so the stories assured her.

That afternoon, Ephanie sat out on the lanai making flower necklaces from fragrant white *pikakee* flowers and green fern leaves for *Keereekayah*, the birthday of the god of hospitality, Keereeka.

For the next ten days, neighbors and relatives would visit each other's houses, bringing gifts and celebrating with fancy meals and special drinks. More than one myth told of Keereeka visiting in the guise of a long-lost uncle and judging a house's worthiness. Everything had to be perfect.

As a grower, tradition dictated that Ephanie's mother give out flower necklaces that were exquisitely scented and beautifully made.

The temple had been preparing all week as well. Ephanie had learned how to make a different type of chalk used to purify a hearth. Prince Aumoe was visiting as part of the celebration. He was a minor prince—the youngest son of King Makani, eleventh in line to the throne—but he was still royalty.

There had been a rumor that Jahaka, the high priestess of the witches, would come to their small island as well, but that hadn't turned out to be true.

Mama didn't take offense to Ephanie's tone, though. She placed her basket of reeds down next to Ephanie and sat down. "I take it that the *pikakee* are being difficult?"

Ephanie sighed. "The flowers keep breaking off from the stems." She'd seen the beautiful flower necklace that Mama had been working on for the prince, full of exotic flowers in more colors than she could name. The scent had filled their tiny house and followed her into her dreams, heaping up on her until she was under a mound of flowers, unable to move or breathe.

"I'm sure whatever you do will be fine," Mama said.

Ephanie knew that Mama would merely coax additional blossoms from the stems for any of the necklaces that Ephanie made that weren't perfect.

"And you'll feel better in a few days," Mama added.

"What do you mean?" Ephanie asked. She wasn't really feeling bad, just frustrated. As always. Her destiny was taking forever to come for her, just like her powers had.

"It's just that time again," Mama said.

"What time?" Ephanie asked. It wasn't her menses. That had happened last week, making her sticky and sweaty and unable to concentrate for a whole day.

Was it maybe because of that old proverb? The southerners had a saying about how madness followed the rise of the red moon, Ty, directly over Kualina Mountain. No one knew what that meant, not even the islanders. Ty hadn't risen directly over the mountain for more than two hundred years, as far as anyone could reckon.

They would all find out what that legend meant though, much later that night.

Since none of the fortunetellers had had visions proclaiming disaster, Seprhya and the other fortunetellers had assured the witches that not much would happen. No directives had come from Jahaka or the council of witches, except to be vigilant that evening.

Mama looked over at Ephanie and blinked. "You're about to have a vision, my dear."

"What?" Ephanie asked. Why would Mama say such a thing?

"You get like this. Irritated. Uncomfortable in your own skin. Just before a vision," Mama explained.

"I do not," Ephanie denied hotly. Seprhya would have told her if that was supposed to happen.

Mama merely shrugged. "I've seen it, every time. It might be because you came so late into your powers. But it also might be something you'll grow out of."

"I don't know what you're talking about," Ephanie said, thinking back. She didn't always feel so out of sorts every time she was about to have a vision, did she?

"I am a grower," Mama said sternly. "I trace cycles, longer than yours." She paused, then added in a softer voice, "You have a predictable pattern, my daughter. You should be aware of it, and use it."

"Thank you, Grower, for your advice," Ephanie said, rising. "I'm sure it will help the others who dig in the dirt."

Where were these words coming from? Ephanie couldn't take them back, though. Horrified, she hurried away, away from her home, back to the temple. Back to the quiet classroom of the fortunetellers, to pray at the altar of Brikalla that this vision would come quickly and be easy to tell.

It couldn't be her destiny, not yet. Ephanie was certain she'd feel more grand if that were bearing down on her.

EPHANIE HURRIED FROM THE FORTUNETELLERS' CLASSROOM, back out into the bright afternoon sunlight. Her classroom had repelled her. It was too stuffy, too sterile.

No life there for her.

She found herself fingering the black obsidian knife that all fortunetellers kept at their waist. The blade had never been bloodied. None of Ephanie's visions had ever demanded a great deal of life. Nearby plants had always been enough. Plus, Ephanie had always been able to push off a vision long enough to prepare, so she'd never had to cut herself and give her own blood to the goddess.

Only poorly trained fortunetellers did that. Their scars marked them as untrustworthy for the rest of their days.

Had Mama been right? Was Ephanie so restless because a vision was about to pounce on her? Seprhya had said that as a witch matured, she'd know when a vision was coming. But her teacher hadn't described the pounding headache that made everything sound too loud, the way Ephanie felt she just had to keep moving, never settling, and how everything irritated her and she couldn't keep a civil tongue in her head.

Maybe Ephanie should go back to the classroom. Collect up some jars of chalk and carry them with her.

But she couldn't go back there. She couldn't breathe in that room. She had to go somewhere, do something else. So she hurried along the path, out behind the temple complex. The jungle grew to her right, dark and dangerous, while the whitewashed wood buildings were grouped together on her left, orderly but stale. She didn't see anyone else on the path, which was good. She'd always remembered Seprhya's comment about lurching as if she was drunk while in the throes of a vision.

Finally, after more than an hour and circling the entire temple complex twice, Ephanie felt as though she could breathe normally. The afternoon sun had sunk further below the trees. Birds sang more loudly as dusk approached and bugs came out in the still humid air.

Something smelled good, there, just ahead. She followed her nose along the dirt path, the large-leaved *hanumau* plants bursting along the edges, bright spikes of birds-of-paradise flowers sticking in between them, along with huge purple blossoms of sea turtle flowers.

The kitchen? No, that wasn't it. She was being drawn behind the kitchen.

Not the smell of fresh-baked fish, no, that made Ephanie's stomach turn. Instead, the scent of fresh blood, some kind of kill—*that* was what drew her.

Behind the plain, white walls of the temple kitchen lay large heaps of compost from the kitchens, buzzing with flies and other insects. They smelled rank, overly sweet with decay. The growers covered the mounds every night with fast growing vines that would help the refuse decompose quickly.

Large wooden barrels, half filled with water, stood beside the door into the kitchens. The pounding in Ephanie's head grew more shrill. She lurched forward, plunging her arm into the rank water of the barrel, coming back with a single fish, a small gray *kapooku*, with a gaping mouth and sharp scales.

Ephanie threw it to the ground and eagerly reached back into the water.

Her hand came up empty.

The others had already been slaughtered, taken into the kitchen for the dinner meal.

The vision pounded at the back of Ephanie's skull, louder than any dance drum or crashing wave. A single fish wasn't enough. Ephanie quickly stepped on its head and slit it from neck to tail, splitting it in two. She rubbed her fingers in the oily "blood" that oozed from the fish, smearing lines across the hard dirt.

It wasn't enough. It wasn't nearly enough to paint the vision in her head.

Whining low in her throat, Ephanie dumped the barrel over, hoping another fish lay hidden at the bottom.

No luck—and the water washed away the first two lines she'd drawn.

Frustrated, Ephanie marched over to the compost heaps. But everything there was dead or dying. She couldn't catch enough flies to take their lives.

She needed something more. Something bigger. And soon, or this vision would overwhelm her, demand her own life for it.

Ephanie looked out into the jungle. One of the trees might work, but she didn't have an ax nor the strength to chop it down. Pulling up plants wouldn't be enough, nor destroying the flowers. And she didn't have wings or patience to try to capture a bird.

She needed something that bled. Entrails. Chalk would help, but she couldn't go back to the classroom to pick it up—she must have something *now*.

Heat poured over Ephanie, threatening to burn her up. She had to find something, *anything*, to paint this vision.

Without meaning to, Ephanie found the knife in her hand turning toward her other hand.

"No," she pleaded quietly, tears already gathering in her eyes. To cut herself, to gain those scars, would mark her as a poor fortuneteller, unprepared. The other witches would always look down on her.

What else could she do? No friendly *poi* dog came crawling out of the woods, begging for her knife, like in the tale of Lalalina. No fish formed out of the water and threw themselves at her.

All she had left was her own life's blood.

The line of fiery pain down Ephanie's arm hurt, but it also brought relief. The blood welled instantly around the cut. Before a single drop could fall to the ground, Ephanie caught it with the dull edge of her blade, the sweep of the knife against the injured skin making her gasp.

Ephanie swung her knife away from her, wide and hard, flinging the blood from the blade. It fell into a pattern on the ground.

It wasn't enough. The picture wasn't complete.

Like all fortunetellers, Ephanie's blood had already started to congeal and the skin to close—they always healed fast. With gritted teeth, she started the second exquisite cut. Pain mingled with joy and addictive release. Her face grew hot with embarrassment but she continued with that superb cut.

"Stop!" came a male voice.

Ephanie didn't bother to look up. Her need was too overwhelming, the pain too delightful. She *must* complete her vision. She was only now fully alive.

Rough hands grabbed hers, pulling the blade away from her arm.

Ephanie gasped, then growled, unable to form words. She struggled to bring the blade back to her skin, but the hands holding hers were too strong.

"It's not worth it. You shouldn't kill yourself," the young man said.

Words would not come to Ephanie's lips. She yanked on her arms, trying to get away, shaking her head.

"I can help," the young man said. He was from the southern islands, with brown skin and soft eyes. Like most natives, he was shorter than she was, his head only reaching her shoulder.

Ephanie didn't care. The blade turned in her hands without her own thought, driven still by her need.

If she couldn't have her own blood, she'd have his.

Using her legs, Ephanie pushed forward, no longer pulling away from the young man, but suddenly driving into him.

Surprised, the young man fell back, stumbling.

Ephanie tried to redirect the blade, to send it into his shoulder. But it was all happening so fast and her need was too great.

The blade plunged into the young man's neck, easily slicing through his soft skin. The blood welled and Ephanie greedily gathered it with both her hands, twisting the knife to get more.

Then Ephanie turned and flung the blood against the ground. It splashed with intent, the vision forming clearly. She sank down to her knees, eagerly reading the signs.

Ships. Many ships. From the west. Coming to attack Hilani, the main island, where the king lived, where high priestess Jahaka lived. At the end of the *Keereekayah* festival. In ten days' time.

The vision required that Ephanie tell Jahaka, the head of all the witches. She must also tell the king. They must both know the attack was coming. But she must tell Jahaka first, this she knew.

As the vision receded, Ephanie sat back on her heels. She knew she'd be able to rest a little, but then she'd have to be on her way to Hilani, the big island in the center region, where the main temple was.

She started planning the journey—it would take two, maybe three days to get from the eastern islands to the center region. Would the temple buy her passage on a boat, or would she be expected to go by canoe, hiring a single rower? How long did she have to tell the people involved before the vision drove her completely mad? Maybe Seprhya would know.

A groan behind Ephanie brought her back to the blood-spattered area.

With horror, she turned.

The young man gasped again, then breathed out his last breath.

Why had he tried to stop her? Why didn't he know about fortunetellers, and how dangerous that was? She hadn't meant to take his life. By Brikalla's Holy Word, not only had she cut herself, she'd killed someone, in the throes of a vision.

No one would ever trust her again.

Ephanie crawled over to the body, too tired to stand. What had he been thinking? What was she going to tell his family? What would Mama say?

Why was he wearing the yellow robes of royalty?

"What happened?" Zakiel, the other fortuneteller student, came rushing forward, out from the jungle. "What did you do to Prince Aumoe?"

"He tried—he tried to stop me," Ephanie said. "I was having a vision and—"

"You killed him?" Zakiel asked. "Why did you kill him? Did the vision need his life?"

"No," Ephanie said. She would never lie about that. "He just got in the way." The vision needed blood and some life. It hadn't required his. Only two or three cuts on her own arm would have gotten her all the blood she'd needed. She shivered in the cooling air, echoes of her own need still resounding in her.

"You'll be punished for this," Zakiel declared. "I'll see to it."

Ephanie looked up, surprised. Why would one fortuneteller turn on another? There were so few of them, and no one really liked them anyway. They had only each other. Then she watched Zakiel tenderly brush back the prince's hair from his face.

Without warning, a new vision poured into Ephanie, showing her what was supposed to have happened. She'd never heard of additional visions striking a fortuneteller after the first had occurred. Maybe it was because she'd used so much life—life she wasn't supposed to take.

The prince and Zakiel were meeting back here, behind the kitchens, without anyone accompanying them, so they could go off into the jungle together as lovers.

"He never would have loved you back," Ephanie said with certainty. The vision kept rolling over her, the years reeling out like fishing nets. "You would have been left here with his child. He never would have acknowledged it. Or you."

Zakiel turned to look at her. "Not everyone takes lovers like your mother," she spat back.

Ephanie laughed, as bitter as a dried orange. "No, most witches just breed." She paused, then added, "But you wouldn't have bred true." She could see the child, a brown-skinned girl, broken and battered by her mother's disappointment.

However, though Ephanie had seen that part, the augury hadn't required that she tell Zakiel more about the child. Or the rest of what she saw, how her own life would change.

Ephanie's destiny had found her. She didn't like it one bit.

"You'll be killed for killing him," Zakiel said smugly as she stood. "The king will have you cut to bits and strewn out across the water, no way for your soul to find a home."

Ephanie looked at the poor prince, dead for no reason other than he'd mistakenly tried to save her from herself.

"No, I won't be," Ephanie said. At least, not at first.

There was no way for Ephanie to explain to Zakiel about her visions, that Ephanie's living would turn out to be more of a curse.

CHAPTER 2

Jahaka hides the midday sun
  And brings the dry, killing snow
  —*Northern children's song, teaching the names of the winds*

JAHAKA TRIED TO PLAY WITH THE OLDER CHILDREN AT THE temple in the courtyard behind the long gallery, next to the jungle. The sun burned hot overhead, while the sky was blue and cloudless. Insects sang in the trees, louder than the temple's trained songbirds. Scents from the ocean wove through everything: salt mingled with beautiful flowers and hot sand mixed with broad green leaves.

The children had a woven ball that they threw from one to the other, far above Jahaka's head. They were all bigger than she was—she was only four—and faster, too.

Mother Rayne merely watched, as always—this time from under the trees, in the shade, away from the sun. She wouldn't say anything about the older children teasing unless Jahaka complained, and Jahaka always tried to be a big girl and not say anything, to make Mother Rayne proud. Mother Rayne was the only fortuneteller loosely associated with the council of witches at the main temple, and Jahaka, even at such a young age, was aware that their position was precarious.

"Hey, over here!" called one of the girls.

Jahaka looked at her, but saw that the ball wasn't actually going to be thrown that way. The boy with the ball was going to throw it a different direction.

Racing as fast as she could on her stubby legs, Jahaka plowed into the girl supposed to catch the ball, knocking the girl to the side. Jahaka tripped and fell. The other girl laughed and leaped back up, snatching the ball with both her hands as it bounced.

The other children cheered as she threw it, far into the trees, away from the courtyard.

Jahaka stayed where she was, her right knee grazed and bleeding, the pain sharp.

No one stopped for her or asked her if she was hurt. The children kept playing their game, now running into the jungle.

It wasn't fair. They were bigger and faster, and Jahaka just wanted to keep up! They should play with her. She could be good at this game. She would show them. She would.

Waves of heat built up inside of Jahaka. It felt as though the huge fire in the outdoor kitchen streamed through her, starting in her belly and spreading up. The trees shimmered in her heat and rage.

Finally, Jahaka's skin couldn't contain the heat anymore. It burst out, flowing off her in waves. Her knee no longer hurt, the pain blasted away. When Jahaka looked down, the skin was merely dirty— the scrape had healed over and the blood had dried.

After brushing her knee off, Jahaka jumped up and raced after the children under the trees.

Only later that night did Jahaka see the satisfied smile of her mother. Only then did Mother Rayne tell her of her plans for Jahaka to become the high priestess of all the witches, the position Mother Rayne, as a fortuneteller, had never been able to obtain.

Jahaka woke with the rising sun, one side of her body

chilled by the cool night breezes, the other warm where it came in contact with Enekai, her latest lover. He was such a boy, so young and eager to please her, the high priestess of all the witches.

But Enekai had surprised Jahaka after their bout of love making by talking of his ambition and his dreams for the western islands.

The southern natives referred to their collection of islands as "Three Hands Full"—named for the fifteen inhabited islands curved in a gentle crescent. The islands were roughly divided into three regions: western, eastern, and central.

Men from the western islands were known for their temper and passion. The bravest fishermen came from this region, as well as the greatest fighters. The eastern islands were known for their artists, the men and women foraging deep in the jungle for exotic flowers, as well as training songbirds and making beautiful feathered cloaks. The central islanders were the beekeepers, and also had the largest farms.

The allegiance of the western islands to the central ones— particularly the main island of Hilani where King Makani lived in his palace—had always been an uneasy thing. The king demanded tribute, as well as an exchange of the sons of the western warlords, returning minor dignitaries in their stead.

As a second son, Enekai chafed at that. His family merely had power, no royal blood, but he felt as though the king was bleeding them, just the same.

Enekai's eldest brother had been raised on Hilani, at the king's court, away from his family. The heir had returned too different for his people to easily follow him. Plus, in the meanwhile, Enekai had worked hard at winning people's hearts.

The previous night, in the dark, Enekai had confessed to wanting to live on more than this small western island, which was growing smaller every year as more children (and fewer wars) occurred.

Jahaka stretched out her hand toward her lover but didn't touch his dark skin. He might be perfect. All she needed now was a sign from the gods, telling her that it was time to lead all the witches from the southern islands back to the mainland. Mother Rayne had never foreseen such a thing, but Jahaka knew it was her destiny, had felt it in her bones since her mother's funeral.

The other witches didn't understand why Jahaka even broached such a topic. The gods had told them to come to the southern islands two centuries before, and until the gods told them to leave, here they would stay.

Jahaka didn't want another disaster to occur like what had befallen Alokai Temple. But still, she prayed for a sign to guide her.

Some of the other priestesses, particularly the ones who ran temples on the other islands, occasionally confessed that their faith had been tested and stretched too far. Jahaka did what she could to help them find their way. She knew she'd surprised more than one by the strength of her own faith.

Without the gods, where would the witches be? The gods had led the witches to the southern islands—after the destruction of Alokai Temple on the mainland, they had sent wave upon wave of dreams to their people, urging them south. Very few witches remained on the mainland, and the ones left behind stayed in hiding, particularly since the mainland peoples persecuted them, burning them at the stake after a "trial."

When the witches had arrived at the islands, they'd found that while one disaster had struck them, another had struck the people here —a horrible volcanic eruption had wiped out more than one island. They'd recently lost their king as well, the great King Kawiti.

Together, the witches and the southern islanders had rebuilt, the witches establishing healing centers and temples on all the islands, and the islanders welcoming the help, while giving them a home. So they'd remained, working side-by-side, yet separate.

However, Jahaka was convinced that it was time for the witches to leave, to go back to the mainland and establish a strong presence there again. They belonged on the mainland. These southern islands weren't good for them.

The pure line of the witches was being corrupted, their powers, even the names and holy days of their gods and goddesses, changing over the decades and centuries, like the hardened Brika becoming Brikalla.

If only Jahaka could get a sign from the gods that her intuition was right, that this was the way to save her people from the creeping changes that infected them.

With a sigh, Jahaka rose from the bed. Standing, she raised her hands up above her head and stretched her nude body, then gracefully folded over and pressed her palms to the floor.

Her healer's body stayed as young as she commanded it. Enekai would have been surprised to learn she was old enough to be his mother—possibly his grandmother—though she looked not much older than he.

Slowly, Jahaka unfolded herself. It would only be a few more years that she could maintain the façade. Then she'd age, possibly quickly. She'd never had that much power as a healer, and certainly never enough to heal more than minor ailments in others.

Or maybe she'd just never cared enough to focus what power she had outward.

Finished with her stretches, Jahaka strode to the window. The fiery ball of the sun rose just above the horizon, casting a long, orange streak across the calm water.

More than one tale from the southern islanders talked of goddesses walking across the ocean on such a beam. But Jahaka had never found any southern island natives with any power. None of the northern witches had, not in all the generations they'd been here.

Just below her, in the garden, the songbirds were already starting their racket. The servants working in the palace had joined in, crooning their own native tunes. This island could use another grower or two, she decided, looking at the state of their garden. It wasn't complete jungle; there was some sort of order there. But the flowers weren't as lush as they could be, and if Enekai was to challenge his brother and his father, his estate needed to be better than theirs, in every way.

The sun continued its searing way up the edge of the sky. Without meaning to, a prayer sprang to Jahaka's lips:

Ekuilli, wise and powerful,
Bring healing to this land
May its people know your strength

May your wisdom calm the storms
May they turn back to the plow
When the shields have been laid down.

"That's beautiful," Enekai said from behind her.

Forcing down her anger at being interrupted, Jahaka pasted a smile on her face and turned around. "It's a prayer of healing," she said truthfully. It was in the old language of the witches, from the mainland, not in the fluid singsong tones of the southern islanders'.

"Tell me more," Enekai said, holding out his hand to Jahaka.

Swinging her hips gracefully, Jahaka walked slowly back to the bed. "It's asking for peace, after the war," she said.

"But not a prayer to keep us from war?" Enekai asked as he took Jahaka's hand, bringing it to rest upon his strongly muscled chest.

"Oh no, not at all, my lord," Jahaka murmured as she bent over the bed to kiss him again.

Yes, Enekai might match her plans nicely.

JAHAKA SAT ON HER CHAIR OF JUDGMENT IN THE RECEIVING room of the main temple on Hilani. She would have denied that it was a throne, though she'd seen King Makani's throne, and her chair was just as grand. The seat had been carved from a single piece of obsidian, sheared and polished so it glowed with its own black light. The back had been made from woven, living vines that grew up from a trough in the floor, intertwined with sweet jasmine, lilies, and hyacinth. Growers kept the flowers fresh and attached to their foreign hosts.

Jahaka wore the yellow robes of judgment that day. It wasn't the same yellow as royalty—the beekeepers—but it was close enough. She knew the colors the witches wore had changed when they came to the islands. The high priestess used to wear black, and fortunetellers weren't accepted at all, allowed to have a voice in council.

All that had changed.

Too much had changed.

No rains were expected that day, so the walls of the room along the western side, to her right, had been taken down and a simple living rope had been strung there to mark the edge. Merchants, farmers, and fishermen crowded together in the outside courtyard, watching the proceedings with great interest.

Jahaka had no doubt they were there just for "the show." However, as long as they stayed quiet—and she had both temple guards as well as King Makani's guard established at the corners to make sure they did—they could watch.

Inside the room, witches from all the professions waited, along with the next batch of acolytes in their bright blue robes.

Yet another change. Robes used to be cover a woman fully, from neck to wrist to ankle. The younger girls all had their hair covered as well. Now, the robes were loose and sleeveless, with either slits up the skirt or even cut off above the knee. They were more practical, given the jungle climate.

Jahaka still longed to go back to the old times, when the witches were more formal, as well as more formidable. Agate, the first of the northern witches to arrive at the southern islands, would never have allowed such a rabble in her chambers.

The first acolyte who came forward was an older girl. While her skin was very pale, her eyes were hazel, mixed brown and green. She wore her worry like a shield, daring for others to cut her down.

"Oh great priestess, I am Nyandar," the girl said as she knelt gracefully.

At least she was showing the proper respect. Jahaka nodded for her to continue.

"I am nearly finished with my eighteenth year, and yet…" Nyandar paused and tears started streaming from her eyes. "Forgive me, but my powers have not come in yet. Please, please, I beg of you, find this unworthy apprentice a new position at your temple. Don't send me away!" She ended by throwing herself on the ground and wailing.

Jahaka sighed, uncomfortable. She wished she could order the girl to get up and show some respect, but she was aware that might appear unkind. Instead she waited until the girl composed herself, her loud sobs diminishing.

It was Jahaka's greatest shame. The witches were no longer breeding true. Even the greatest healers couldn't cure the powerless. And more powerless girls were being brought for judgment every season. Out of every one hundred witches born, maybe five now were powerless girls.

When the girl—Nyandar—finally looked up, Jahaka told her, "I'm sorry, my dear." And she truly was.

However, the witches' laws about powerless witches were clear. They couldn't live at the main temple lest they contaminated the younger girls, those who hadn't come into their power yet. It was shocking that this Nyandar had been allowed such close access to them. She would have to leave. She could go back to her family if they would take her. If they wouldn't, and no one else stepped forward, she'd be turned into the jungle. The temple had no facilities for taking care of powerless girls, and no one would want regular interaction with them, afraid for their own powers.

"No!" Nyandar called. "You can't send me away. I'm good with the little ones. And the caremother needs help. I'm good for the temple. My family won't take me. You must let me stay!"

"We can't," Jahaka said, conscious of the outsiders watching the proceedings.

It was time for Jahaka to make these judgments private. Mother Rayne had warned against this, though—that people might accuse her of making biased judgments if there was no one watching her.

Maybe Jahaka needed to set up a watch group of carefully selected advisors who would always agree with her decisions.

The girl raised her tearstained face. "The temple needs workers. And I'm a good worker. Not everyone in the temple has magic!"

"True. But you're a witch. You were born to a witch who didn't breed true. That means you're imperfect, unclean." Jahaka kept her tone even as she said the words—gentle, perhaps, and not flinging them as accusations.

"Where will I go?" Nyandar asked.

Jahaka had no response. The girl couldn't be the temple's responsibility. They didn't have the resources. She had no power, not even a glimpse of magic.

And there were too many like her, too many flaunting the purple robes of the powerless, even here on Hilani. If her family wouldn't take her, none other would either, no matter how good she was with the little ones.

Yarrow, one of the senior priestess and Jahaka's main advisor, stepped forward. "My lady, I've heard of a compound, on one of the smaller islands in the eastern region, Mokolani, that's been set up for our poor brethren like Nyandar."

"We'll give you safe passage there," Jahaka promised. She'd heard of this island before as well, a wretched, isolated place with little contact from the other islands.

Maybe that would be better than being forced into the jungle alone, since Nyandar, like most witches, had never lived deep in the bush and probably wouldn't survive.

It was the best Jahaka could do for the poor creature.

"Thank you, thank you," Nyandar continued, bowing over her hands and still weeping as two temple guards helped her to her feet and directed her out of the chamber area.

Jahaka took a deep breath. She would talk to Yarrow and some of the others, about creating a separate council for apprentice issues. The council would have the power to pass judgment themselves, with her final approval, of course.

That way, if that separate council made a mistake about a powerless girl who later came into her magic, they could be blamed. Jahaka would be able to stand clear, keep her reputation spotless.

The next girl who strode forward was obviously of mixed blood. Her skin was the color of wet sandstone walls, her eyes were as dark as a fortuneteller's robe, and her hair was wild and black and hung in strange curls. She wasn't as short as the natives, but she was still short for a witch.

However, she also proudly wore the robe of a grower. She stood tall, staring defiantly at Jahaka.

An older woman walked up beside her, also in blue-green grower robes. She stepped beyond the girl, coming closer to the high priestess. She had clear gray eyes and skin browned by the sun, with wrinkles deeply etched in her temples and around the corners of her lips. Her nose was upturned, not to snub others, but to turn her face upwards toward the living sky, so her prayers would more easily flow out.

"Greetings, high priestess Jahaka," the older woman stated. "I am Ivy, the head of the growers on Nanalani, the island directly east of here."

"Greetings, Ivy," Jahaka said formally. "What can the court do for you today?"

"You decreed that those with differently shaped powers should be brought before you," Ivy said. "I present Daisy, one of our growers who has just come into her power."

"High priestess," the girl said, with a mere nod of her head to Jahaka.

"Daisy," Jahaka said, her tone as chill as the wind she was named after. "Show me."

The girl looked around. "There's no dirt here," she complained.

"There, then," Jahaka said, pointing to the courtyard outside.

The girl strode to the roped-off area, then gestured to the crowd there to part. They split easily before her, revealing the trampled dirt of the courtyard.

Daisy clenched her fists tightly, raising them up to her neck. Then she opened her fingers, flinging her hands out.

Even from her seat, Jahaka felt the wave of power that flowed from the girl.

Plants sprang up, as they would for any strong grower: Simple *mamapo'o* bushes, hibiscus trees, and tall palm grasses.

Jahaka was about to ask what was special about that when the crowd standing outside started shifting and moving, shuffling their feet and muttering. Jahaka left her seat to walk closer to the edge and see what was happening.

Daisy wasn't merely growing plants in the dirt that lay out there. She *moved* the dirt, directing it like living rivers, to support her plants.

Jahaka shivered. Such a display of power was unnatural. She'd never seen anything like this before, had never even *heard* of it before.

This was something new.

Jahaka turned from the display back to the older priestess, Ivy who watched her apprentice with apprehension. Fear-filled eyes turned to look at Jahaka.

At least Ivy understood just how dangerous Daisy was.

"Thank you for bringing your apprentice to me," Jahaka said, bowing her head low to Ivy.

"I am eager for your guidance in her training," Ivy said, staring desperately at Jahaka.

"I will pray for guidance, as well as consult with my council," Jahaka promised, though she knew it would be futile.

No one had ever seen anything like this before

Mama had warned that this would be just the start.

More witches, with stranger powers, would be born, if they stayed here in the islands.

The witches were changing.

Daisy was much more frightening than poor Nyandar. Powerless girls could be shunted off, isolated. Daisy represented something different—a new power—to witches who hadn't seen a new power in centuries.

She represented change.

And change was never good.

JAHAKA PROSTRATED HERSELF BEFORE HER PERSONAL ALTAR, praying to Ekuili, the god of healing, to Brikalla, the goddess of foretelling, to Hynla, the god of luck, and even to Miatlu, the god of the underworld, begging for a sign.

The witches were changing. Would the children born to those like Daisy even be recognizable?

All the traditions they'd fought so hard to save would die. They'd carved out a space for themselves in this hot, wet land, where the winds they'd cherished no longer existed, the snows never came to purify them, where half of their prayers had to be taught by rote because the children didn't understand what they referenced.

Jahaka knew how to save them. Mother Rayne had told her of the problem so long ago, and the answer had come clear to Jahaka in the evening after her mother's funeral.

In order to become pure again, the witches had to move back to the mainland.

However, the mainlanders would never accept them.

They would need to set up their own kingdom, carve out their own space.

Enekai would help. Jahaka knew he was part of the puzzle. He'd be glad, once he took over as king of the southern islands, to move onto the mainland. They'd have to harness the most clever fishermen, the bravest of the warriors, to fight the currents and the wind to make it back to the mainland.

But how would Jahaka justify this war? Particularly to the healers and the growers?

The fortunetellers were no help. Who could predict what they'd see? Even Mother Rayne hadn't been able to direct or control her visions.

All Jahaka needed was a sign from the gods that her intuition was true.

No one came to Jahaka's door with news—they knew better than to disturb her prayers. However, something changed in the air, making her look up, kneel back from her position on the floor and look out the window, toward the ocean.

Beyond the darkened room, across the bay, a tall column of black smoke rose.

Someone among the royalty had died.

Had the madness already started? The southerners had an old proverb that when Ty, the red moon, rose directly over Kualina Mountain, madness would follow.

But no one knew what the madness would be, or how it would manifest. None of the fortunetellers had reported any dire visions, so there wasn't anything Jahaka could have done about it, except to order more guards that night around the temple complex, and to tell the other island temples to be vigilant.

Besides, it was the start of the celebration of *Keereekayah*. Witches had spent much of the day preparing for visits from all their neighbors and their relatives, to bring fortune and good luck for the new year with all the wishes traveling past their thresholds.

How much could they celebrate if King Makani had died?

Though Jahaka doubted it was the king. The palace wasn't that far from the main temple: They would have sent runners, not a smoke signal, if it had been someone really important in the royal line who had passed.

Then who had died? And how could Jahaka use it for her advantage?

With a sigh, Jahaka bent her head in prayer again. She would just have to be patient, as Mother Rayne had taught her, as she'd always been, waiting for what was sure to finally be her sign.

CHAPTER 3

When the red moon rises directly over Kualina Mountain, madness
follows.
—Southern Islands proverb

HINANULI, THE GREAT GODDESS OF KUALINA MOUNTAIN, LOVED
to throw her red necklaces high in the air, above the mountain, up into
the clouds. The land shook when she danced, and she often made the
people cry with the smoke from her fires.

Haikili, the god of thunder, was disturbed by Hinanuli's dancing.
He warned her to not throw her red necklaces so high. The stones her
mountain threw would strike the islands and the people, and would
hurt them.

But Hinanuli didn't care. She danced and threw her necklaces
higher and higher, until they landed on the table of the god of thunder
himself, disturbing his evening meal.

With great anger, Haikili raged down on Hinanuli. He struck her
mountain with torrential rains and lightning, tearing up the edges of
the great peak, spiking the stone that had been flat, so that Hinanuli
could no longer dance.

Then Haikili threw Hinanuli herself into her mountain. The red fires, unable to escape past where she blocked their chimney, tore into her. Hinanuli couldn't escape the fire's rage. The flames burned the goddess, turning her smooth skin into pocked black obsidian, her flowing hair into ash.

Ashamed, Hinanuli stayed hidden in her mountain, never dancing again.

It is said that she only creeps out at night now, whispering to women in their dreams.

If you listen to Hinanuli, you may gain great power.

Or you may gain great madness.

Or both.

MAHINA SAT STILL IN HER HUT, THE SOUNDS OF THE JUNGLE songbirds and the screeching crickets washing over her, lulling her eyes close. She rested her heavy head on her fist, her elbow pressing into the hard table.

Did she have a table, though? Perhaps it was the cutoff stump of a tree, butchered for its wood to feed the temples and the strange white witches.

A baby cried in the corner, or maybe that was just the *moomaki* bird. Flies buzzed around Mahina, drawn by the fish scales she'd sheered that morning, or maybe the day before.

Time didn't matter to Mahina, not anymore. It flowed like wind through the jungle leaves, barely touching some, rattling others. She remembered that at one point she had cared, when she'd been clever and small and young.

But now, Mahina was old. She moved at the pace of the mountain and was just as strong, shambling through the jungle of her home.

No, there was no child crying in the corner. The young ones had left, gone deeper into the trees, to hide in the rivers and caves there, too destitute to even build huts, clothed with the glory of the trees, draped with the deep red and green clusters of sea-turtle flowers, wearing necklaces made of flowers not just on feast or celebration days but every day, ropes made from vines to tie up their feet, not proper sandals.

Ah, her children were grown, long gone, moved into the towns where the priestesses were, looking always for children like hers and never recognizing them.

The witches didn't understand that her children were born strong but wouldn't remain that way. The years would weaken their power, not strengthen it. Their spirit would seep away.

Mahina turned her head—she was sitting in her hut after all—and spat on the pounded dirt floor. King Kawiti had cursed them, cursed them all, so long ago, all her sisters and all her people, too.

So Mahina and her children turned dumb, powerless, growing weaker as they aged from mewling infant to standing child.

The jungle filtered the bright afternoon sun, baking the small hut. Winds didn't make it past the threshold, and if they did venture inside, quickly left through the small back window. A mound of leaves and woven ropes, thick with moss, lay in the corner, the shape of Mahina's large body imprinted on them from when she remembered to sleep.

Thirsty, Mahina stood. She remembered how to stand, remembered her feet dancing on the sand in the moonlight, light and quick once. Now, she remembered thirst again. She slowly made her way out of her hut. There, around the back, stood the first toe of the mountain.

First, Mahina reached out and rubbed the pad of her thumb against the stones there, the rock worn smooth from the years, decades, lifetimes of her touch. These stones were important, blessed by the goddess. They held power and dreams and remembered more than Mahina did most days.

Trickling down beside the rocks was a tiny creek, full of clear water, clean and pure all year round.

Mahina stuck her fist into the cold water that was still chilled from its trip down the mountain, then brought it to her face to lick it off. There had been something else, once, for gathering the water, but she didn't remember what it was, or what it was called, or how long since she'd used one. Her hand was all she knew how to use now.

She stuck her fist into the water a second time, her knuckles grazing the pebbling rock at the back of the tiny flow.

And Hinanuli, the goddess of Kualina Mountain, started to speak.

Mahina found herself walking down a jungle trail. The day had shifted. It was later, the sun coming closer and the heat pressing in. Why was she here? Why had she left her hut? Was it time to go into the village already? To steal another dead rag to replace her living garments, so that she could pass among the towns folk again? To beg for bread she would never eat? To maybe trade her body for fish from the merchants, instead of catching her own in the stream?

Her fist throbbed by her side. Mahina brought it up to see the red marks that flayed her dark skin. She put it to her mouth, licking the flaming marks, trying to soothe them.

Now, Mahina remembered. Hinanuli had spoken to her, told her it would be time, soon. The goddess had directed Mahina to go to the village, to cover herself in the clothes they used, put dead things on her feet so that she wouldn't track the mud of the jungle along their useless white paths, wouldn't cut her soles on their sharp stones and edges.

But what was she supposed to do after she bathed herself in the streams and dressed herself as they did?

The thought itself dazzled Mahina so much that she had to stop.

She remembered something more than just her hut, just the children who'd been lost and found in dreams. She had a plan, things to do, in a particular order.

For the first time in a very, *very* long while, Mahina could think beyond: *be hungry, find food; be tired, find bed.*

She recognized that her thoughts, such that they were, were still slow and not as bright as when she'd been younger.

But they were so much more than she'd had in her hut.

Mahina shivered in the heat of the afternoon. Her hut. Had *that* been where she'd lived? For all those years? Walls barely woven together, supported by the trees growing around them, the refuse building in the corner until it became a wall itself.

No wonder her children had left—fleeing into the jungle, until it took their minds from them as well? Or did they go into the village, to grow pale like the puny white women there?

Mahina shook her head. Had she actually ever had children? Or were those memories merely dreams from her sisters? Maybe she just remembered the goddess Hinanuli's children, how they'd scattered after she'd been thrown into the mountain for dancing too strong.

With a deep breath, Mahina started moving again. She, too, was strong.

The descendants of King Kawiti wouldn't be able to stop Mahina and her sisters this time, or so the goddess assured her.

MAHINA WASHED HER HAIR AGAIN IN THE RIVER. THE HARSH dreads would never unwind. She'd have to shave her scalp and let her hair grow out again if she wanted to be rid of them completely. But at least her hair felt clean to her fingers now. The bugs had all left and her skin didn't itch anymore. Quickly, with fingers that were almost clever, Mahina tied flowers into the ends of the long black strands, fragrant purple and white *pahina* with their draping petals and leaves.

It didn't take long, this time, for Mahina to wash her body. Dirt no longer caked into every wrinkle. How long had she been walking in the world? She couldn't count the nights—too many had been lost, long ago, to madness. Maybe a handful of sunrises, maybe more.

The time before the goddess had spoken to Mahina was endless and confused with the dreams of her ancestors. She could never be sure of her age, what had actually happened to her, and what events her sisters had lived through.

None of that mattered, though.

In only a few more days, the red moon would rise directly over Kualina Mountain. Mahina had to be at the big witch temple by then. Not on the island of the king, no, but here, on Ailani Island.

Mahina didn't understand why Hinanuli insisted she go to the witch's temple. Weren't her own people's temples good enough?

However, something was about to happen there, something that

Mahina had to witness. Something strong enough to draw her out of the jungle, leaving behind her leaf dress and dirt and wild hair.

Something to force Mahina into the world, if only for a little while.

Mahina wondered if she would die at the witches' temple. It felt that way sometimes. The goddess marked her path strong and true, but without explanation.

Only a few days ago, Mahina wouldn't have known or been able to wonder enough to ask for an explanation.

After Mahina finished bathing, she quickly put on the *sulluu* she'd stolen, wrapping it around her waist and up over her chest. Not because she was ashamed of her body, like the stupid white witches, no. Her people, before the witches had come, had worn cloth only wrapped around their waists, proudly showing their breasts.

Her children, the ones who lived in the jungle, wore only skirts of leaves and nets of vines across their chests.

But the goddess had instructed Mahina to appear like the others, which meant covering herself. So she dressed in the *sulluu* and held her head held high. She was a big woman, tall and heavy, like the mountain.

Stupid northern witches were thin and frail compared to her. Despite their great height, they couldn't stand in the ocean without being bowled over by the waves, couldn't sink their feet into the sand and pull the power of the mountain to them.

They had no idea of the power of the islands, couldn't use it.

Mahina would show them. She knew it. Her dreams had told her that the power was there, not just in dreams, but under the earth, just waiting for her to reclaim.

Mahina watched the witches making their flower necklaces, weaving them in the old way, but out of unfamiliar flowers, vines, and leaves. She stayed in the jungle, away from their sterile white walls and hard, white stone paths.

Was next week the new year? Did her people not celebrate that anymore? Mahina hadn't seen any of the southerners weaving necklaces or baking the special cakes or making offerings of *puapua* leaves to Keereeka, the god of hospitality.

Then again, they mainly worked either in the kitchens or in the laundry of the witches at their temples. A very few dyed cloth or wove. She had seen at least one of the witches wearing a traditional cloak made of bird feathers, and recognized the pattern from her ancestors.

The few fisher folk kept to themselves, away from the temple, their village half a mile away, down the beach.

When Mahina had walked down the dirt path between their huts, they'd whispered to each other, calling her *Koro Haiku'ee*, Old Mother, an aspect of Hinanuli. A few had turned their hands sideways to her, to stop the evil eye from visiting them. The women had kept their children away, not letting them come closer to either pester her or be cursed by her.

Maybe they saw that the goddess had talked to her, whispered to her, but not in a dream. Given her the power to leave the jungle, though her sisters and her children had remained behind.

Soon, Mahina would call to all her people. She would bring them out of the bush and into the light, to stand in the ocean and laugh at the waves trying to knock them over. They'd climb the mountains and bring the stones down. Or dance on the flames and throw their fiery necklaces high, disturbing the thunder god again.

Even without the goddess whispering in her ear, Mahina knew that tonight was the night. Ty would rise directly over Kualina Mountain later that evening. The folks in the village watched the horizon uneasily, as if they sensed it, too.

Mahina didn't remember when the proverb about the moon and madness had arisen. Sometime after King Kawiti had cursed them, a proclamation of the king's curse abating. Of her sisters coming back into their power.

Redness tinged the evening sky as the sun set, and the air held onto its electric feeling. Mahina watched the sky, then the shore, unsure where to go.

Coming out from the jungle, Mahina walked over the sand to the open ocean. Across the bay stood the lonely Kualina Mountain.

Hinanuli had always danced alone. The other gods had been jealous of her power and her beauty. That was why the god of thunder had thrown her down—not because of her dancing, but because she'd refused him, laughed in his face when he'd tried to court her.

The red moon rose in the dark sky, barely visible. It never cast much light. Gulik, the greater white moon, just threw a sliver over the dark water, ready to eclipse its little brother.

But tonight, Ty would reign.

Mahina hummed to herself as the moon climbed past the horizon. The goddess stayed silent, but the ocean wind spoke to Mahina of the coming night, the great depths of the water, the wide spaces between the islands.

As Ty slowly climbed closer to the peak of the mountain, more of the fisher folk joined Mahina on the beach. The women broke into a song of welcome, though the men tried to hush them. They believed the proverb, that merely madness would follow, while her sisters knew better.

By the time they reached the chorus, Mahina remembered the words and joined in. Her voice sounded strong among the others. She hadn't spoken for so many years, it surprised her how loud her voice had grown.

> *Welcome, oh friend*
> *Arrived here today*
> *Good health I wish*
> *Good food as well*
> *I had heard*
> *That you were coming*
> *I have mourned*
> *That you were away*
> *Welcome, oh friend*
> *Welcome.*
> *Please stay.*

As the song circled back to the beginning, Mahina found herself turning away from the swelling ranks of people. Row upon row now stood on the sand, some holding hands, singing from their hearts as they greeted Ty, singing it a clear path through the sky.

Mahina didn't belong here. This wasn't where she was supposed to be. The goddess whispered at her to flow away, back to the temple.

Away from the beach, Mahina's feet grew unsteady, her steps became shambling again.

Where was her hut? Was it in the jungle, there? The paths were too clean here. Anyone could follow her. She needed to get away, hide in the shadows, into the bush and away from the clear trails. Mahina raced beyond the path, breaking free of the areas with people. She had to get away. No one could see her, no one could know she was there.

King Kawiti might come after Mahina again, curse her and her sisters. Or had that been her grandmother, or her great-grandmothers?

Mahina was no longer certain. Her brilliant thoughts dripped from her like new rain and old habits took over.

Being in the bush brought Mahina relief. She stripped off the stupid woven plaits tied to her feet, squishing her toes down into the cool mud. Snakes slid along the branches, hissing their songs to her. Flies danced around her head, buzzing like thoughts that were no longer there. The *sulluu* clung to her, flattening her breasts, binding them like she was some kind of man.

A clear stream interrupted Mahina's flight. She put one foot into the warm water, splashing the water all the way up her arm, to her fingers.

Suddenly, Mahina stopped.

The goddess had spoken to her, first, in the water.

Crouching down, Mahina thrust both her fists into the stream, pressing them down all the way, touching the stones at the bottom.

Her hands washed clean, the words came again.

Back to the temple. Back, back. Before it was all cleaned up.

Before it was too late.

With a bellowing rough cry, Mahina turned and raced back to the witches' temple.

Later, she would learn that her scream was the first in the night of madness.

THE SPOT WAS EASY TO FIND, NOW. EVERYONE HAD LEFT IT AS the moons had grown strong.

It wasn't the stench of blood, though it would have been easy to mistake for that.

No, it was the smell of power.

Mahina marched out of the jungle, across the white stone path that separated the buildings from the land, and past the refuse piles creeping with strangling vines that would leach out all that was useful from the riches the stupid witches piled there.

But Mahina couldn't stop there, collect the treasures others had thrown away.

There was a greater prize to be had.

Dark spots covered the ground just beyond the piles. They'd been painted in a pattern once, but not one that Mahina could read.

Not until Ty peeked up above the edge of the temple roof.

Finally, Mahina saw what had happened here.

A prince, a direct heir of King Kawiti, the king who had cursed her and her sisters and all her kind, had been killed here, his blood spilled across the ground.

The silly witches had used only a part of this bounty, to paint their pictures and see only a little ways into the future.

They had no idea how to use it to *change* the future, the course of all.

Mahina scooped up the large lake of blood, where it had pooled as the prince had lost his life. She gathered it into the skirt of her *sulluu*, like a woman collecting berries, picking up each crumbling bit. The sand and dirt didn't bother her, nor lessen the power of the blood.

Blood of a prince, spilled just hours before.

After gathering up as much as she could, Mahina hurried off. She knew where to go now.

Back to the foot of the mountain to cast her spell.

MAHINA TRAVELED ALONG THE JUNGLE PATHS, PACED BY THE snakes and the *poi* dogs. They kept her on the right trail, always moving east.

It wasn't the foot of *her* mountain that she stopped at, just the closest one. It, too, had a stream tumbling down the edge. But it was covered in moss and ferns, while hers had worn spires and flowers. Bamboo clinked hollowly around her as the breeze up high in the canopy made its way through the trees. The songbirds were silent— probably all stolen by the temple by now. Instead, the flies sounded loudly, like the wailing shells the priests blew to chase away the demons of the underworld.

Finally, Mahina stopped, her sides heaving. When had she last rested? Had she stopped at all during the night? It was just dawn, now.

Did it matter?

Mahina dropped to her knees, still holding up the edges of her skirt. The blood had caked the sand more solidly together, the grains taking on a dull and heavy hue. Slowly, Mahina removed the sand from her skirt, kneeling in the dirt at the foot of the mountain with the trees singing beside her and the water laughing with her, for once.

At first, Mahina prayed, silently asking the goddess for guidance. How could this blood scrub clean the curse that affected her and all her sisters?

She didn't understand at all, just that she needed to use the sand to scrub herself clean.

With a steady hand, Mahina reached out for a chunk of the bloodstained sand. With sure movements, she sat back, no longer kneeling, but sprawled on her back, easy and open like a child, as she scraped the soles of her feet with the sand, rubbing off the jungle mud and getting down to flesh.

As soon as the blood seeped into the soles of her feet, Mahina knew how the king had cursed her and her sisters.

They'd dared to use the power of the mountain, so he'd cursed them to *become* the mountain.

No wonder they all grew slower as they grew older! With every step they took, the dirt of the mountain seeped into their skin, slowing their thoughts and stealing their magic.

Tears in her eyes, Mahina scrubbed harder, using her nails to claw at the tough skin of her soles, pushing the blood into the pores.

She felt it drawing out the poison that had been placed there generations ago by the great king.

Mahina separated out a part of the bloodstained sand, then stood on it. She stripped off her *sulluu,* the cloth that had let her pass through the towns without too much comment, then she started to dance.

She danced for the moon Ty, who had shown her the way. She danced for the flies who had buzzed in her head when it stood empty of thoughts. She danced for the laughing water that reminded her of the goddess' true words. And she danced for the goddess, who had given her back her power.

By the time Mahina was finished, she'd pounded the sand away, until it was mixed in with the mud at the foot of the mountain. Then she stomped harder, pushing the sand further into the ground.

Let the mountain soak up its power. Let the stones help her bring down the descendants of King Kawiti.

Then Mahina gathered up what remained of the sand, slathering it over her skin like the oil from *mahiki* fish. She let it cake on, thick, to draw out the rest of the poisoned spell. She laughed when she looked down. The blood had soaked into her skin, while the sand had turned white.

She almost looked like one of the stupid northern witches.

With a second great, booming laugh, Mahina leaped up, grabbing hold of the first set of boulders above her head. She climbed, one foothold at a time, up and up. The jungle sang around her, the trees rustling high above, the cicadas cycling up and down, and the bees and the flies buzzing their merry tune.

It didn't take long to reach the first outcrop. There, she paused, looking out over the vast greenness of the jungle. To the right stood the village, its temples a bare blight, biting into the jungle. The ocean sparkled blue beyond that, and off in the distance, she could see Kualina Mountain, the source of all their power.

Hinanuli didn't really live inside the bottom of the mountain, thrown down there by the thunder god. She understood that now.

Hinanuli lived in all of them, her sisters and her alike.

She shook herself once, twice, like a great orca whale when it shoved itself out of the water, dancing above the waves. The sand flew from her, carried on magical winds and the power of the goddess, each grain flying across the jungle, across the ocean, to the three handfuls of islands and beyond, seeking her sisters. She continued to shake and dance, the sand flying from her, each grain charged and carried away.

Such a tiny thing, a grain of sand. An irritant, an ant to be crushed.

But one by one, by gathering those grains together, a beach could be built.

Or a mountain.

With one last great shake, she shed the last of the poison, along with the name that the people had known her, the name they'd given her, and truly became herself again.

Uli, the great witch of the south, stood laughing on the mountain.

CHAPTER 4

Only the blind grope in the dark.
—*Southern Islands proverb*

Ephanie walked with Mama across the cool morning sands. The ocean beyond the beach lay calm, its blues matching the sky. Only a teasing wind played with Ephanie's curls, as if it were sad, too, that she was leaving. The sun shone brightly, promising another warm day. It would be many months before the winter rains came. A large number of boats and canoes were moored in the bay and on the sand. Maybe the fish weren't biting that morning, and the fishermen had come back early.

Over her shoulder, Ephanie carried a small bag with a few essentials. She wore her pots of chalk tied to her side: she was never going anywhere without those again. Her black robes absorbed every bit of heat the sun beamed down, and Ephanie felt as if everyone stared at her.

At her scarred arm, that she kept firmly at her side.

Signal fires had spread the news of Prince Aumoe's death. The actual news of what happened would have to wait until Ephanie reached Hilani Island. King Makani had sent his fastest rowers to pick her up and bring her to him; she would get there early tomorrow morning. First, she would meet with Jahaka, the head priestess of the witches, then she would meet the king.

Ephanie knew she had to tell the truth. She was as clever with words and lies as she was with her hands, which was not at all. Her vision of what happened to her at the hands of the king didn't depend on lies.

As they neared the water, Ephanie spied a group of southern natives sitting to one side, under hastily constructed fabric shades, temple guards standing all around them.

"What happened?" Ephanie asked Mama.

"You remember that old proverb, that when Ty rose directly over Kualina Mountain, madness would follow?" Mama asked.

"Yes," Ephanie said. But no one knew what type of madness, or why it would cause madness in the first place. None of the fortunetellers had had any visions of dire consequences, so no one had known what to expect.

"I'm surprised the noise didn't wake you last night," Mama continued.

Ephanie shook her head. She always slept deeply after a vision, and nothing, not even her guilt, could have kept her awake the night before.

"The villagers gathered on the beach to watch Ty rise over Kualina," Mama continued. "At first, it was peaceful. They sang songs and chanted."

"But then?" Ephanie asked when Mama didn't continue.

"I don't know why the madness didn't affect us. But it didn't. However, fights broke out. Many fights. You remember Ipo? The old cook at the temple?"

Ephanie remembered the old woman. She'd been round and large, bigger than even Nawai, her mother's lover, though short, maybe coming up to Ephanie's chest. Ipo had talked with a slow, sure voice, like she'd swallowed the cooking smoke. Ephanie had been fascinated with her as a child, always going and begging for sweets and tidbits. As

Ephanie had grown older, though, she'd stopped visiting the old woman, tired of her stories and slow ways.

"Ipo nearly killed a man. She grabbed his face and twisted his neck. Our healers were barely able to save him. Then she stole a spear and fought off the guards, before she ran away and escaped into the jungle."

"Really?" Ephanie asked. Ipo had always moved at her own pace, slower than a dry creek. How could she have suddenly gotten so fast?

"That was the worst, though several women, as well as men, beat each other severely. They all say they're sorry this morning. We don't know whether to let them go or not," Mama confessed. "We really have no say. It's a matter for King Makani, but he doesn't have enough guards here to keep them."

"That's why there are so many boats on the beach this morning!" Ephanie said. She paused, then added, "I'd think that holding the fishermen away from the ocean would be the greatest punishment we could give them. They live to be on the water. We should let them go."

"Normally, I'd agree with you," Mama said. She sighed. "But some have this look in their eyes. It's like the madness still lurks. Others, no." She gestured toward the group of men sitting on the sand, all downcast. "Some of these tried to take women off to the jungle, use them against their will."

"I don't believe it," Ephanie said. She saw Kahanu and Eowi and other men she knew, good merchants and skilled craftsmen. They would never threaten anyone.

Mama shrugged. "We stopped them. Once we got the men and women separated they stopped fighting, though they still yelled at each other." She gave a dry chuckle. "I think we learned some names and words we'd never heard before."

"What are you going to do with them?" Ephanie asked, stopping at the edge of the water. Off across the blue, she could just make out the thin black line of a boat arrowing into shore. Her stomach dropped. She dreaded the crossing: not just because of the judgment that lay waiting for her, but because she often got seasick.

"Many of them claim not to remember the night, and seem

confused," Mama said. "We don't know what to do. According to our laws, if a man forces a woman, his life is forfeit."

"But you stopped them, right?" Ephanie asked.

Mama shook her head. "Not all."

Ephanie shivered in the warm sunshine. Very rarely did the witches enact their laws, and never over the laws of the king.

But this was one time when they wouldn't make an exception.

Healers gave life—and could take it away just as easily.

Ephanie turned back to look at the men. What would be their fate? Would the temple kill all of them for even attempting violence? Or would the excuse of the madness free them?

Then she looked further back, toward the temple. They were preparing the body of the prince there, to be taken out into deep waters and lowered, his soul prayed away to the four winds. His family would have their own wake after they learned all the circumstances of his death.

But no one else came from the temple to see Ephanie off. She would have thought at least her old teacher would stand by her. Ephanie swallowed down the bitterness at that.

Her life—that shining destiny she'd been sure she would have—had been set off course with a single cut of her blade.

At least her arm didn't hurt any longer. Just the memory of the pain, and the clarity it had brought, how alive she'd felt, curled at the back of her head like a snake waiting to strike.

"Don't worry about them," Mama said after Ephanie had looked back toward the temple possibly one too many times.

Ephanie sighed. It hurt that no one from her guild would support her.

"You weren't prepared, that's true," Mama said, blunt as always. "But I've always believed that everything happens for a reason. You were there, unprepared, because that was how the goddess meant for you to be."

Ephanie crossed her arms across her chest and looked out over the calm ocean waters. She'd had a choice, she knew that, from her vision. It could have gone a different way.

But the prince had blundered into her augury, forced her hand, forced *fate* down another path.

"I will take you back," Mama stated stiffly as the silence grew. "If the high priestess gives you a choice to return to your family, and if the king lets you live."

Ephanie looked at her, surprised. "Why?" she asked. She was a failure. No witch would ever trust her. And the king would…she couldn't think about what the future held for her.

Also, Ephanie was certain that Mama would have sent her away if she'd never developed any powers, if she'd remained a powerless girl. Why would Mama take her back now?

"Nawai has taught me to look beyond the cycles and patterns of the plants and seasons, and see what's in my heart," Mama said. Her tone was almost soft.

Mama still wasn't looking at Ephanie, though, but staring out at the calm waters and the ever-nearing boat.

"You're part of my family. It's important that we stick together. Remember that. We're always stronger together than apart," Mama said earnestly.

"I'll remember," Ephanie said, if for no other reason than she'd never expected Mama to say anything of the sort.

"In the oldest tales, witches worked together, blending their magic with one another," Mama added.

Ephanie shook her head. No one would work with her. Not as a failed fortuneteller.

"You might still have great things ahead of you," Mama said as they both watched the long, sleek black boat make a beeline for the shore. "Not everything happens in your dreams as you think."

"No," Ephanie said. "We pay the price of life so that the visions will come true." She knew that from her teachings and all the myths.

"You always have a choice," Mama said. "And I will give you another one. Come home, when you can."

Ephanie nodded, too choked up to reply. Mama wanted to see her again? She'd never known.

"Goodbye, daughter," Mama said after Ephanie silently handed her bag to the second rower while the first held the boat steady. They both wore just a simple cloth skirt around their waists, with vests beaded with bright red and orange beads done in swirling patterns. Yellow feathers hung from their short hair, showing that they were messengers from the king.

"Goodbye, Mama," Ephanie said. She pulled up her black robe easily and stepped into the water, then onto the boat. It rocked and she gulped, telling herself sternly that she wasn't going to get sick this time.

Ephanie watched the shore pull away as the rowers swiftly moved them along, faster than a seagull diving into the water. Mama stood there, alone, her blue-green robes marking her as foreign against the white sands.

Only when Mama had blended into the background did Ephanie turn forward. The boat shifted slightly from side to side as the rowers worked diligently, moving them across the water.

It was still too much motion, though.

Ephanie got seasick almost immediately.

THE NEWEST SET OF ROWERS HAD TAKEN PITY ON EPHANIE AND stopped at a little outcrop of coral. It wasn't much of an island, just scrub grasses and spiny bushes bravely clinging to the rock pushed up along the center ridge. With the right wind, Ephanie could have thrown a stone from the tiny beach where they'd come in and had it land in the water on the other side.

Waves rolled softly against the jumbled rocks and the wind wasn't too strong. Ephanie scrambled up and over, breathing deeply and trying to settle her stomach. The rowers had even given her more water so she could wash out the bitter bile taste still in her mouth.

Because there wasn't a village on this island, the rowers had let Ephanie walk alone, stretching her legs. She knew she wasn't supposed to, but moving felt so good, so she kept going once she reached the end of the island, walking across the point then back along the other side.

There was more of a beach here: stronger winds as well. Stringy brown grass stubbornly marched against the sand, trying to get a foothold. Seagulls whirled above her head, bobbing in the steady breeze. The waves crashed just ahead, past the peaceful point.

The land dipped down here. Ephanie was surprised to see that what she'd thought of as a small ridge on the other side was in fact the back of a cliff.

Ephanie paused, taking a deep breath of the fresh sea air. The steady wind on this side of the island felt good, cool, against her throbbing head. Her stomach was almost settled. If only she didn't have to get in that damned boat again.

After two more breaths, she turned to go back. The rowers had been kind to stop for her—she didn't want them to regret their decision and not stop again the next time she asked for a break.

Wait—was that a moan? Over the sound of the wind?

Ephanie turned back around, scanning the beach. It was hard to tell, sometimes, since the birds often mimicked the cries of children.

But no, there, something moved. A large dark boulder…except it had arms and a head.

Ephanie hurried across the sand, her sandals not giving her enough purchase in the loose ground. She called to the rowers, hoping the wind would carry her words, "Hey! Over here! There's someone here!"

It was a woman, a southern native, big like Ipo. She rolled in the sand, moaning, the white grains covering her dark skin. She didn't wear any clothes, and her large breasts hung down to her waist while black hair curled over her sex.

"Are you all right?" Ephanie asked as she came up.

The woman didn't reply. She stood up and looked around, blind— her eyes had rolled back into her head, and just the whites showed. Her large hands moved restlessly over her body, rubbing the sand into her skin. Wild black hair hung down to her waist. Streams of green seaweed hung from the ends, along with shells and flowers.

Ephanie took a step back when the woman started to laugh.

The woman threw her hands up to the sky while her entire body undulated with sheer joy. Then she started to dance, the sand flaking off.

Was it darker when it touched the ground? What had the woman been rubbing off?

But Ephanie knew the woman was lighter now. She skipped merrily on her feet, singing a low song that Ephanie didn't recognize.

Before the woman finished, the two rowers appeared next to Ephanie.

"We go. Now," the first one instructed.

"But she may need our help," Ephanie protested, though she knew the woman didn't.

"No. We must go. Now," the second one said, wrapping his hands around Ephanie's upper arm and pulling her back. Despite his short size, his hands were like iron, unrelenting.

The woman finally looked up. Her eyes had returned to normal, though they were darker than most of the southern natives Ephanie knew. She glared at the men and in the native tongue ordered them, "Let her go!"

The rowers ran, dragging Ephanie between them.

With a loud growl, the woman raised a hand, then made a slapping motion with it.

A large wave leaped from the ocean and soaked them all to the waist.

Was it also tugging on their feet as it fell back?

The rowers cut across the point of the island, pulling Ephanie and racing toward their boats. Ephanie could feel the power of the woman behind them, crackling with anger.

Another wave came out of nowhere, threatening to swamp the boat. "Get in! Get in!" the rowers urged.

Ephanie didn't want to get in the damn boat again.

However, she wasn't sure if it wasn't better to do that, then to be abandoned here on a hunk of rock with a strange southern witch who had powers none of the northern witches had ever heard of.

One of the rowers scooped Ephanie up and threw her into the boat before she could make a decision.

The waves suddenly calmed and the rowers paddled with all their might.

Words carried on the wind blew into Ephanie's ear. She knew she was the only one who heard them.

We will come and find you, the woman promised.

Ephanie had no doubt that the woman meant what she said, that she'd track Ephanie across the waves using power Ephanie didn't understand

And that chilled Ephanie more than the wind on her soaked robes.

HILANI—THE LARGEST ISLAND OF THE THREE HANDS FULL— didn't look like much as they approached from the east. Ephanie had expected the witches' temple, or maybe even the king's palace, to be visible from the ocean. All she saw were the big palm trees, marching all the way down to the shore. There wasn't even a bay where boats could moor. She tried to swallow down her disappointment as her anxiety built.

Maybe only parts of the island were inhabited. That would make sense, actually, as most islands were only partially populated, with both the natives and the witches sticking to the edges of the land and a few calm bays.

It wasn't until they drew much closer that Ephanie could see a road cut through the trees, curving along the side of the hill. Then a bay opened up to the left. Ephanie caught glimpses of the palace—yellow stone rising out of the green trees, its back still buried in the rock— before the edge of the hill cut off the view.

Ephanie thought it made sense for the palace not to be directly accessible from the water—that would keep it safer during times of war.

Before the northern witches had arrived at the islands, the southerners had constantly fought, each island proclaiming its own king. However, since the time of the witches, the Three Hands Full had been united.

Would that last, given her vision? Ephanie had only seen the attack, not the battle's ending. Or was the vision a warning, so that King Makani could rally and bring his people together again?

Finally, they passed another sheltering arm of rough boulders and cut to the left, darting into a protected cove. It was much larger than the bay on her home island, at least three times the size. Not only that, it had three huge, wooden piers built out into the water, for larger boats to tie up to.

It took Ephanie a moment to realize she recognized them from her vision. They'd all been burning, though.

A colorful group stood at the end of the closest peer. Ephanie finally realized that it was a large group of witches, with every discipline represented.

Was Jahaka there? Would Ephanie have to give her confession in public?

At least Ephanie knew she wouldn't be put to death immediately. Her visions had assured her of that.

But what was to come…wasn't much better, at least not as far as she could see. It was only a few more hours' time, though, that she'd seen. After that she didn't know how long her life extended, though she had a feeling the worst was still to come.

She knew the bindings of the king were going to hurt, and they were coming soon.

The rowers took the boat straight to beach, ignoring the group gathered at the far end of the pier.

Ephanie almost laughed as the witches hurried down the pier to meet the boat on the sands. They didn't understand the type of boat the king had sent her, that it wouldn't be able to dock where they'd been standing. The pier was only for the longer merchant ships, which had two hulls and would go from island to island for weeks at a time, never docking but with smaller island canoes paddling out to trade.

Given the powerful woman Ephanie had met on the tiny island, how much did the witches understand the southern natives at all?

The rowers pulled the boat far up the sand, letting Ephanie step out gracefully. They held her bag and looked resigned as the group of witches surged forward.

Ephanie turned to the rowers. "Tell the king my vision dictated that I tell the head of my temple first, before I talk with him. But I cannot live and not tell him. I will be there as soon as I can, or die trying."

The rowers nodded mutely, the yellow feathers tied to their hair blowing strangely. They both had a far-off look in their dark eyes. Their beaded vests were sweat-stained from the effort they'd put in rowing her to the island.

Did they have a type of magic, too? Men with power? Ephanie shivered. Had the witches missed everything? And would anyone believe her if she told them?

Now that Ephanie thought about it, she realized that every island where they changed rowers, the men had been ready for them before they'd arrived. As if they'd known they were coming.

Maybe it was just because the islanders knew how long every ocean crossing took. That must have been it.

But still…

The temple guards arrived on the beach before the rest of the witches. Two of them took hold of Ephanie's arms. They wore brass and stone breastplates, with a red streak painted down the center of each—the red of the healers. All the guards trained with healers present, primarily to accidental prevent deaths.

However, healers were also trained to take life, like the guard.

The rest of the witches soon joined them, swelling around Ephanie like a colorful sail, all at least a head taller than the tallest guard. The fishermen on the beach stayed next to their boats, fixing nets or untangling lines, but they watched from the corners of their eyes, never staring directly. Ephanie still felt as though everyone looked at her.

Just beyond the beach, exiting the trees, a row of the king's guards marched. They wore similar armor to the temple guards, though their breastplates were marked with yellow, and they kept a strict order, walking with a precision Ephanie knew the temple guards couldn't match.

The temple guards let go of Ephanie and joined their fellows, out in front of the witches.

The two groups of guards would clash in just a few more feet.

Would the temple guards and the king's guards fight over Ephanie?

She couldn't allow that, couldn't let another life be taken for her mistake.

How could she stop them? She'd assured the rowers that she would see the king, or die trying. She'd meant that. If she couldn't fulfill that part of her vision, she'd be driven insane by the goddess. She *had* to tell the king.

She also had to tell him second.

The king's guards spread out, locking their spears and shields together, blocking the path of the witches and their guards.

"We need to take the prisoner to the king," the guard in the center called out as they approached.

"She reports to her order first. Then to the king," an older witch called out. She wore the bright orange of the high court, her importance no longer tied up in just her profession.

"We must take her to the king," the guard said stubbornly.

"I must report to the high priestess first," Ephanie called out before anyone else could say anything. "I must. Then I will go to the king. And again, I must see him, too."

"No. It was his son you killed." The guard's dark eyes bore into Ephanie's, blazing with anger. "You must talk with him first."

"I can't," Ephanie said, trying to explain. "The vision—"

"It doesn't matter," the priestess said. "She is a witch, one of ours. She talks with Jahaka the high priestess first."

No! Ephanie wanted to call out. It wasn't because she was a witch. Brikalla had shown her the order she needed to carry out the fortunetelling in, whom she must talk with first.

"We will take her. Now," the king's guard said.

"You will not," the priestess replied.

The king's guard started a deep chant that rumbled Ephanie's bones. Though she'd never heard it before, she knew it was a war chant—calling on Kuu, the god of war—to see them to victory.

Ephanie didn't want this fight—they didn't need to battle at all. "Wait! Wait!" she called. "Please, just come with us, to the temple. I will walk with you easily. After I tell Jahaka, I will go straight to the king. Please, no more madness."

The king's guards continued their rolling chant. The temple guards braced themselves, forming two lines.

"Stop! Stop!" Ephanie called. No one was holding her. Without hesitation, she pulled her knife from her belt and slipped between the lines, going toward the guards.

The older witch reached out to stop Ephanie. Without pausing, Ephanie slapped away her hand with the back of her knife.

Standing directly behind the line of temple guards, Ephanie spoke to the head of the king's guard. "I promise I will go with you. Please, just let me tell the head of my order first."

The head guard raised his hand. The rumbling change died down. "You don't go anywhere," he said, pointing his spear at Ephanie. "The head of your order needs to come here, to the beach, to speak to you. Then you come with us, to the king."

Ephanie nodded. "Yes." Finally, there was a solution! She turned to the older witch. "Can someone fetch Jahaka? So that we don't have any more bloodshed?"

The old witch glared at Ephanie. "Your high priestess should command you. Not some rabble guard."

"I'm not commanded by anyone but the goddess Brikalla," Ephanie told her, the stiffness she'd learned from her teacher lending her spine some bone. "I need to tell Jahaka of my vision, then King Makani. But I don't want anyone else killed. No more life should be taken for this vision. I'll turn this knife on myself first."

The older witch sneered at Ephanie. "Couldn't control yourself, could you? Now you have the taste of pain in your bones." Without turning away from Ephanie, she called out over her shoulder, "Yarrow, bring Jahaka here, with my apologies."

Ephanie trembled inside. How had the old witch known? But yes, that was exactly what it felt like. She knew that for every vision, for the rest of her life, she'd always be tempted to turn the knife on herself.

No wonder no one trusted a fortuneteller with scars.

EPHANIE KNEW JAHAKA WAS OLDER THAN MAMA, THOUGH SHE

looked the same age as Ephanie, perhaps just a few years older. She was tall, like most of the witches, with pale skin and very fine, delicate features, her dark hair pulled back tightly into a bun. She wore the yellow-orange robes of the high court, not the red of her healer's robes. Her blue eyes reflected the sky above.

Both the temple and the king's guard stood stiffly at attention as Jahaka approached. She walked easily between them, dipping her head and giving them a woman's smile before turning her attention to Ephanie.

All the coldness of winter winds focused on Ephanie. Her mouth grew dry and her heart pounded in her chest.

But Ephanie was of the fortunetellers. She was here because the goddess Brikalla had chosen her to bring forth this augury. Ephanie shifted her weight, spreading her feet slightly wider so she felt more grounded, even here on the shifting sands.

Suddenly, the day darkened, as though a cloud had covered over the sun. Ephanie knew not to look up—no one else saw it but her.

"Jahaka," Ephanie called out, her voice grown as deep as the chant that had come from the king's guards.

All those around Ephanie drew back. They recognized the voice of the goddess even if they'd never heard it before.

"Ships are coming from the west, to attack this island. They come on the last day of the feast of *Keereekayah*, nine days from now. They bring armies of men to swarm the land, fire to burn the piers and the boats. Many will die. You must prepare as only you know how for this."

Ephanie swayed, the augury released into the world, her body her own again.

"Thank you, fortuneteller," Jahaka said with a simple bow of her head. "Do you know how many ships?"

Ephanie tried to bring the vision back and count. "Dozens and dozens," she said. "The bay was full of them. Plus canoes and smaller boats. All carrying men. With weapons. And sticks that they light, to blow apart things." Ephanie had never seen such things before. She hoped that Jahaka and the guards already knew about such things.

The guards around Ephanie shifted. Were they starting to plan?

Were they already counting the deaths ahead? Or did they only think about victory, one that Ephanie hadn't foreseen?

"You have told no one else of your vision?" Jahaka asked.

Ephanie shook her head. "You are the first." It was custom for a fortuneteller to only inform those involved in the augury their fate. Many fortunes bound the tongue of the teller, so that she could only tell those whose fate was involved.

"We heard that a prince died for this prophesy," Jahaka asked.

"Yes," Ephanie dropped her head in shame. "He tried to stop me, from…fueling the prophesy." She didn't want to speak her shame out loud. "His life wasn't required," she added truthfully. "His death was a mistake." One the goddess would make sure Ephanie paid for.

"Good, good," Jahaka said. "Yes, that's good."

Ephanie didn't understand why the head priestess said that. Ephanie had been unprepared—she'd failed her teachers, as well as all the other witches.

But it didn't matter. She was now on the same island as the other person who the augury regarded. "Now I must tell the king." Her voice held deep undertones, the prophesy still guiding her.

"You must?" Jahaka asked. "Was he part of your augury quest?"

"Yes," Ephanie said. Finally, someone who understood what she was going through! How she had to get to the king, soon, or risk more madness.

"I know you must speak to him," Jahaka said. She paused, looking sharply at Ephanie.

Ephanie didn't shift her weight from one foot to the other like a mere apprentice, though Jahaka's gaze made her feel that way.

With a single nod, Jahaka seemed to come to a decision. "After you see the king, and face his punishment, you may return to the temple."

"Thank you," Ephanie said, though the words tasted bitter. On the one hand, she was glad that even though she was a failed fortuneteller, at least Jahaka would speak to her.

On the other hand, Jahaka wasn't about to stop the king from whatever punishment he deemed necessary. Even if that meant Ephanie's death.

No one would stand by her. So much for her grand destiny.

With a sigh, Ephanie turned from Jahaka and toward the king's guard. The temple guards let her slip through their ranks. She slid her knife in her belt, then walked up to the head of the king's guard. "Take me to King Makani," she said.

The king's guards grabbed her. Ephanie cried out as they tied her hands.

The bindings hurt very much, indeed.

CHAPTER 5

You can't make bread from grain alone.
—*Northern proverb*

JAHAKA IMPATIENTLY PACED THROUGH HER ROOM. REMNANTS OF her sacrifice still burned on the altar in the corner, the smoke sweetening her vision. The bed in the corner lay unmade still from the morning; Jahaka wouldn't allow another into her room, not since the girl had been taken. Instead, she'd fasted and prayed, leaving the running of the council to her advisors for the rest of the day.

Jahaka had needed the time to think, to put together plans and more plans.

Finally, she had a sign from the gods.

The fortuneteller—what was her name? Ephanie—had confirmed Jahaka's intuition, the one she'd gotten at her mother's funeral.

All the royals must die. Jahaka would see to it.

Certainly, Ephanie had said that the prince's life hadn't been required. But she was young. Maybe it hadn't been, but maybe it had been. She was still learning her craft.

It would be easy enough to spread the rumors that perhaps the prince's life had been required. After all, the girl had been unprepared, and had tried to fuel her vision with her own blood. She was obviously unreliable.

But if Jahaka claimed that her mother had had a similar vision, with many deaths among the royalty....

Maybe Jahaka shouldn't have given up Ephanie so easily. King Makani would have to punish her to maintain face. But Ephanie was a witch. The king shouldn't be allowed to kill her. Jahaka could see her mistake now, in letting the girl go off to the king's palace without insisting that the temple guard accompany her.

Jahaka needed to question Ephanie in private, to see if she had any more details about the attack. As far as Jahaka knew, Enekai didn't have that many ships to attack Hilani Island with. Was there a second force that he'd been able to harness? Some agreement he hadn't told her about?

Even with such a warning, King Makani wouldn't be able to overcome the attack. His alliances were weak, weaker than he knew. From her window, whenever she'd glanced up, she'd seen the king's messenger boats darting off. They'd return with bad news: few of the other islands would promise men: fewer still would deliver them.

And was the purpose of the vision? To warn the king, so he could prepare? Or to let him know that his days as ruler were numbered?

Ephanie hadn't seen the warriors coming in on the other side of the island as well. She'd only seen the main attack, from the north. Not the second, from the south.

And the girl had said only that many people would die. Not many witches. Which meant that Enekai had kept his word and instructed his warriors to kill only the guards, not the healers working with them. Because surely if many witches were to die, the goddess would have stated that.

Jahaka was going to have to rescue Ephanie. The king couldn't be allowed to keep her, or to kill her. That was Jahaka's first step in her plan. She made herself stop pacing and forced herself to look out the window over the bay. Long clouds gathered across the sky, purple and dark, hiding the moons and the stars.

Would there be more madness that night? Jahaka couldn't count the number of fights put down by both her guard and what had remained of the king's guard. The pens behind the king's palace overflowed with victims of the madness, and the witches' courtyard was also getting full.

Tomorrow, Jahaka would sit in judgment over the southern men who had forced women to their will that night. How should she judge them? They'd been taken by a madness. Some of them had already taken their own lives, ashamed of what had overcome them.

Others, though, appeared to be ready to do it again.

Jahaka also didn't know what to do with the southern women, particularly the ones who had attacked and beaten the men. Her healers had saved all of the men, but it had been close. Many of the men would bear scars for the rest of their lives.

And what were these women now? Power ebbed and flowed around them. They weren't witches, but they were…something. They didn't seem to know what to do with their power, either.

When the witches had arrived in the southern islands two centuries before, they'd never found any native witches, though the people had seemed familiar with magic.

What had caused their magic to disappear? And would it go away again? Were the women here only powerful for a short while?

Jahaka had more questions than answers at this point.

But finally, she had a plan. Or at least the first steps. She must steal Ephanie back.

As Jahaka suspected, two acolytes—older girls who hadn't come into their powers yet—stood waiting outside her door. Yarrow would know better than to place temple guards, would understand that Jahaka wouldn't have wanted to be distracted.

Luckily, Jahaka already knew one of them. Did Yarrow know of the secret vows and training Jahaka had with some of the acolytes? Or had the girl volunteered?

"You," Jahaka said, pointing to the unfamiliar girl. "Run to Yarrow. Tell her to gather up as much of the council as she can and for them to meet me in the judgment room. Quickly!"

The girl ran off gracelessly.

"And you," Jahaka said, turning to the girl she knew. "Go and fetch me some water."

Jahaka stood in the hallway, watching as the girl scurried away to the end where a large pitcher sat, carefully lifting it and carrying it back, using both hands.

"Good," Jahaka said, drawing the girl into her rooms. "I'll help you pour it, here," she said out loud.

Anyone listening—and surely, Yarrow, if not the guard, had hidden ears near her rooms—would only hear that.

As the girl splashed the water from the pitcher into Jahaka's washing bowl, Jahaka whispered urgently in her ear. "After you're finished here, go to the market, to the wide well on the north side. You know what I'm talking about?"

"Yes—" the girl started.

"Hush," Jahaka said as she fiercely twisted the girl's ear, getting her to stop talking out loud. "Drop this shell into the well," Jahaka said, slipping the shell into the girl's palm. "And call out for Aleekona. Can you do this? Without telling a soul?"

The girl opened her mouth, then shut it again and merely nodded.

"Good," Jahaka said. This girl may be showing promise. So many of the ones she'd tried training were useless. "When you get back, tomorrow, I'll have other errands for you."

Yarrow may be paying the girl to spy as well, but maybe not. It didn't matter—the name would mean nothing to the older priestess.

And the plan would have already been put in motion by the time she did figure it out.

Jahaka took her time sluicing water over her arms and neck, time Aleekona would need to set a guard in place.

Then all Jahaka had to do was speak carefully, and be heard.

"The king is holding one of ours," Jahaka announced as she walked into the judgment room. The other priestesses of the council were already waiting there, as instructed. They all wore their council robes, vibrant orangish-yellow that wasn't quite the same yellow as royalty, but it was close.

The western wall had been put up for the night, but the windows had been left open and the ocean wind swirled through the room.

Anyone crouched below the openings would also hear every word spoken by the council, something Jahaka was counting on.

Oil lamps sat every foot or so on a shelf on the inner wall, dancing in the breeze. However, they cast enough light that Jahaka could see everyone's face clearly.

The council women stirred together, following their own currents before settling as Jahaka marched to the front of the room and sat in the judgment chair. From there, she could see the patterns and groupings the women formed. Interesting. She hadn't expected Vine, the single, token fortuneteller, to side with the growers. She'd expected her to either stand apart, or with the healers, the other takers of life.

The representative from the merchants of course stood with the fishermen. The healers stood alone, something else Jahaka hadn't expected.

But in the end, all that mattered was whether she could bend them to her will.

"The king is holding the fortuneteller, Ephanie, the one who told me the prophesy of the boats coming from the west," Jahaka explained.

Vine, the sole fortuneteller, stepped forward. "She killed his son. The prophesy didn't demand his life."

"So we're just going to let the king take hers?" Jahaka asked earnestly. She had to let the unseen listener know that she needed Ephanie saved.

The witches murmured uneasily. The balance of power between the witches and the king was always a delicate issue.

"We are holding some of his men," Yarrow said, stepping forward. "The ones from the night of madness."

"True," Jahaka said. "They hurt more than one of ours, though."

"They were insane," Yarrow pointed out. "Not themselves."

"And what will happen the next time madness strikes them? Do we just forgive them again?" Jahaka challenged her. No man should be able to force his will on a woman. It wasn't to be allowed.

Because if a man could do that to a woman, what would the guards believe they might be able to do to the witches? Would the king try to take more power from them?

All of the women in the council understood the implications.

"What would you have us do? Set up an exchange?" Vine asked. "She's a young fortuneteller. Inexperienced. And unprepared."

That sent a chill through the assembled group. Jahaka had seen the scars as well. The girl had cut herself to power her vision. She'd do it again, possibly taking her own life in the throes of prophesy.

"Which means she needs our help, our guidance, even more," Jahaka pointed out. "She needs more training," she added, stroking Vine's ego. "We need to rescue her."

Yarrow turned and looked sharply at Jahaka, while Vine merely shook her head. "There are other girls," Vine said, "who are more powerful. We could lose this one."

"There aren't as many girls in this generation as last," Jahaka said. "More and more girls are being born powerless."

The group of women grew very still.

Everyone knew about the problems they faced. No one had ever talked out loud about them.

"It is time we spoke the truth," Jahaka said earnestly. "Our race is fading." She wasn't saying anything she hadn't already bitterly complained about to Aleekona at least once, so nothing she was saying would be new or inappropriate for a hidden listener. "Too many are being born without power. At least one in ten, now. Our blood is also…*mixing*." She counted the number who responded with disgust —easily two-thirds. Good. She could persuade the others easily enough.

Or replace them, before she revealed her final plans about moving the witches back to the mainland, carving out their own territory. Becoming pure again.

"We need to stop these things," Jahaka said firmly. "And I have a plan." Again she paused, taking the temperature of her council. About the same two-thirds seemed curious.

It wouldn't be too difficult to bring them along.

"However, tonight, we must save one of our own," Jahaka continued. "We need to rescue Ephanie. We cannot appear powerless, particularly now. It was bad enough that the king's guards forced me to go to the beach to meet the girl."

That drew a murmuring assent from everyone in the room. All of the council agreed. They had all felt the sting of that.

Jahaka would have to remember that. Pride would draw these women along faster than anything else.

"Therefore, because the king wouldn't expect it, I shall go to call on him. Tonight," Jahaka announced, standing. The unseen listener would report that, and Jahaka knew they'd accompany the party, still hidden and out of sight.

"My lady, do you think that's wise?" Oak, the head of the growers, asked. "The last few nights have brought madness to more than one of the southern people. Plus, the king may be in grief over his son and unable to be reasoned with."

"I don't want that girl waiting in their prison pens with the people who were put in there because of the madness," Jahaka pointed out, telling Aleekona where she thought the girl might be held.

It was a real fear of hers, that the girl would be placed with the men and women who had been driven mad by the moon, and would get hurt.

That would require a level of retribution that Jahaka wasn't ready to deliver. Not yet.

"I shall go anyway," Jahaka said. "None can hurt me." It wasn't quite true, but true enough: she did have fantastic control over her own body, better than most healers, who were more outwardly focused.

Vine took a step forward. "And I shall go with you. She is of my profession. Someone who knows what she's going through should be with her."

That almost sounded…motherly. Jahaka glanced over at Vine, but she still wore a stone cold expression.

Maybe she just wanted to teach the girl to better control her powers. The goddess knew she could use it.

∾

Jahaka arranged for only four of the temple guards to accompany them. When Yarrow had asked about taking more, Vine had answered her, "Do you think this blade on my belt is only for show?"

Jahaka took another look at the old fortuneteller. She had more backbone than Jahaka had expected. Interesting. Maybe Jahaka did need to make a change in her council. Vine wasn't officially part of the council: fortunetellers were still not allowed. Only members of the council could become high priestess, and no one was prepared for a woman whose powers came from death to be placed in such a high position.

But maybe Jahaka could make the relationship with Vine more formal, an "official" as opposed to unofficial liaison with the council.

Except that after taking one last look at that cold face, Jahaka knew that she never would. Vine would never bend to her will.

The six of them walked through the quiet village square toward the palace road. The usual night market had been shut down early by the guards, afraid of more violence, both from the passing of Ty overhead as well as rumors of the coming battle.

Woven grass huts hung cloth over the doorways, indicating they didn't want visitors: Most weren't rich enough to afford proper doors. Though Jahaka also recalled that some didn't like doors? Some sort of tradition about welcoming guests?

It was a shame, though. It was supposed to be the celebration of *Keereekayah*. The streets should have been full of visitors, bearing presents and good luck as they called on their neighbors and relatives.

Quiet chants carried on the soft winds, melodious and fluid. The rich scent of spicy fish stew, a traditional dish, floated by as well. Jahaka hoped that people were at least celebrating on their own.

The small village almost seemed peaceful, if not for the guards placed every fifty yards or so, watchful and waiting.

As they neared the palace road, the path narrowed, pushed closer by the numerous palms and beech trees, until they could only march two abreast. On the side of the road, guards had already started piling logs: before the battle, the road would be completely blocked.

A *huo* bird called out into the quiet night, and its mate responded just a little up the path.

The two guards in front of Jahaka stopped.

"What is—" Jahaka asked, purposefully loudly.

"Shhh," the main guard said, raising his hand.

"It's just the *huo* bird," Jahaka pointed out. "Calling its mate at the palace."

"It might have been a signal call," the man replied, holding himself stiff, listening hard.

Jahaka was impressed. She hadn't realized any in the temple guard would be that professional and cautious. "I commend you for your wariness," she said after nothing out of the ordinary happened. All they heard was the distant surf, the wind rattling the leaves, and the shuffle of feet from the other guards. "But none of the madmen we've captured in the pens would be so organized as to attack us here." The place the road narrowed was the logical place for any attack.

The guard grunted and nodded, then started walking again.

Jahaka was going to have to warn Aleekona to be more careful about his signals to her in the future.

EVERYTHING WAS GOING ACCORDING TO PLAN.

After they'd passed through the palace gates, Jahaka had heard a *huo* bird call again for its mate, letting her know that Aleekona had also made it there.

If Ephanie was in the pens, Aleekona and his men would get her, whether the king acquiesced or not. It was a calculated risk; the girl might not be in the pens. But Jahaka was betting that the king wouldn't torture her, would think she was too highly placed among the witches, wouldn't understand the significance of the scars along her arm.

King Makani needed to realize just how isolated he was. His

despair would influence his generals and his troops in ways he couldn't combat.

The waiting room Jahaka, Vine, and the four guards were taken to was nearly as grand as the throne room: two stories tall, with windows that ran from the ceiling to the floor. Colorful murals covered the stone and wooden walls, showing the southerner's stories of the gods, the birth of the sun by the grand eagle, how the shark god clove the world in two, creating earth and water, as well as the rising of the mountains and why there are so many different types of fish and beast.

The witches had never bothered trying to convert the southern people, just as they'd never questioned the gods of the witches. They shared a few, like the gods of hospitality and the underworld. However, their birthdates were different, as well as their celebrations.

It was another thing Jahaka had seen happening: the blending of the gods. Soon, they wouldn't have two separate, distinct lines. And as the high priestess of the witches, she couldn't stand to see that pollution occur, either.

The door opened at the front of the room, cleverly hidden by the painting there. A crier strode in, wearing long brown pantaloons with a white vest, with a yellow sash across his partially bare chest. He strode to the center of the room and announced in a deep voice that belied his thin stature: "King Makani and his trusted counselor."

The king walked in the door, smiling. He wore the standard long skirt of the southern islanders, with a black and white geometric pattern on it. His chest was bare, although he wore a yellow vest and necklace of white flowers. He still wore his crown, made of twisted gold wire with large black, red, and pink pearls set in it. The king was about the same age as Jahaka, and showed it only on the slight graying at his temples and the many laugh lines around his eyes. He was tall for a southerner, coming up just past Jahaka's shoulder, but also nearly as broad as the door he came through.

"Jahaka!" the king called as soon in his booming voice as soon as he saw her. He strode forward, holding out his hands to her. They clasped forearms, as was the tradition among warriors of his people.

"King Makani," Jahaka replied. "Thank you for seeing me so late tonight."

"Of course," the king said expansively. "Only together can we make our way through these troubled waters."

Jahaka bit her tongue and merely smiled. The king was always using old proverbs to make his point. He was more traditional than she was, hidebound without ever looking for better opportunities.

"May I introduce one of our sisters: Vine, teller of prophesies," Jahaka said, giving the traditional title, something that the king would understand.

"It is my honor to meet another of your *teeka*," the king said, bowing his head to Vine.

"The honor is mine, great king," Vine responded.

"And you've met my councilor Oka'u," the king said, turning.

Oka'u was the color of burnt wood, much darker than most of the southern natives. He was thin as a reed and very short, maybe coming up to Jahaka's chest. He kept his head shaved and it glistened like an oiled nut. His face was perfectly round, with clear brown eyes and white teeth in a mouth that rarely smiled.

"Always a pleasure," Jahaka murmured, though a little annoyed. Oka'u was a shark, with a strong bite and a warrior mindset. Normally the king kept the little man at arm's length.

Maybe the madness had disturbed him as well.

"May we offer you any refreshment? Plum wine? *Ikilaki*, made from the palms?" the king asked.

Inwardly, Jahaka sighed. The formality of offering and refusing was necessary, and often, she quite enjoyed the word games. Tonight, though, she was impatient.

"No thank you, none for me," Jahaka said.

After the same offer had been made to Vine as well as Oka'u, the king finally asked Jahaka, "How may I help you this evening? It's late, so I assume your deed must be urgent and some of the demands of courtesy should be set aside."

"Thank you for your clear vision," Jahaka said truthfully. Because after asking about refreshments, tradition demanded they inquire about close relatives, how the fishing went, as well as their various interests like the beehives the king and his family kept, or the songbirds the temple bred, before they could talk about business.

"First, again, accept our deepest sympathies for your family and your son," Jahaka said. It had been a few days since the boy had died, and the temple had already sent their condolences, participated in some of the declared grieving.

"The loss of one so young is always difficult to bear," King Makani said with a huge sigh.

How much of his grief was real? How much was a show for Jahaka? She doubted she'd ever know.

"It is, truly, especially when coupled with a disturbing prophesy," Jahaka said.

"Visions like that have never been granted to my people," the king said. "But I trust this girl. How she spoke—how she looked as she revealed the vision from her goddess—truly she'd been touched."

"Yes," Vine said, stepping forward. "The words came directly from the goddess Brikalla. The images as well, drawn out with living chalk, blood, or life. A foretelling is never complete until the ones who the fortune affects are informed. In the order the goddess decrees."

The king and Oka'u glanced at each other. "We understand that she was unprepared for this vision," Oka'u said.

"She's young," Vine said. "Inexperienced. She needs more training."

Jahaka nodded. "Again, we are sorry that her inexperience caused your family any pain. However, why did Prince Aumoe try to stop her?" While it was true the girl had been unprepared, nothing would have happened except her to bear the scars of her mistake if the boy hadn't interfered.

"It's one thing to be told to stand by while someone desecrates their body," the king said. "It's quite another to actually do it. Aumoe had a good heart. He was trying to help."

"He shouldn't have interfered," Vine said coldly. "The girl isn't to be held responsible for her actions."

The king nodded thoughtfully. "So would you say she was mad while receiving her vision? No longer sane? Like the men on the night of madness, who attacked the women?"

Jahaka sighed inwardly. So the king was looking for an exchange.

But they couldn't release the men. Too many had a clever look now, lurking around the edges, as if they were planning on doing it again.

"She wasn't mad, no," Vine replied. "She was divinely inspired."

And that was the difference, wasn't it? Just the moons causing madness, versus a goddess pouring her visions into a willing vessel.

"But some say the madness was caused by Hinanuli," Oka'u said. "She who lives under Kualina Mountain. The moon carried her words and madness with it."

Vine blinked and looked at Jahaka. "A goddess who was thrown down, into her mountain, burned by the fires there, until her skin turned to black obsidian and her hair to ashes. It's said she only comes out at night, whispering to women in their dreams, turning them mad."

"Or giving them great power," the king added.

"Or both," Oka'u said.

"So the madness was inspired by one of your goddesses?" Jahaka said.

The king merely shrugged. "It could easily be laid at her feet. So the men weren't responsible for their actions. Just as your fortuneteller wasn't."

"And the women? Who nearly beat the men to death? What will you be doing with them?" Jahaka asked. The temple guards had only held onto the men, but had allowed the women to go. The witches had very few rules when it came to that sort of violence, as it normally only occurred in times of war.

"They will be treated appropriately," the king said dismissively.

Jahaka wasn't certain what that meant, if they'd be punished or released.

"Will the madness continue?" Jahaka asked.

"No one knows," the king confessed. "We assume it will pass, as it has in the past. But how long will it stay? Our legends only predict the madness. Not if it lasts for nights or years."

"It is the first time the red moon has passed over Kualina in generations," Oka'u said. "Since before the coming of your people to the islands."

"It's been that long?" Jahaka asked. No wonder no one knew how to prepare for it.

"And it will be that long before it happens again," King Makani assured her. "But for now…"

"Now, we'd like to retrieve our sister," Jahaka told him bluntly. "She's inexperienced, untrained. She needs guidance. She can't get that from your people."

"She killed a prince," Oka'u said. "The penalty is torture and death."

"The prince has already paid the price for interfering with a prophesy," Jahaka replied. "If she hadn't killed him, we would have put the same penalty on him."

"He was just trying to stop her from hurting herself—" Oka'u said.

"He interfered with the word of the goddess," Vine replied harshly. "Tried to divert a prophesy."

"He didn't know what he was doing," the king said. "She should have been better prepared."

"We can all agree on that. But the only way to give her better training is to give her to us," Jahaka said.

"No," King Makani said firmly. "She must pay, as my son has paid."

"Then must all your other men pay as well?" Jahaka asked sweetly. Surely the king would give her the one girl's life in exchange for the dozens she held?

Not that she'd give them all away. Not the ones who she was certain would do more evil.

"Our men—" the king started.

A loud explosion rippled through the room, startling them all.

Jahaka kept the expression of surprise on her face, though inside she exhorted Aleekona to get the girl, and soon.

More shouts followed and outside the room they heard the pounding of men's feet.

"I'll go see what's happening, my lord," Oka'u said, racing out the door.

The four temple guards came from the corners and surrounded

Jahaka and Vine. The king's guard poured in from the hallway, surrounding their king and the temple guard.

"Do you think the attack has already come?" the king asked Vine. He seemed more curious than anxious or worried.

"No, my lord, not the attack the girl saw," Vine assured him. "It won't happen for nine days, at the end of the *Keereekayah* festival." The word from the goddess was always accurate.

"Maybe a preliminary attack? To test our defenses, perhaps?" King Makani looked thoughtful.

Did he really have that much faith in his guard? Or did he think his allies would come to the rescue before he was taken? Did he have allies that Jahaka didn't know about?

One of the king's guard rushed into the room. He gave a fluid report in the native's language.

Jahaka didn't bother trying to follow along. Instead, she concentrated on the expressions darting across the king's face.

Surprise, mainly. Then shock.

"The pens holding the madmen were attacked," the king said slowly, turning to face Jahaka.

"By other madmen?" Jahaka suggested. It would be best if everyone believed Aleekona and his men had also been driven mad.

"No," the king replied.

Only now did Jahaka notice that the king's normally dark brown skin had turned ashy.

"By the *Mahinapo*."

"The who?" Jahaka asked, turning to Vine, who shrugged. She'd never heard the term either.

"The southern witches," the king said.

CHAPTER 6

To forget one's ancestors is to be a brook without a source, a tree without roots.
—*Southern Islands proverb*

THE GREAT SOUTHERN WITCH ULI STRODE THROUGH THE jungle, hungry. She stripped a banana tree of all its fruit, green and yellow, as well as the *mamapo'o* plant of its berries. Normally, people didn't eat that fruit, but she could eat bones and leaves and twigs that her tamed brethren shunned. Birds streaked rainbows through the branches, flying beside her. Stinging bushes rolled out of the way on the swell of ground Uli brought with her.

A dancing brook called to Uli above the sweet sounds of the jungle. It would hold small creatures, maybe a fish or two.

The goddess Oenonu—the true goddess of the jungle, not the faint Kalluka who never battled a jungle demon or fed the heart of her enemy to the base of the mountain—provided such bounty for her children.

The people would have to be re-taught her name, as well as her dances and her ceremonies.

So much had been lost when the mountain had exploded, Hinanuli sending her fiery necklaces far into the sky.

Uli followed the call of the stream, wishing to worship the goddess as well as slake her thirst and hunger. Unashamed, she knelt and drew the clean water into her mouth. Why had the king taught that only animals bent their head to eat or drink? Only those stupidly proud would pass by such a stream if they were thirsty and didn't have a cup.

Her people would have to learn to use their hands again.

A crashing noise disturbed Uli's pleasure in the water. She turned slowly—any beast that attacked her would deserve its fate.

Another woman came through the brush, her chest bare, her ponderous breasts hanging low. She was older than Uli and she wore her gray-streaked hair short, in the northern style. A modern skirt was tied around her waist, made from fancy cloth, instead of a traditional *sulluu.* Her fingers were short and stubby, like her nose and chin, while her eyes were wide and wild.

Without pause, the other woman walked directly into the stream, upstream of Uli, to drink her fill, muddying the water streaming down toward Uli.

"Why do you ruin my drink?" Uli challenged the woman.

"I do not," the woman said without looking up. "I saw you there, but didn't notice you."

The old insult stung—it implied that a person was only as important as a single tree or a vine in a large jungle, which was to say, not at all. An individual tree or vine didn't matter as much as the full jungle.

"I was here before you," Uli said, her anger surging. This was the first sister that Uli had met since she'd broken free of the curse. It was probably a woman whom Uli had freed with the sand. Why was she insulting Uli this way?

"No, I was." The woman finally turned and looked directly at Uli. "My children outnumber yours, and my years as well."

"Hmph. They're all soft, living in villages, fed every day," Uli replied, refusing to pay respect even if she was supposed to give homage to her elders. The woman had a village feel to her, and was probably as soft as the others.

But instead of being insulted, the woman threw back her head and laughed.

Only then did Uli realize she'd been smiling the whole time.

"It's a joy to give and take in a proper *leeleen*." She walked down the stream, arms open wide. "Sister. It's good to see you."

Uli swallowed down her anger. It *was* good to have a proper trade of insults, though she hadn't been able to do such a thing for most of her life, and her dreams of them were confused. "Sister," she said, making herself open her arms and hug this stranger.

The stranger's skin smelled spicy, like the peppers that grew in the shaded places low on the mountain. Her skin had never been cracked and dirty like Uli's—she'd always been sheltered.

"I am Ipo," the woman introduced herself.

"Uli," she replied. "Welcome to the world," she added, the traditional greeting for a girl when she reached womanhood.

"Do you know what happened?" Ipo asked. "I was, I lived—but I didn't know myself. Not my true self. Then Ty rose, over Kualina Mountain, and the wind carried my name to me."

"Ty helped you remember your name?" Uli asked, surprised. She'd assumed her spell had returned all the southern witches to themselves.

At Ipo's nod, Uli continued. "That's good. But the others—I freed them. I took the blood of the dead prince to break the spell cast by King Kawiti, then flung the sand out to the rest of my sisters."

"The dead prince, yes," Ipo said with a sly grin. "I'd fed the child who'd killed him. She used his blood for her vision."

"Did you use his blood, too?" Uli asked.

"I think the smell broke those at the temple free, when Ty rose," Ipo said. "I didn't know what it was, at first. But why? What bound us, that his death broke?"

This, Uli could answer. "King Kawiti cursed us to carry the mountain within us. With every step, we drew more of its weight inside, until our thoughts were slow and our pain, lessened."

"I remember being slow," Ipo admitted. "But I didn't know it was the ancient king who had cursed us. How could he? Men have so little power."

"The king can bind men to him. He used something else to bind the mountain to us," Uli explained. "I don't know if it was one of those northern witches who helped him, or one of our own sisters. But he gained the strength to curse us all, for all our generations."

Ipo looked away from Uli. Her gaze would have burned the stream if she'd directed it down. "What are we going to do?" Ipo asked after her chest stopped heaving and her fists unclenched.

"We kill the current king," Uli said simply.

Ipo turned and looked at Uli, her eyes still blazing. "Not good enough. Not just King Makani. We must kill them all. All those with royal blood."

Uli smiled at Ipo. "Yes. The king is just a start."

WITH GREAT WAVES OF POWER, ULI *PUSHED* AT THE EARTH UNDER palm, beech, and *manuhali* trees on her side. Ipo matched her, also walking in a circle, but she set fire to everything blocking in her path. The trees cracked as their trunks split, making dull thuds as they fell over, their roots quivering, exposed. Bushes and spiked thorns rolled out of her way. Birds fled, the snakes slithering out of the jungle as fast as they could. The flies followed suit, but would be the first to return.

Uli cackled as the jungle moved for her, the earth conforming to her desire. For so long, it had worn her down. Now she was in control of it, as she was born to be.

Once the two witches had cleared a space the size of half a dozen large huts, together they chanted the old prayer of the mountain makers:

> *Oenonu, green goddess,*
> *Make way for the mountain.*
> *It grows taller than the plank tree*
> *Wider than a waterfall.*
> *Bones of the earth—rise!*
> *Oh mountain,*
> *Make yourself known.*
> *Come kiss the sky*

And set the stars
Dancing above your head.

Uli reached deep into the ground, finding the roots of the mountain beneath the layers of soil and *pulling*. The stone felt cold and solid in her magical grasp. At first, the rocks resisted; they followed the flow they'd had for millennia, hiding from the air.

But Uli would have her way. She wrapped her grip around the stones and pulled harder, dragging the rocks upward.

With a great creaking groan, giant boulders churned against each other. They rolled to fill the clearing the witches had made, pushing against the boundaries of the jungle. Then they started piling up, one on top of another, higher and higher. Foot by foot, the mountain thrust above the ground, its black rock shining with its own light, the sides smooth and hard as glass as the magic sheared off the dirt and pebbles.

Uli danced as she worked, directing the stone to be solid and sure as it impelled its way to the sky, above the trees, into the night. Ipo joined her, singing hymns to Hinanuli and the other mountain goddesses.

Soon, the new mountain stood higher than any of the temples of the northern witches, though lower than the first mountain on the island.

Uli didn't want to make her jealous.

Light reflected darkly off the sheer sides, a black beacon. It would be visible from the ocean to the east, as well as from most of the island. Those who couldn't see it would hear about it from their neighbors.

All the southern witches on the island would know what it meant. It was a sign of their power returning.

And that they should all gather at the source.

ULI GRUNTED AS SHE HEFTED HER END OF THE LOG. IT WAS heavy, but she would never complain. Not to Ipo. Ipo would just laugh at Uli. Again.

At least it was the last log Ipo wanted. They threw it on top of the other two already lying in the center of the new clearing they'd created. The sun already approached the horizon, and slanted through the trees that edged the rough circle.

"Now, watch," Ipo said, giving Uli a mischievous grin. She started to chant, an everyday prayer merely asking for the blessings of her ancestors. Suddenly, Ipo threw her hands out.

The green wood caught fire instantly. The flames grew high, dancing above their heads.

"You're a powerful fire dancer," Uli told Ipo.

Ipo didn't respond, her attention fully on the flames in front of her. She reached out one hand, making a claw, then twisting it. A curl of the fire separated and twisted up like a living braid.

Uli didn't know what it was for, but she assumed it would be useful in a battle.

Then Ipo sculpted another section, creating a ladder shape. "I remember," she whispered as she played with the flames. First she formed a wild bird out of the living fire, then a hopping turtle, and finally a great tree.

"I'm impressed," Uli told Ipo.

"There's more," Ipo said. "But I'm still dreaming it."

Uli nodded. She, too, still dreamed of the old days, in her hut, by herself. She would never be able to remember if her children were real or not, or if she just dreamed of all of her sisters and their offspring.

"That's all?" came a voice from behind them.

Uli turned slowly. Three women stood there. The one in front was unnaturally thin. Her skin was clear and clean, but the whites of her eyes were hazed with red, and her gums were swollen and stained black.

Had she been one of the poppy maidens in the jungle village far from the witches, trading her body for the drug?

"I'm Lakawoo," she announced, clawing out a ball of fire that separated into two figures. Uli caught her breath when she recognized herself and Ipo, dancing and raising the mountain.

"Welcome, sister," Ipo said. "Not even in my dreams have I seen stories in the flames."

Uli shivered. How powerful was this Lakawoo?

But Lakawoo just laughed. "I couldn't set such green wood to flames. So in that, you must teach me, grandmother."

Uli turned to the other two, standing back out of the flame's reach. "And you?" she challenged.

They laughed as one, sending shivers down Uli's spine. How could two of her sisters be so similar to one another, though they looked dramatically different?

"I'm Nila," said the taller one, the seashells tied to the ends of her long dreads catching the light. A skirt of seaweed hung from her waist. She was ponderous, like Uli, a powerful warm force.

"And I'm Hinan," said the other. Dirt still caked her long hair, and her face was gaunt from not having enough food. She wore a necklace of seaweed between her small breasts.

"If it were to rain, we could take that fire," Nila boasted.

Ipo scoffed. "Not likely," she said. "Not against the two of us." She shuffled closer to Lakawoo and the pair of them stood, defiant, staring at Nila and Hinan.

Uli assumed from the witch's boast that she and her sister were water shakers.

Nila and Hinan reached out and grasped hands. They sang a melodious chant, full of nonsense syllables.

The air shifted around Uli, growing cooler and more dry. Strange winds licked her face, sending birdflesh up across her shoulders.

The fire diminished.

Ipo and Lakawoo turned to face the flames. Ipo raised her hands, her arms straining as if she lifted a great weight.

The fire grew smaller still.

Ipo redoubled her efforts. Power swirled around her. Lakawoo shook, sweat dripping down her face.

Suddenly, the flames burst up, reaching the tops of the trees. A loud *boom* filled the clearing. The blast of heat forced Uli to take a step back. With a flick of her wrists, she reached far into the earth, ready to dump soil onto the flames if the fire dancers couldn't contain it.

But the fire shrank back down. Ipo turned to the two water shakers, her joy flowing from her. "Well done, sisters!" she boomed, bouncing over to them and wrapping the pair of them in a great hug. "Well done!"

Lakawoo still stood next to the fire, her eyes wide, her hands still shaking. "I've never felt such a powerful force," she whispered. "Not even in my dreams."

Uli nodded. Her sisters had changed.

Was it for the better? She didn't know.

AFTER THEY'D EATEN THEIR FILL OF FLOWERS, BANANAS, SMALL birds, and fresh fish, Uli stood before them, the flames from Ipo's fire still leaping high in the dark night.

"Welcome, my sisters," Uli said, though she'd greeted them before, when they'd arrived. "We have come back into the world. And those who cursed us need to feel our retribution."

"But I just re-awoke!" Hinan complained, the smaller of the water shakers. "I don't want to go into battle. I want to live in my cave near the ocean. I can do so much more now," she added. "Like call the fish from the ocean into my net, or draw the water from the well without a bucket. My life is my own—I don't have to rely on others to feed me." She shuddered.

Uli tried to control her own shivering. They'd all been reduced to needing either their children or their neighbors to care for them. They'd lost too many of their wits to survive on their own, grown dependent on others as part of their curse.

And possibly that was why there were so few of them left: people weren't as kind now as they once had been.

"There's another reason why the royals should die," Lakawoo said quietly as the witches came back from their memories. She'd refused to say where she'd been living, only that she hadn't been actually living before two days ago. "Not all our sisters are free."

"What do you mean?" Ipo asked, turning from the fire to stare at Lakawoo.

But Lakawoo stared into the flames, ignoring the others.

Both fire dancers did that, would get lost in the flames. Uli hoped it wouldn't happen when they battled.

"See?" Lakawoo said, reaching out and taking a living flame, coaxing it into her hand. It stayed the shape of a small ball, burning brightly. "Your spell freed many of us, for which we thank you," Lakawoo said, glancing at Uli, then back to her palm. The light highlighted her chin and the bottoms of her cheeks, hiding her eyes. "But some still bear the curse of the mountain."

Lakawoo flung the ball of fire down to the ground, where it took the shape of a large woman. Uli stifled her gasp when she recognized the hut the woman lived in. It looked just like hers, with the refuse pile in the corner and the children screaming silently without shoes while the woman just sat with her head supported by her fist.

The image disappeared as quickly as it had formed. Lakawoo sighed and sagged, her head dropping down. "There are others like her. Still cursed." Then she looked back up at Uli, her bloodshot eyes boring into Uli's soul. "You must free them, too. And they can only be freed by blood. Royal blood."

"Then we will kill all the royals," Uli replied sincerely. "I promise to be as tireless as the stones in hunting them all down."

"And I," Ipo said. "Let my flames wreathe their bodies before their souls are prayed away to the four winds."

Lakawoo laughed, bitter and cackling. "I'll go with you, but I don't know how much good I'll be. My gifts have changed—I don't know if I'll ever be able to light a fire such as you," she said, indicating Ipo. "But I can see things in the flames that others can't."

"You defended your flame well enough," Uli told the young witch. "I accept your service." She'd take another fire dancer any day. She needed all the skills of the southern witches in order to take on the king.

"I have to rescue the young northern witch, first," Nila said.

"A white witch?" Uli sneered. "Why would we rescue one of theirs?" They'd done nothing to help her sisters who'd been enslaved.

Their time would come, too.

"She was the one who killed the prince. She's been taken by the king," Nila replied. "And I promised I'd come and get her. She tried to help, when she saw me changing. Before the guards took her away. Before I'd come into my full power."

"So?" Uli asked. "She left the blood. The stupid white witches have no idea what to do with that power." Why should she rescue someone so foreign? It wasn't as if she could teach the girl how to use her power.

Ipo stepped forward. "I fed the girl as a child," she said. "Ephanie. She doesn't deserve to die being tortured by the king."

Uli shuddered. She had memories from one of her sisters, from long ago, of the king's torture pens, where they hung her by her arms until her shoulders snapped out of place, while beating the soles of her feet, breaking all the bones in her ankles, until she could never walk again.

"If the king has her, wants her, then maybe we should take her back," Uli said slowly. She wanted to deny the king everything.

The other witches nodded in agreement.

They'd save this stupid girl witch, then. Deny the king access to her, then whittle away at everything else he held dear.

Besides, maybe this northern witch could be of use to them as well.

Uli stood with the others on the beach, waiting until dawn. Strong winds blew in from the water, bracing and refreshing. Waves rolled softly, breaking at their feet. The far horizon pinked with the coming sun. Most of the fishermen had already gotten into their boats and left. The ones who remained sat watchful on the beach, repairing their nets and waiting to see what happened.

Nila and Hinan had assured Uli that they could take them all all the way from Ailani to Hilani over the water, without waiting for a boat.

They just needed the right sunbeam.

The salt in the air soothed Uli's nose. She remembered this scent, from when she'd been a child. Recalled dancing in the moonlight on clear sand, the torches flickering high, chants rising up to the top of the mountain and beyond, all the way up to the stars. Then racing into the waves, the surf cool against her skin, her body angled and sleek as it dove under the waves, swimming strongly into the deep.

Or maybe it was one of her sisters who still missed this smell, could swim as well as any dolphin.

Finally, the sun crested the horizon and the beams formed, reaching across the gray waters. Nila and Hinan crooned to the rising orb, reaching out with their hands and pulling, their actions softer than Uli's when she'd pulled the rocks up from the ground, but with just as much power.

The light streaked closer, coming faster now. Nila and Hinan sang louder, words of power that stirred in Uli, like old roots reaching down through the loam for fresh water.

When the two stepped aside, Uli could clearly see the path over the water, like one of the white roads the witches had built on the island.

But this road wouldn't last, whereas theirs were scars in the earth.

Nila and Hinan gestured for the others to step forward.

For a moment, fear rose over Uli, like a shadow overtaking the mountain. She wasn't used to the water. It was someone else who loved it, cherished it, could live in it. She was of the earth and the stones. Surely the water wouldn't support her.

She was going to sink.

However, the other witches had faith in her. And Uli was *never* going back to the little hut in the jungle again, only vaguely alive and no more aware than one of the slugs living in the roots of the banana trees.

Swallowing down her fear, Uli stepped forward.

Cool water splashed over the top of her foot, and the light beam buckled, dropping further under the waves.

Uli took another step. The light grew solid, supporting her great weight.

After two more steps, Uli knew that she couldn't merely walk. No, the light demanded something more from her. It wasn't the pounding dance she did on the earth, a dance that would shake the trees and cause the ground to move in waves.

This was a lighter dance, a sliding, slippery movement, one foot gliding after another, like paddles dipping down and thrusting forward, propelling her forward, faster, smoother.

Uli threw her head back and laughed as she danced across the ocean, her sisters in a line behind her, quickly slipping out of the bay and across the open sea. The light turned, and they headed west, for Hilani, the large island in the center region.

The king would never see them coming.

"Will we get there before the light fades?" Uli asked as the sun broached the far horizon. Darkness gathered above them, while a few stars poked through, shining behind them. Her leg muscles hurt from gliding all day. Nila had called fish out of the water to her hand, slicing it quickly with her stone knife and handing them fresh strips. But she couldn't take the salt out of the water, and so Uli was thirsty as well.

Uli couldn't see any land in front of them, just smooth, black-glass water. Their beam would disappear soon.

She didn't know how to swim.

"We're turning, just here," Hinan said. They made a sharp left, the light thinning to a mere thread.

Cool water splashed over Uli's feet, and with her next step, up to her ankles.

"Do you feel that?" Nila called. "The coral underneath?"

Uli shook her head. There was merely water, and more water—too much water—between her and the solid earth.

"The reef is just below our feet," Ipo said. She called up a ball of fire in the center of her palm and threw it in front of Uli. As it sank, Uli saw the black rock.

It really wasn't that far down.

With a quick thrust of power, Uli reached down and touched the coral. It had never known the light. It wasn't really earth; made from sea creatures, it was more like sand.

Still, Uli could use it. She could force the creatures to grow, adding soil from the seafloor far beneath them.

Pulling hard, Uli rose up the rock. The water lapped at her thighs as she sank, the reef growing slowly toward the surface.

Finally, sharp edges kissed the soles of Uli's feet and she started to rise.

"Thank you," Ipo said, the relief making her voice ragged.

Maybe Uli hadn't been the only one afraid of drowning.

Uli's feet cried out as the rock took her weight. Her bones compressed as all the weight of the world came back.

But Uli also felt good, solid, again. She couldn't stand to be so light all the time.

Uli took one step forward onto the harsh rock, then another. She heard Ipo whimper as she walked: her feet had never been toughened by the jungle; they were still village-soft. Uli couldn't blunt the edges of the coral, though.

They needed to get to land, quickly. The coral wouldn't stay above ground for long. She'd forced it too fast. It was brittle and would break off and dissolve, going back to its original state soon.

Only earth and true stone kept the shape Uli cast them into.

The coral path curved around the edge of the bay, taking them to the far southern point. Uli saw the hated palace cut into the hill. It was far too grand, with carved pillars and rock walls, instead of the humble woven reeds, leaves, and wood of the ordinary person's house.

It would all have to come down.

And why had the king built out of stone? Didn't he remember her strength? The power of her sisters?

Foolish man.

Uli breathed a sigh of relief once they stepped complete away from the water and onto the sand. Even its uncertain surface was better than the water she'd been on all day.

She didn't rest there, though. Instead, she walked up the short beach and stepped up, onto solid rock.

Finally. She reached down and nestled her thoughts deep in the ground, the cool earth soothing her, nourishing her, replenishing her.

Uli turned back, looking the way they'd come. No trace remained: the water hid the coral Uli had raised.

But they'd made it safely to shore. She didn't know how far they'd come in a single day. It had been a great journey, one her people would remember in songs, later.

When they started to sing the praises of her sisters again.

"We should go," Uli said, trying to rouse the others. "Rescue this northern witch of yours." They sat together in a small cave in the side of the cliff that Uli had carved out of the rock. Ipo had set a fire dancing on only a few twigs, then had "tamed" it, so it burned brightly while barely consuming its fuel. The cave was cold and damp, but Uli found it comforting to be completely surrounded by rock.

Nila and Hinan shook their heads, moving in unison.

It still gave Uli the chills to see her sisters working together this way.

"We can't," Nila said with a great sigh.

"It took too much effort, too much work, making such a water crossing," Hinan added. "We need to rest."

Uli hadn't needed to rest after raising the mountain. Then again, the very earth sustained her. Maybe Nila and Hinan should go swimming, get the water to support them, maybe refresh them.

"But without you, how will we find the northern witch?" Uli asked, frustrated.

"I know the child, too," Ipo said, standing. "I can help you find her and free her."

Lakawoo rose and stood beside Ipo. "I am also tired from the crossing," she said. "But I will join you, and add what damage I may with my flames."

Uli grinned, happy that Lakawoo understood what they were about to do.

It was time to cause mayhem.

"We will get the girl," Uli promised Nila. Then she turned to the others. "This way."

Uli led the two fire dancers out of the cave, then up, forcing a set of steps into the side of the cliff. She didn't need them: the stone would provide her with enough hand-and-foot holds to easily climb to the top. But the fire dancers didn't have the same affinity for the rock. As the water shakers had had to provide a path across the ocean, so Uli now needed to provide a path across the earth.

Jungle came all the way to the edge of the cliff. This was just a different path that Uli needed to provide, raising the earth and cutting a swath through the dense bush.

But after only a short while, Uli stopped.

Someone had built a *road* here, covered with foreign white stones not from this island. The road cut into the sweet earth, stifling its power.

It wouldn't take much for Uli to disrupt it, to draw the earth up in a ridge down the center of this manmade thing.

Ipo gripped Uli's arm before she could call up the rocks. "Later," she whispered. "We should visit the king and his prisoner pens first."

Uli nodded and sighed. Sometime she would return and destroy every single road on the entire island. But Ipo was right. First they needed to get the girl, as she'd promised Nila.

They walked north through the trees, avoiding the roads, then swerving around the small collection of darkened huts they discovered.

Why were her people not celebrating the new year? Why were curtains over the doors, instead of having them open for all to come and visit? Were her people scared? Had the king done this?

Or had the northern witches?

As they grew closer to the palace, more nettles and stinging thorns grew. Uli suspected they'd been planted to discourage people from passing this way.

Had the king thought such a ploy would really stop Uli and her sisters?

He really had forgotten.

Ipo put her hand on Uli's arm, then pointed to the left. "The pens are this way. I can smell them," she added, wrinkling her nose.

Uli paused and sniffed, but she didn't smell anything beyond the freshly turned earth and the dry jungle leaves. She nodded and burst another path through the bush in the direction Ipo indicated.

After only a short while, Uli stopped. Just beyond the jungle, she could see torches burning.

Had that been the scent Ipo had caught earlier?

The witches crept up the last few feet to the edge of the clearing. The stinging nettles were tightly bunched here, making any escape from the palace impossible.

Torches stood every few feet around the wooden fence that surrounded the pens. The pens themselves weren't built that solidly: just wood planks notched together at the edges. However, none of them were tall enough for a man to stand inside. In fact, even sitting, most would have to bend their heads. They weren't long enough for a short woman to lie down fully. And all of them held three or more people, with no room to move, no privacy.

It was so much worse than the hut Uli had once lived in.

It wouldn't take much to disrupt the fence, bring the earth up and cause it to topple.

But there were guards with long spears on all the sides. How to distract them?

"Let me," Lakawoo said, noticing Uli's hesitation. She reached out to Ipo, who put a lump of fire into her palm.

None of Uli's memories showed her sisters working together. They were always separate, alone.

No wonder they'd been defeated.

Not this time.

Uli would string them together like a flower necklace, each more brilliant and destructive because of the support of her sisters.

Lakawoo stood and walked closer. Two of the guard noticed her approach, but before they could call out, Lakawoo threw her fire at them, living ropes that bound and burned them.

Now they screamed.

Uli called up the earth, disrupting the fence posts, then sending a ridge down the center of the pens, raising the structures up, causing them to wobble.

One good push and they would topple over. Most of the prisoners just called out, not taking the opportunity to free themselves.

"Here!" Ipo called, leading them to a pen closer to the center.

At least the girl—Ephanie—had some sense. As soon as the pen holding her had started tipping, she'd kicked at it with her feet.

Men's voices called out in the dark, calling out for them to stop. More guards, from the trees? Why had they been hiding there?

Then they screamed, and the scent of burning flesh filled the night air.

Ipo quickly hurried over to the pen holding the witch and tugged at it, stripping one wall from another. "Come with us!" she insisted, holding out her hand.

The skinny, tall, white girl looked at her in shock, eyes wide and wondering, then she grasped Ipo's hand. Her face was tear-smudged and her arms poorly bandaged, long cuts running from the inside of her elbow to her wrist.

What had they been trying to do? How had they been torturing her?

With a roar, Uli shoved her power *down*, into the earth. That was it. She was going to tear apart the king's palace. No one should suffer like the people here.

But instead of spreading through the earth, the force of Uli's will came up against what felt like a wall and abruptly stopped.

Something—someone—had bound the earth, deep underground, and set it to sleep.

It would take more than just Uli's power to wake it and make it move to her will. No wonder the king had felt it safe to build here.

Cursing, Uli turned and left the pens, blasting rows of earth at any who might follow them. It was easy for them to escape down the hill and into the woods, hidden by trees and rocks, her sisters following.

CHAPTER 7

Even a future long foreseen pains the living.
—Northern proverb

EPHANIE COLLAPSED ON THE HARD FLOOR AS THE LAST OF THE prophecy's words left her. Finally, she could rest. She'd done her duty to the goddess, told Jahaka her fate, and now the king.

The ships were coming. She could still see them, dancing across the waves. Dozens and dozens of them, all bearing men with spears and knives.

All coming to attack the island of the king.

The throne room at the palace was grander than any place Ephanie had been before. It stood as tall as two palm trees, one set on top of the other. White rock rose up to the ceiling, which was made of beautiful light brown wood. The room was longer than it was wide, and carved pillars decorated both of the long sides. Windows open to the bay opened along one side, while doors to other parts of the palace opened on the other side. The entire back of the room was filled with people, all southern islanders: the court and the king's family.

King Makani sat before Ephanie on a throne carved out of

limestone from the Hilani Island cliffs. The top edges of it were still rough, almost like coral growing up out of the ground. Circular patterns of red, black, and pink pearls worked down the tall sides of it, in waves.

The king himself was a broad man, wearing a brilliant yellow vest that set off his dark brown skin. Gray spiked the hair at his temples, which he wore very short. His brown eyes had looked kindly on Ephanie when she'd stepped forward, though he hadn't asked the guards to remove the rough bindings that cut into her wrists.

Now King Makani asked, "Were they men from the west?"

"They floated in from the west," Ephanie clarified, still slumped over, though she could hear her mother's voice at the back of her head telling her to sit up straight. "I don't know if they were men from the western islands, or from somewhere else."

Though Ephanie truly didn't know, she suspected they weren't from the western islands, at least, not all of them. However, it was merely a feeling she had. She knew better than to say anything about that. Seprhya her old teacher, had warned often against such foolishness.

It wasn't right for a fortuneteller to give her opinions. Only the word of the goddess mattered. Besides, the one carrying the fortune might be wrong, she could be biased.

Only the words of the goddess were accurate, her prophesies always true, paid for with life and blood.

"How many men, how many ships?" the king asked.

Ephanie looked up and shook her head at the king. She had no idea. "Many," she responded. "The harbor was full of ships. And more men kept coming."

The king thought for a moment. "When does the attack start? Dawn? Midday?"

"I don't know," Ephanie replied. She had only seen the attack after it had started. For all she knew, it could have begun the day before, though it didn't feel that way.

"What types of winds are blowing?" the king asked.

"It's still," Ephanie answered. "The smoke from the fires rises straight to the sky."

"And the attack happens at the end of *Keereekayah*?"

"The last day," Ephanie replied.

"How do you know?"

Ephanie opened her mouth, then closed it again. There wasn't anything in the vision to tell her what day it was. She just *knew*. "The goddess told me."

"And your goddess is always right?"

"Visions from the goddess Brikalla are always accurate," Ephanie said, pulling herself upright and standing, swaying. "Paid for with life and blood."

Her vision had showed her this part. But she was aware only of a bit more of her future. Then she'd fall back into ignorance.

"And how did you pay for this vision?" the king asked, his kind voice turning harsh.

"My mother had told me that a vision was coming, but I ignored her good advice," Ephanie admitted. She knew she needed to tell the king the truth. "I went outside, unprepared for when the vision arrived. I needed blood—life. And I accidentally took the life of your son."

The entire room was silent.

"Why did you take his life?" the king asked, his voice ringing out like a booming wave.

"I'm so deeply sorry for that," Ephanie said, sorrow filling her voice. She truly was. "It was a mistake. I was unprepared, so I began to use my own life, my own blood, to draw the vision out. Your son— your son found me cutting myself." She took a deep breath, but she had to tell the truth of this as well. "He tried to stop me. The goddess turned the blade in my hand. I only meant to cut him a little. But the knife plunged into his neck instead of his shoulder." Ephanie paused, then added, "I'm so sorry."

A undulating wail of mourning sprang up behind Ephanie. The court could finally mourn their lost son now that they knew how he'd died. They could tie up his life in a song, chant it with the departing tide as they threw flowers and fish into the waters, to go decorate his body already lying in the deep.

The king nodded to the guard standing to the right. They directed the crowd out in a large wave, sending them through the doors, their mourning cries echoing through the hallways.

Ephanie didn't have to look behind to know that after a few moments only half a dozen guards, the king, and his one advisor, were still in the room.

"Oka'u," King Makani said.

The little man stepped forward, giving Ephanie a smile that was all teeth and bite which chilled her very soul. He was darker than most of the southern islanders, small and compact, though his bare chest rippled with muscles.

"How were you drawing your blood?" Oka'u asked, stepping closer.

Ephanie shuddered and showed him the inside of her left arm, gently tracing the long scar there. "I would have drawn enough blood from myself," she pleaded. "If only he hadn't interfered."

Oka'u came over to examine her. "It healed quickly," he said. "Was it not very deep?"

"It was deep," Ephanie assured him. "We heal quickly, though." She didn't bother to specify that it was just the fortunetellers: better for them to think it was all witches.

"Do you?" the little man asked. He drew a blade from his own belt. "Just how quickly can you heal?" With a grasp stronger than a riptide, he darted out and grabbed her arm, then, just as quickly, sliced through the skin, all the way along.

Ephanie gasped at the pain. There was nothing soothing here, no relief, not even knowing that she'd already seen this, lived through at least the start of it.

"My," Oka'u said. He watched, fascinated, as the skin curled back up together, the blood dripping down around her white skin, forming rivers that quickly dried. "And there is power there?" he asked.

"No," Ephanie said truthfully. "Only the vision has strength, and can be drawn out with blood."

"Let's see what else we can draw out from you," Oka'u murmured.

Guards suddenly surrounded Ephanie, moving her toward the door.

Though Ephanie knew it was useless, she still struggled, trying to push back. She didn't want to go to the torture pit, no matter how inevitable it was.

King Makani sat silent on his throne, his face as expressionless as if it were carved out of stone.

While Oka'u watched her with greedy eyes.

He'd drink up all her pain, and then demand more, she knew.

EXHAUSTED WITH CRYING, HER THROAT ACHING WITH SCREAMS, Ephanie finally rested against the table holding her. Oka'u had cut strips of skin from her arms, scarring her far beyond her first single cut, the one she'd inflicted on herself.

But each slice of the knife had healed quickly, cleanly.

Tomorrow, she knew that Oka'u would start again, tear apart her freshly healed wounds repeatedly, measuring the time it took for her to heal. While they waited, he'd pet her hair, dry her tears tenderly. Ephanie couldn't squirm away from him, suffered his administrations, shuddered when she realized she was starting to look forward to them, as it meant at least a temporary respite from the cutting.

What would Oka'u do with the information of how long it took for her to heal? Was that what really mattered? Or was it just her pain, her screams, that fed his soul?

At least Ephanie had survived the day. Her vision hadn't told her that. She had no more foreknowledge.

An old man came in, bent over, with fingers that had once been broken and never healed properly. He roughly bound Ephanie's arms in strips of cloth, clearing away the last of the dried blood. Then the guards were back. Ephanie happily followed them out of the torture chamber. She never thought she'd leave that room.

Fear spiked through Ephanie's confusion and she started to struggle, though she had no strength. They weren't going to kill her, were they? She'd pleased Oka'u enough with her suffering, hadn't she?

Then they stepped outside. Relief made Ephanie sag in their grip. She took a deep breath, breathing in the night air.

Then she gagged. The stench of human filth and fear rolled over her. Both men and women cried out in pain and fear.

On the edge of the flattened courtyard stood an enclosed area, filled with rough wooden structures. Vines and strong nets were strung between posts dug deep into the ground.

Only when Ephanie drew closer did she realize that each of the small boxes held people, generally three or more. No one could stand or even fully lie down. They reeked with feces and urine. During the day, the sun would shine down brightly on them all day, and no water was in sight.

Ephanie struggled again to get away, but she was weak from the loss of blood as well as the horror and pain she'd experienced all day.

There was no getting away.

One of the guards lifted up the short wall of one of the pens, while two others stood with their spears ready to stop anyone from trying to escape. But the two women stayed cowed at the back of the pen, the long wounds sliced in their backs oozing and buzzing with flies.

Without warning, another guard grabbed Ephanie by her arms and pulled down, forcing her to her knees, then pricked her butt with his spear.

Hate blinded Ephanie's eyes as she crawled forward, whimpering as she put her weight on her injured arms.

She didn't know if she could ever get revenge on these men, on the king.

But she would dream of it tonight.

EPHANIE SAT WITH HER LEGS CROSSED UNDER HER, HER HEAD bent. She couldn't sit up straight, couldn't stretch her legs out and lie down fully either. She'd tried talking to the other two women in the pen, but they'd ignored her, refusing to answer any of her questions, urgently whispering at each other instead.

The only thing they'd showed her was the single corner they'd used for their bathroom, instead of refuse being smeared the length of the pen.

Full dark had come, and the moans of the prisoners had died down. Ephanie didn't think she'd ever get used to the stench, however; she'd have nightmares about it for the rest of her life, whether that would be very short or very long, she didn't know.

As the night grew more cold, her two companions seemed to arrive at a decision. One of them finally turned to her and asked, "Witch?"

"Yes," Ephanie said, relieved. "I'm Ephanie."

The woman grunted but didn't reply with her name. "Why here?" she asked.

Ephanie didn't want to admit her guilt. She couldn't defend herself from these two. Though maybe it would be better to die here in the pens, rather than on Oka'u's table. "I accidentally killed someone," she confessed. It was the truth.

"Oh, yes, yes," the first woman said, nodding. "Me, me, yes." She paused, then added, "He was bad man."

This tiny woman had killed a man? Ephanie was certain if they could stand up, her head wouldn't come much higher than the middle of Ephanie's chest. Her hands were tiny and fluttered like a hummingbird as she talked. Her dark face was mostly hidden in the night, but her voice was high and sweet, making Ephanie think her features must be delicate and laughing.

Ephanie turned to look at the other woman.

"Hurt," she said, nodding. Her voice turned fierce. "Hurt and hurt and hurt." She was a larger woman, with solid legs and thighs that she slapped as she talked. "Hurt and more hurt."

Ephanie shivered, glad that whatever look the second woman had on her face was hidden in the darkness.

These women were here in the pens because of the madness. They didn't seem sorry at all, or like they'd stop hurting people if they were let go.

What had happened? Why had the southern islanders, who were generally so peaceful, turned so violent?

It couldn't have just been the rising of the moon. It had to be some kind of magic. But what would cause this sort of change?

"Oka'u hurt?" the first woman asked, pointing to Ephanie's arms.

"Yes," Ephanie said, nodding.

The woman turned and showed her back. Strips of skin had been peeled off it as well. "Me. Yes. Me." She turned back to Ephanie. "You help?"

Ephanie shook her head, her hands useless in her lap. "No. Not help. Not my magic."

"Ah," the second woman said, nodding. "You, fire?" she guessed.

"Fire?" Ephanie asked, confused. She had no idea what the woman was asking for.

"Witch, yes?" the first one said. "Water. Mountain. Fire."

Ephanie still had no idea what the woman was asking. "I'm sorry," she said. "I—"

A man screamed in the night. No, two. The earth rumbled under the pen, growling like mountain cat.

"What is it? What's happening?" Ephanie asked.

The women shook their heads and started chanting. Ephanie could barely make out the words above the screams of the other prisoners, something about saving them from the walking mountain.

When the earth erupted under their pen, tilting it to one side, Ephanie stopped asking questions and instead started kicking the edge that had come up out of the ground.

It was better to die standing than hunched over like a beast.

Suddenly, the pen flew open. It took Ephanie a moment to realize that she recognized the woman—Ipo, the old cook from her island.

But Ephanie had never seen such a light in Ipo's eyes before, intelligent and cunning. "Come with us!" she called, holding out her hand to Ephanie.

"Yes," Ephanie said, reaching up. Ipo's strong, large hand grasped hers and pulled her to her feet.

The former prisoners of the pens rushed toward the fence, which no longer stood. Guards ran forward, trying to stop them, only to fall back, screaming, as flames danced across their chests and down their arms. The earth kept moving like a living thing, fanning out and coming back up again, almost like wave, toppling the remaining pens.

Then Ephanie realized there were two other southern island women, like Ipo, inside the fence. They moved slowly, with effort.

And power emanated from them.

One was casting flames at the guards. She was smaller, and the firelight reflected her bloodshot eyes. The other, much larger woman, stood in the middle of the pens and pushed her hands down, the muscles on her arms straining.

All at once she rocked back, as if she'd been struck. She shook her head as if trying to clear it, then saw the others. "Run!" she called, moving faster and more gracefully than Ephanie had thought she would have been able to.

Ipo started to run as well, leading Ephanie through the night. The other followed, through the stinging bushes surrounding the clearing, into the trees.

Ephanie had never raced through the jungle like this. The first woman forced a path through the bush and trees by raising a swath of earth, causing the plants to topple to the side. Behind them, the ground sank back down, the trees sometimes falling back over, blocking the way so none could follow them.

Before long, the adrenaline wore off and Ephanie struggled to keep up. She wasn't about to ask them to slow down, though.

She'd escaped, alive, from the torture pens.

THE CAVE THE SOUTHERNERS LED EPHANIE TO WAS COLD, DAMP, and rough. It smelled of wet earth and dead fish. Boulders moved into place after they passed, blocking the entrance. A small fire already burned in the middle of the cave. Ipo walked over to it. After passing her hands over it, the flames leaped up.

When had Ipo learned to do that? Had she always had that ability?

Two other southerners moved out of the shadows and into the firelight. Did they have power like the others? With a gasp, Ephanie realized that she recognized one of them—the woman she'd seen on the beach, with the seashells tied to the ends of her long dreads. A skirt of seaweed hung from her waist.

What had the women in the pen said? Fire, mountain, and water? Were these the powers of the southern witches?

"Thank you," Ephanie said. "For saving me. For coming to get me.

I am Ephanie, teller of fortunes and prophesies," she added, addressing the sea women.

"I am Nila," the woman whom Ephanie recognized said, nodding her head to Ephanie. "I saw you taken. They hurt you."

"Yes," Ephanie said. "But I'll heal." She would always bear the scars of her torture, and the deep places in her mind that had opened to the pain. Ephanie looked around to the other women.

"Uli," said the big mountain woman. Twigs, flowers, and moss were entangled in the long curls of her hair. Her eyes burned with a black fire that made Ephanie want to step aside, get out of the way. She was naked like the others, wearing only a necklace of obsidian, each piece the size of Ephanie's fist. "Fortunes?"

"Yes, when the goddess grants me her wisdom," Ephanie replied.

"You kill prince," Uli said, nodding. Her accent was thick. She obviously didn't speak much of the witches' language, and Ephanie only knew a few of the southern island words.

"Yes," Ephanie admitted, suddenly wary. What did this large, powerful woman think about that? Was Ephanie in more trouble now?

"Not use blood," Uli said.

"I used his blood," Ephanie assured her. "For my vision. But it was too much life. I took too much." She still regretted his death, and she hoped the goddess was finished with punishing her for it.

"No," Uli said. "Not use all blood. Wasted."

Ephanie blinked. Uli thought Ephanie had wasted the prince's blood by not using all of it? What did that mean? What was she supposed to have done with the blood?

"I used what I needed. For the vision," Ephanie said.

"Not all. I use," Uli said proudly. "Free sisters."

Ephanie looked at the other women, who were all smiling and nodding. They'd been trapped?

"How did you free your sisters? What had trapped them? Who?" Ephanie asked.

"Spell," Uli said. "Curse. King Kawiti." She paused and spat.

Ephanie recognized the name. King Kawiti had died just before the witches had reached the southern islands, in the great disaster, just after the volcano had blown up. The southerners still mourned his passing and celebrated his birthday every year. On some of the islands, he was almost a god.

He'd cursed the southern witches? No wonder none of the northern witches had never found any women here with power!

Had he also enslaved the rest of the southern islanders, somehow? So that they were peaceful? And now the spell had broken by Uli, or been weakened by the rising of the moon, and so the people were coming back to their natural state?

"Are all your sisters free now?" Ephanie asked. "Or has the king still enslaved them?" And how much power had it taken to bind all these powerful women?

Uli shook her head, obviously not understanding the question.

Ipo answered. "No, they're not."

Ephanie turned to face her old cook. She looked younger, and her eyes held a cleverness that Ephanie didn't remember. Ipo idly toyed with the fire, sending a flame up, then bringing it back down again, directing it without touching it. How could she do that? None of the witches from the north had such a power.

"They're still trapped," added another of the witches, the other one Ephanie had seen before. She had bloodshot eyes and her gums were etched with black lines. "I'm Lakawoo." She gathered up a handful of Ipo's flame and threw it to the ground.

Ephanie gasped. She held out her hand to the burning vision she saw there—an older native, dully making her way up a jungle trail, unaware of herself and her surroundings. Buried deep inside the woman was a power as great as any of the other southerners.

The vision didn't have the certainty that came with one of Ephanie's visions. That didn't mean it wasn't true.

How had Lakawoo created such a picture? It wasn't the future, not a true prophesy, but something happening on another island, in the western region. It was akin to one of Ephanie's visions, though how it was related, Ephanie had no idea.

Was Ephanie's power somehow similar to that of Ipo's and Lakawoo's? She couldn't think about that now.

"How do we free them?" Ephanie asked, turning back to Uli.

The final witch came forward before Uli could reply. With a twitch of her hand, water came from nowhere and splashed out the small ball of fire. She was also nude, and wore a necklace of seaweed between her breasts. She was more gaunt than the others, and dirt caked the wrinkles of her knees, streaked the insides of her arms.

"I am Hinan," she said. "You were the start of our freedom. Now, we must go kill them all."

Horror trickled down Ephanie's back. "What do you mean, kill them all? Kill who?"

"The king. And all his sons," Ipo said, standing to join Hinan. "They've cursed us, stolen our power. The only way to free ourselves is to take their lives. To take the *power* of their lives back to ourselves."

Ephanie swallowed down the bile that suddenly filled her mouth. She'd only ever killed at the goddess' bidding. And only the once taken a human life. Now these women were going to ask her to take more.

They had rescued her. She did owe them something. And she wasn't sure that taking the lives of the king and his sons was wrong, not given how these women had suffered, not knowing themselves or their power, like that unaware creature that Lakawoo had shown Ephanie, like how Ipo had been all of Ephanie's life.

What would it have been like if Ephanie had never know the visions of the goddess? If she'd always been kept in the dark?

"There is a battle coming. Men will attack Hilani Island," Ephanie said, dragging each word out slowly. To tell another of a fortune that didn't directly belong to them went against everything Ephanie had been taught. "At the end of the *Keereekayah* festival. In nine days? Eight days?" She wasn't sure—had she lost a day in the torture chamber? So much had happened.

"The king will be harder to get to," Ipo said. "If he's worried about an attack."

"But he'll send more of his heirs away," Lakawoo pointed out. "Keep them out of harm's way."

"We will get him," Uli said firmly. "And them."

The others seemed to look at Ephanie, expectantly.

"I'm not sure how I can help," Ephanie said slowly. "But if I can, I will."

Ipo turned and said something to Uli, in their flowing language

Ephanie didn't know what they'd said. If she could guess, though, she would bet it was something like, "I told you we could use her."

It made Ephanie straighten her back and lift her chin defiantly. She would only be used by the goddess' will. None other. They'd soon discover that. She would only help them as much as she decided to. No more.

~

DAWN CREPT SLOWLY ACROSS THE MOUTH OF THE CAVE. EPHANIE sighed and turned over again. She'd slept badly. Uli's snores had grated like the cries of the *moomaki* bird, which always sounded like a child crying. The rocks under her back and side dug into her and she couldn't find a comfortable position to sleep in, her arms still hurt and the memory of Oka'u chased her dreams.

Was Ephanie really going to help the southern witches kill the king and all his sons and daughters? He hadn't been the one to curse the witches.

But he'd hurt her. Sent her to be tortured. Sent her and others to Oka'u's tender care.

Ephanie shivered, her stomach rolling. She'd never hated like this before, or felt such fear. She longed for her quiet room with all of Mama's plants softening the edges of the rooms, the sweet and earthy scent of growing things filling the air.

Ephanie rolled over again. Damn it! The rocks were shifting, she was sure, just to stick into her side more.

"Maybe we find you a feather bed and a warm man so you sleep, eh?" Ipo asked Ephanie.

"No, thank you," Ephanie replied coldly. "I will find my own way." She stiffened when she heard the words.

If Mama had been right, Ephanie was on the verge of another vision. She sat up, closed her eyes, and tried to gauge how close the vision was, how long she had before she cut herself again.

Curling excitement filled her belly at the thought of her knife on her skin. She would have thought that Oka'u had cured her of wanting to cut herself, but no, she just wanted to replace his pain with pleasure.

How much life did she need? Could she get by with a single cut? Or were there enough plants around to forestall her own pain?

"What is it, *uuka*?" Ipo asked.

"Vision," Ephanie said through gritted teeth. "I need life. Something strong. To fuel it, paint it out." Plants wouldn't do. She opened her mouth and breathed through it, trying to settle her stomach so the bile there wouldn't spew out.

When Ephanie opened her eyes, she found all the southern witches watching her.

"Life," she croaked. "Or blood. A knife." She shivered. She wasn't supposed to cut herself, to draw out that exquisite pain, to be truly alive.

But what else was there in that tiny cave?

"Come," Nila said, holding out her hand.

Ephanie bit her lips together so she didn't tell Nila that she could get up on her own. Instead, she took the hand offered her. It was warm, rough, and strong, and steadied Ephanie more than she'd thought possible.

Uli moved the rocks to the side so there was a small path for them, down the beach and into the ocean. Nila led Ephanie, drawing them both into the water until it lapped at Ephanie's knees.

"How many?" Nila asked.

"How many what?" Ephanie asked in return, exasperated. Did these women read each other's minds or something? How could they expect her to know what they meant?

"Lives," Nila replied. She reached her hand out, then made a pulling motion.

Ephanie didn't understand what Nila was doing until she looked down.

Black shapes came closer, under the water, swimming around Nila's feet. Large ocean *jakalala,* each about the length of Ephanie's arm.

Fish! Ephanie could use the lives of fish. She eagerly reached for the knife on her belt, but it was gone, taken by Oka'u and used on her.

But the vision was upon her. Ephanie reached into the water and plucked up one of the strangely docile fish. It struggled once it was above the air, its mouth gaping. With hands grown strong and clever,

Ephanie gripped the fish and twisted, pulling the head from the body. She threw both pieces onto the shore and eagerly reached for another.

It only took half a dozen of the large fish to satisfy Ephanie's need. She turned and rushed back to shore, eager to rearrange the bodies. The scales cut her fingers and she smiled, the blood so pretty and red next to the gray fish parts.

The vision exploded in her head, in all its blood and glory.

"I'm so sorry," Ephanie said, turning to Uli.

CHAPTER 8

Never give a woman the power of the mountain.
—*Southern Islands proverb*

JAHAKA STARED AT KING MAKANI IN AMAZEMENT.

Southern island witches? What was he talking about?

Men and women screamed in the night. A great roaring followed, like a wave crashing nearby. A sickeningly sweet smell followed it: burnt flesh. The grand throne room suddenly seemed closed in.

Jahaka swallowed down the bile that filled her mouth. "What do you mean, southern witches? Your people have no magic!" There were tales of gods and goddesses, those who moved mountains, walked on water, or threw flames. But no women—no witches—had ever been mentioned or found.

The king sagged, color returning to his dark features. His eyes remained haunted, though. He pulled his yellow vest closer across his chest, as though he were cold. "My ancestor, King Kawiti. After the great battle."

Oka'u returned to the room. "My lord, perhaps—"

"No," the king said. He turned to the little man and spoke a harsh phrase. "We will need their help," he added, turning back to Jahaka.

Jahaka nodded slowly, though inside she crooned, *The king would topple so easily now.* "Who are the southern witches? What did King Kawiti do to them?" How had he hidden them for so many centuries?

"The witches fought among themselves, always," King Makani said. "Taking the *leeleen* too far. There were never many, so despite their great power, there was only so much damage a single witch could do before exhausting herself." He sighed, licked his lips, and continued. "Then the two greatest of them, Hinanuli and Kilihai, formed alliances with their sisters. Hinanuli had the power of the mountain—what we call a mountain mover. She could control the earth, bring rocks out of the ground, make the stones do her bidding."

Jahaka had heard the name Hinanuli before—that was the given name for the goddess of Kualina Mountain. Were all the southern island goddesses and their deeds actually tales from older times, of their witches?

"Kilihai was a water shaker. She could call fish to her, walk on sunbeams across the water, and raise the waves," the king said.

No wonder Jahaka's ancestors had never thought these stories to be tales of witches—the southern island witches' powers were too foreign from their own.

"The two battled, calling on the elements of earth and water. Hinanuli also had a partner who was a fire dancer, and could cast flames as well." The king paused, shaking his head. "According to legend, it was they who caused Kualina Mountain to erupt, when she'd slept peacefully for lifetime upon lifetime. They killed whole islands with their hatred."

Jahaka shivered. She'd never heard of such magic before, or such power.

King Makani looked up and stared directly at Jahaka. "My ancestor, King Kawiti, had some magic himself. It is the power of all the kings, the ability to bind the people together. He worked with a witch—who asked that her name never be used—to curse the witches, bind them to the mountains, slow their wits so they could never come to power again. Then he bound the people of the islands as well, calming their warlike nature, bringing peace and prosperity to the Three Hands Full for generations."

"But the curse—the binding—has ended?" Jahaka asked, her head spinning. What power these women had!

She needed to find them. Maybe she could bend them to her will or make them her allies.

"It's been unraveling for some time," the king admitted. "We've been searching for a way to extend it, but so much was lost."

Oka'u spoke up. "The madness has brought back many memories of the old times. I've been trying to see if there are other memories stored in the heads of those who went mad, to see if they remember how to be bound."

Jahaka nearly snorted. As if the ones who were suddenly freed would tell their captors of how they'd been originally caught. Then she looked more closely at Oka'u. He hadn't been asking kindly, she realized with a shiver.

"What do the southern witches want?" Vine asked, stepping forward. "Why did they attack here, and more importantly, why did they stop?"

The king and Oka'u looked at each other. Jahaka could see them preparing a lie. "We can't help you if we don't know the truth," she said, hoping to avert them.

Oka'u nodded, opened his mouth, then closed it again and sighed. "They took the fortuneteller," he admitted. "As for why they stopped, who knows? They're all mad."

Jahaka noticed that the king very carefully didn't add anything to Oka'u's story.

He knew why the witches had stopped, but he wasn't saying. She suspected Oka'u knew as well.

"Why would they take the poor girl?" Vine asked, sounding as perplexed as Jahaka. "She's untrained and very young. She can't help such powerful witches."

"She killed Prince Aumoe," Jahaka said. "On the night of the madness. She weakened your line further, didn't she?"

The king nodded slowly. "Yes, that was my thought, when I'd heard she'd been taken." His eyes bore into Jahaka's. "This is why we need your help. They will be coming for me, for all of my family, soon."

"Of course, King Makani," Jahaka said solemnly, though she wanted to laugh. "We will help in any way we can."

The king would bring her witches closer to him, to all in his family.

And at the right time, Jahaka and her witches would purposefully fail him.

First thing in the morning, after a restless sleep, Jahaka hurried over to the storyteller's rooms in the temple complex. She'd always found the old tales fascinating, and had encouraged the women who remembered them and taught them to the children to interview every old priestess who came to the main temple to see if they could recover any stories they didn't know.

The main room was one of the few with a polished wooden floor and many rugs, so the little ones could gather and comfortably listen. Murals of the witches' history covered the walls and were always being added to. Hieroglyphs accompanied the pictures, telling the stories in more detail.

Jahaka had tried to change the curriculum of all the children, so everyone at the temple would be able to read the old characters, but the council had always balked, not wanting to give up any of their perceived power, so the girls were required to learn only a few characters. Maybe now she'd be able to force them to teach more, after pointing out how much had been lost among the southern islanders.

"Robyn!" Jahaka called as she walked in.

The old storyteller rushed from the backroom. She wore a storm gray robe, indicating that she'd retired from using her powers and moved onto teaching. Had she been a healer at one time? She didn't look as though she had been: wrinkles covered her entire face, and her skin had that soft look, as if age had worn it thin and smooth. Age spots covered her forehead and dotted her cheeks, and her once-blue eyes were faded. Her smile showed gaps in her teeth but her grip was strong as she held out her hands to Jahaka.

"To what do I owe this honor?" Robyn asked as Jahaka kissed her old teacher's cheek.

Quickly, Jahaka told Robyn of the southern witches. "We need to sift through all their stories," she instructed. "Their myths. Not all of them are tales of the gods."

Robyn stiffened. "What do you mean?"

"The story of Hinanuli!" Jahaka exclaimed. "It was actually about a southern witch. Not a goddess."

Robyn slowly drew her hands back. "You understand the implications of what you're asking," she said flatly.

Perplexed, Jahaka shook her head. What was upsetting her old teacher?

"If the stories of southern people's gods and goddesses aren't real, but are about powerful women and men instead, who's to say that ours aren't as well?" Robyn asked plainly.

Jahaka gasped. "No! Our gods are real. The goddess Brikalla, and the gods Caduk and Ekuilli—they can't be witches." She'd seen the power of the fortunetellers, the growers and the healers. These abilities didn't come from the witches themselves, but from the gods.

Robyn sighed and shook her head. "I know you're almost as old as I am, but you don't listen to your old body. These questions, once asked, cannot be unasked. To study the southern island myths is to ask for comparison, to study our own as well."

"No," Jahaka said immediately. "Our tales are true. Not myths." The gods had always guided her, led her along the right paths through the jungle as well as the village. How could they not be real?

After a few moments of silence, Robyn finally replied, "I can limit my searches. Be clever in how I ask my questions, so that no priestess or storyteller starts to question her own faith."

"Be your cleverest," Jahaka said. "Like Hynla, the trickster."

"Yes, my lady," Robyn said.

Jahaka left the storyteller's rooms, uneasy. Her faith had never been shaken, not like the other powerful witches whom she'd counseled.

The tales of the gods were true. They were pure, unlike the southerners.

And if Robyn asked too many questions of the wrong people, raised too much doubt…well, she could be dealt with as well.

JAHAKA MET WITH VINE IN HER PRIVATE CHAMBERS, THE SAME AS how she'd been meeting with witches all day, determining their temperament, seeing whom she could rely on, who could be trusted to do the right thing and step aside when the time came to help the king and his family.

Luckily, Jahaka had found more than a few who were happy to do her will. They agreed that the king must die. The fear that their own powers might be bound had proven to be very useful.

It was late afternoon when Vine came to Jahaka's rooms. The window overlooking the bay was open, the wind filling the room with the fresh scent of the sea. A bowl filled with small, sweet oranges, purple plantains, and red *okoku* berries sat on the table between the chairs Jahaka had set up. Clear water, two beautifully carved cups, and a tiny statue of Brikalla filled out the carefully set scene.

Jahaka didn't want any to forget that their own gods had set them down this path, bringing them to the islands, saving them from the mainland. That their own gods were powerful and always present in their lives.

"Good day, my lady," Vine said as she crossed the threshold. She stayed at the door, her head bowed, as if she were afraid to step closer.

"Come in, please," Jahaka said. "I have fruit and water, and could send for wine, if you'd like."

Vine looked up, her clear eyes taking in everything. "Thank you, my lady, for inviting me here," she said, slowly crossing the room but not sitting. "How may I serve you?"

"First of all, sit down," Jahaka said. "This isn't a formal meeting."

Vine sat carefully, but she stayed at the edge of her chair, her back stiff, her hands folded tightly in her lap.

"I didn't call you here to chastise you," Jahaka said, trying to ease the old woman's fears.

"Really," Vine asked dryly. "Then why did you call me here."

"I'm meeting with many of my top advisors, in private, today," Jahaka explained. "I'm trying to determine who will be best to send with the king's heirs as they scatter to various islands." Though the king hadn't specifically asked for such help, Jahaka knew it was just a matter of time. He needed them, the power of the northern witches, more than ever.

As a bonus, getting off Hilani Island before the attack would be a sure way of staying alive. Jahaka had had to deny more than one petition for suddenly leaving, disgusted at the lack of courage and faith her priestesses had shown.

Their healers, temple guards, and faith would protect them.

Vine nodded to show she was listening, but she didn't say anything.

Perturbed, Jahaka asked, "Do you think any of your guild would be appropriate?"

Vine gave a dry, bitter laugh. "To fall on their own knives when you ask? Or to turn them against the heirs? Oh yes, my lady, I know many who would be happy to do that."

What was Jahaka missing? Something else was going on with the old fortuneteller. It couldn't have been a vision. News of a new augury would have been told to her.

"Why do you think I'd ask for such a thing?" Jahaka hadn't been that straightforward with any of the witches who'd agreed, and she was certain none of them would have talked, particularly not to a fortuneteller, no matter how close to the council she might be.

Vine merely shrugged. "The king or one of his kind could bind us, too," she stated. "And we can't allow that."

"Yes, exactly!" Jahaka said, pleased that Vine understood why Jahaka was asking such things.

"Of course, it wouldn't have anything to do with your recent trips to the west, or that young upstart, Enekai," Vine continued.

"What do you mean?" Jahaka asked, pleased with how casual she managed to sound. Enekai was just someone she had diplomatic relations with, not a lover whom she still dreamed about, alone in her bed.

"As you've said, we northern witches have lost a lot of power since coming here," Vine replied. "Not just in my guild, but in all of them. For example, more than one fortuneteller knew of the doom of Alokai Temple so many generations ago, because the telling was so powerful. Anyone with any ability could feel it."

"So there's been another foretelling?" Jahaka asked. "Another prophecy?" If it involved her, why hadn't she been told?

Vine shook her head. "We've grown weak. Soft. There have been dreams, but dreams only. And we've been taught never to pay attention to our dreams. They don't always come true."

Jahaka nodded. All witches were told that from a young age: to ignore their dreams, particularly if they were members of the fortuneteller's guild. Only the fortunes fueled by life were guaranteed to come true. More than one myth told of a disaster that occurred when a witch followed a dream rather than a prophesy.

"But maybe our dreams shouldn't be denied," Vine said, suddenly turning and staring at Jahaka. Her voice lowered and took on a singsong tone. "I've seen the tops of mountains blow, and waves that swallow islands. Fire that dances on the wings of birds and living nets to contain them. Whole islands covered in deadly spiderwebs and jungles that are silent."

Chills ran down Jahaka's spine. This wasn't the same as a vision. Vine didn't speak with the voice of the goddess.

But it was very close. Something of power lived in Vine's dreams.

Vine took an abrupt breath and sat back, shaking her head. "There are too many things this old witch has dreamed of, some that came true, and too many that didn't." She paused, then addressed the floor. "We're headed into times of true chaos now. No one, not even the gods, can guide us."

"What do you mean?" Jahaka asked. Had it also occurred to Vine that the stories of their gods and goddesses might be myths? How far had this poisonous idea spread?

"In times of great crisis, the goddess won't speak until after the tipping point has been reached. As I said before, everyone knew of the doom of Alokai Temple. *No one* knew the outcome. No one could have predicted that the witches would migrate to the islands."

Jahaka shook her head. "What do you mean?"

"The battle that's coming. Ephanie saw it, and others, too, have now had inklings of it. But no one has seen beyond the battle. It's too great of a turning point. Too many factors affect the outcome." Vine paused, then added, "So yes, I know of witches who will help you get rid of the royalty. It's something I won't be a party to, and that I would advise against, because no one, *no one*, can predict the outcome of the battle, whether the king will win or lose. No one knows if that will weaken our position, or strengthen it."

With that, Vine stood. "Thank you, my lady, for letting this poor advisor speak clearly." She bowed her head and strode out the door before Jahaka could call her back.

The afternoon sun still rode high in the sky, but Jahaka shivered as she sat thinking. Then her chin rose defiantly.

It didn't matter if no one could foresee the final outcome, if the gods couldn't guarantee it.

Jahaka would just have to do everything in her power to make certain the king lost. With Enekai ruling here, under her thumb, the power of the witches would grow, not diminish.

Sneaking out of the temple proved to be easier than Jahaka had anticipated.

While on one hand, this made her life easier, on the other, she didn't like what it said about the security of the temple. She really was going to have to talk with Yarrow and the head of the guards about tightening security. There was a battle coming. They should be better prepared.

That night was even quieter than the previous one. More guards stood on the corners, but none stopped a healer in her red robes, carrying a basket of herbs and hurrying. Jahaka had used this disguise before when she'd needed to slip out of the temple. No one would stop a healer on her way to help someone. Anyone who dared would be put to death.

The only way to test whether a woman was a healer or not would be to cut her, for her to prove she could heal herself deliberately, not just quickly, like a fortuneteller. There had been talk of the healers all growing some sort of mark or easily recognizable birthmark, but it had never gone too far.

But maybe it didn't matter that much. A southern witch couldn't pretend to be a white healer any more than a northern witch could pretend to be a fire dancer.

And besides, the northern witches would have nothing to fear from the southern witches, once they realized they were all on the same side of the war, all wanting to be rid of the current royal regime. Plus, the southerners had rescued Ephanie.

It didn't take long for Jahaka to arrive at the little hut off the market. Aleekona didn't live there; Jahaka wasn't sure who did, perhaps one of his followers. But they always met there, once Aleekona had moved out of the temple.

The call of the *huo* bird greeted Jahaka as she pulled aside the curtain hanging over the doorway, stepping into the darkened room. She widened her eyes so that she could see without the aid of light.

Aleekona stood on the far side of the room, in the doorway, his sword ready. He really had turned into a fine man, with a broad chest and strong arms. He wore his hair down just to his shoulders, braided in a fisherman's knot. He'd been born to a northern witch and raised at the temple with the other children.

Jahaka remembered how soft his skin had felt the first time she'd seduced him, flowing under her fingers like the smoothest sand.

Once she'd become his patron, though, he'd moved out of the temple and remained at a firm but polite distance.

She wondered sometimes if he'd used his own body against her, putting himself in her way so she'd notice him and take advantage of him. Then moved away and denied all contact, even when she'd made it obvious that she'd like to continue their liaison.

"So are we just going to talk in the dark, like old times?" Jahaka teased as she unerringly made her way to a chair on one side of the table sitting in the center of the room.

A rich chuckle greeted her. "I prefer the light now," Aleekona said, reaching down and uncovering a small, already lit oil lamp. He picked up the clay lamp and placed it in the center of the table before sheathing his sword and sitting down. He sat straight and tall, ready to leap to action at a moment's notice.

Jahaka could barely tell Aleekona was of mixed race—a son born to a witch—unless she was looking carefully. Then she'd see that his eyes weren't as dark brown as most of the natives, his nose was wider and longer, and he was taller than many as well.

It suited him, though—the wider reach and more muscular stance —particularly as part of Jahaka's private guard.

"I am glad to see you safe and unharmed," Jahaka said truthfully.

"That's just because you don't want to have to train any new guards," Aleekona teased.

"True," Jahaka admitted. "But also because I would have missed you, old friend." She closed her mouth abruptly. What was going on with her? Why would she admit to such a weakness here?

At least Aleekona didn't seem to catch it.

"I am also glad to see you unhurt, particularly after all this madness." He grew more serious. "I've had to discharge some of men from my guard. They weren't all…stable. After the moon passed over Kualina Mountain."

"I'm glad you were able to replace them," Jahaka said, disturbed.

"Easily," Aleekona said. "From your generosity, I can offer more money than they'd get anywhere else, even on the deep sea fishing trading routes."

"Good," Jahaka said.

"But what can I do for you this evening?" Aleekona asked. "You surely didn't come here just to ask after the state of my men."

"What happened, last night?" Jahaka said. Aleekona had seen the southern witches attack first hand. She wanted a report.

"Ah." Aleekona shifted in his seat. "We would have gotten the girl," he said earnestly. "We were just too late. The others got there first."

"I don't blame you for not retrieving her," Jahaka said gently, knowing she was giving her old lover too much. She should pretend to be cross with him, to keep him on edge. "I just need to know what you saw. Who you saw, what they did."

"The southern witches," Aleekona said, nodding. "You want to know about them." He seemed relieved.

"Yes. Or we can talk about your failure," Jahaka added, only partially teasing.

"There were three of them," Aleekona said earnestly. "One was a mountain mover. She caused the earth around the fence to raise up, so the posts fell over. Then she sent lines of earth through the ground, breaking up the pens." He paused and swallowed.

Even in the dim light, Jahaka could tell that the memory bothered him.

"The other two were fire dancers," Aleekona continued. "One would set a guard on fire, then the other would take the flames, make them into ropes and vines, snaring anyone else who came near." He took a deep breath and shook his head.

Jahaka couldn't imagine the power that these woman used. What was the cost? How did they harness such elements? How ancient must they be, to have such magic?

Could they teach her people?

"Can you describe them?" Jahaka asked, wanting to be able to recognize them if they came to the temple.

Aleekona laughed and shook his head. "You'd recognize them. They're naked, wearing only necklaces and belts to indicate their power. They're powerfully built women, large old mothers, wearing their years heavily on their skin."

Jahaka blinked and shook her head. Naked women? Old, and probably fat? And powerful? This surprised her. "Really?" she asked.

"Yes, my lady," Aleekona replied, a slight reproof in his tone. "My people have different measures for power and beauty."

Jahaka sat back, stung. Was that why Aleekona had rebuffed her? Because he turned back to his people? To their ideals? She looked down at her thin hand, pale, with the bones just under the skin. She'd always thought her white skin was so beautiful, especially when her hand was stroking his.

It didn't matter what Aleekona thought. Jahaka clenched her fist. "How can I contact them? Where would I find them?" She had to stay focused.

"There's a report that on Ailani Island—near where the prince was killed?—a new mountain has been born," Aleekona said. "The witches may be gathering there. Or maybe it's just a distraction, and they've gone elsewhere." He paused, then leaned against the table and earnestly added, "No one knows where they've gone, where they'll strike next, or what they want. They're not the same as my people, and are very, *very* different than yours. I know you want to find them, to make them allies, but they are madwomen, each and every one of them."

"Really? Because tearing up the prison pens to rescue my fortuneteller sounds pretty organized to me," Jahaka pointed out. They couldn't be that crazy—she should be able to bend them to her will.

"Old stories are being retold in the marketplace," Aleekona said. "And when the king's guard tried to stop the storytellers, the crowd turned against them. The people want to be prepared. They remember."

"They remember what?" Jahaka prompted when Aleekona didn't continue. The king had said something about people remembering as well. And Oka'u was probably torturing others to see if they'd spill those memories.

"The *Mahinapo*—the southern witches. They nearly destroyed all of us, battling each other," Aleekona replied. "No one remembers what the battle was about. Just the aftermath. Not just the lives that were lost, but entire islands."

"I see," Jahaka said, pondering.

The southern witches were unstable? Good. Maybe Jahaka could use that as well, to help persuade the northern witches that it was time to move back to the mainland.

CHAPTER 9

There is no light burden when walking a long trail.
 —Southern Islands proverb

"Sorry?" Uli asked. She cursed her past once again. Her slow thoughts had stopped her from learning the witches' language when she'd been young.

This foreign witch—Ephanie—had power that Uli had never seen before, not even in any of her sisters' dreams.

Through her blood and the lives of the fish, Ephanie had cast a fire that held pictures only she could read. They were similar to Lakawoo's images of what was happening far away. But these images were different—not of today, but tomorrow and beyond.

No wonder the witches thought they were so special if they had such abilities. But Uli was certain that she and her sisters were stronger, and would show these skinny women.

The girl's voice deepened and her words flowed clear. No matter how little Uli knew of the witches' language, she still would have understood this prophecy. She shivered. Were these really the words from a goddess?

143

"I see you standing by yourself in the final battle," Ephanie predicted. "Your sisters have all left you. Too many fights, too many differences. You cannot work with them as they work with each other. Instead, you face the king, alone, dirty, unkempt, your wits woven again into the stones, your very name lost to you. You stand alone."

Ephanie fell down to her knees after the words of her goddess left her.

Uli shivered in the cool morning air. Was this a curse the girl had given her? It felt like one, wrapped in a prophesy.

"I'm so sorry," Ephanie said. She gave her tears up easily, her body wracked with pain.

Uli looked to Ipo, who nodded and walked over to the girl.

"Here," Ipo said, "Come with me." She raised the girl up and led her away to lie down again in the cave.

Uli looked at the other witches standing there, staring at her. "What does she know?" Uli asked, defiant.

"Their prophecies always come true," Lakawoo stated. "They pay for the truth with life. Frequently their own."

Uli turned to look out over the water. Did it matter if she was alone? She'd always been alone. It was harder to hear that she'd lose herself again to the stone. Was it easier knowing the betrayal was coming? Or harder?

"I will lead us as far as you'll have me," Uli stated. Alone, she could stand. But slow again, and deserted in that nightmare hut? She'd kill herself first.

"And I will stand next to you, as long as you'll have me," Ipo said, coming to stand beside Uli.

"I will as well," Lakawoo said.

Hinan and Nila looked at each other before walking over to stand in front of Uli, not beside her. "We aren't leaving you now," Nila stated clearly. "But our own sisters call to us. The other water shakers. We hear them in the waves. In the end, we will stand with them. But not against you. That we swear."

Uli nodded. That was more than she could have asked for.

The other witches left Uli then, to stand and watch the day begin, the canoes darting across the water, the world turning around her as her thoughts sought a path through the densest jungle.

~

"You said your sisters called you?" Uli asked Hinan and Nila when she walked back up into the cave. The girl lay curled up on her side, dozing, but awake enough to listen. Ipo and Lakawoo stood to one side, while the water shakers stood on the other.

Were they already turning against each other? Did none of them remember that was what destroyed them the last time?

Hinan nodded slowly. "I can hear them." She turned her head and looked out the cave toward the water. "On the waves. They're meeting together. Near Kualina."

"Do you know how many?" Uli asked.

"Four, maybe six," Hinan said. "Their voices are hard to make out," she added, apologetic.

"You should go to them," Uli said. "We need to stay here."

"Why?" Ipo asked.

"The king is here," Uli replied. Wasn't that obvious? Maybe they could aid in the attack as well. Distract the king's guards, guarantee their defeat.

"He'll send his heirs away," Lakawoo predicted. "Not the younger ones, but the eldest. He'll send them to far islands, well protected, so we can't reach them."

Uli snorted. There wasn't anywhere she couldn't reach. Given time, she'd figure out how to dig deep enough to pull up the palace stones.

"This may be what Ephanie saw," Ipo said. "That we separate to go after the heirs."

"Maybe," Uli said, though she doubted it. She'd been alone all her life—her dreams of children were just that. It was just her in the jungle. It would be just her at the final battle, too.

"How do we attack the king?" Lakawoo asked. "Why did you stop attacking the palace?"

Uli sighed. She didn't want to tell them, but maybe they should know. "The stones under the palace are bound. I couldn't tear them out." That didn't mean she would never be able to. She'd figure out a way.

"How did King Kawiti bind the stones?" Hinan asked. "I thought his only power was over people."

"Another must have worked with him," Ipo said, turning to Uli. "Didn't they? One of the mountain movers."

Uli shuddered at the thought. Not one of her sisters! But it was the only thing that made sense. "I don't know why any of my sisters would work with him," Uli said quietly. "It wasn't one of the northern witches. They don't have the power."

"It's possible, though," Lakawoo said. "The witch who worked with him might not have had her will," she added.

"What do you mean?" Hinan asked.

Lakawoo gave a bitter laugh. "Poppies make everything sweeter, until there isn't anything else. Until you can't live without that sweetness." She glanced over at Ephanie, then back to Uli. "Pain is an unsubtle torture. There are many other ways to control someone."

Uli glanced at the skinniest and smallest of the southern women. Lakawoo was starting to fill out, but she'd never have the same power or stand as firmly as the rest of them.

"Thank you," Uli replied softly. "I will hold onto that thought, but I know better than to hope it was the truth."

The southern witches never stood together for long enough to conquer the kings. One of her sisters could have turned against them by standing with the king.

"So how do we attack the king?" Ipo asked. "How do we get into the palace and kill the younger heirs? There will be guards. They'll be watching for us."

Uli looked over her shoulder at the young white witch lying there, listening but not understanding what they said. "There may be a way."

"I KNOW. SCARED," ULI SAID, SITTING BESIDE THE SHAKING GIRL, Ephanie. If only there were a power of languages, so Uli could speak better, could understand this northern witch! But that only happened in myths, where the gods and goddesses could understand all creatures.

The evening had drawn up close, with purple and pink clouds gathering at the horizon. Hinan had called fish for their dinner, and Ipo had cooked them to perfection. The girl had seemed uncertain about how to eat the fish at first, but she'd caught on quickly enough, using her fingers like they did, plucking out the bones and tossing them into the sand, where Uli buried them promptly.

How long would they be able to stay there? Uli was surprised they hadn't been found yet, that she hadn't had to turn away the king's guards. The spot they were at was inaccessible, but she still thought he would have sent climbers down the rocks. Or maybe they were all busy preparing for the upcoming battle.

It didn't really matter: they'd move the next day when they separated. The water shakers would leave to go to their kin, while only Ipo and Lakawoo stayed behind.

"Where the king sends his heirs? We must know," Uli added.

The girl could get into the palace unnoticed. Uli, Ipo, and Lakawoo, on their own, would be questioned by the guards.

"But they'll catch me!" Ephanie complained, her pale skin whiter even than the *maui* fish.

"We get you out again," Uli assured her.

Ephanie shook her head. "No. He'll kill me. Oka'u. The king's *advisor*."

Ipo came and sat next to the girl, taking hold of one of her hands. "We could kill him first," she said softly.

"No," Ephanie said.

"Why?" Uli asked. The man had hurt her. He deserved to be killed.

"I'll kill him," Ephanie said firmly. "Not you."

Uli nodded, pleased.

Maybe the northern witches could be useful beyond issuing curses disguised as fortunes.

~

THE PLAN WAS FOR THEM TO MEET AT THE PALACE CLOSE TO sunset. Ephanie and Ipo would come in along the village road, while Uli and the others would approach from the shore.

Uli would spend the day studying the palace stones, seeking a way to make the very foundation shake.

Ephanie and Ipo would gather information, first from the village, then from the palace itself, finding out how many heirs were still on Hilani Island. Where they hid themselves.

Ipo was the right choice to go with the girl; they'd both been raised in a village, and Ipo's hair was still short. She could pretend to be the girl's nurse. Hopefully that would hide her in the village. She'd have to make her way alone on the road to the palace, though, because the guards might still recognize her power and stop her.

The water witches would wait in the cave until Uli came back for them.

Uli led the way for Ipo, Ephanie, and Lakawoo. The rock felt good under her hands and feet, but she made an easier path for the others to follow, going south, around the base of the island. The steps she forced out of the rock crumbled into nothing after the last of them passed by; Uli didn't want anyone to spot them.

The cliffs were formidable, Uli knew that. She also knew that it wouldn't stop her or any of her sisters.

There were other mountain movers, she was certain of it. She wasn't sure if she wanted to meet another of her sisters or not.

When Uli reached an accursed road, she stopped. "You can follow the white path," she said, trying to keep the disdain from her voice.

Ipo just grinned at her. "Thank you, sister, for all your labor today. You can go lie in your hammock for the rest of the afternoon, dreaming and watching the clouds go by."

Uli smiled at Ipo and tried to make her voice as casual, playing along with the *leeleen*. "Don't work too hard going to market, to *buy* the goods other people have made."

Ipo put her hands on her waist and replied, "Most claim money makes you harder. But nothing could make *you* less soft."

"I think all that fire has addled your brains," Uli replied hotly.

"Enough," Lakawoo said, coming between the two women.

Uli backed away, ashamed. Ipo had just been playing, trying to say goodbye without tears, because for all their plans and strength, there was no guarantee they'd see each other again.

Ipo stepped around Lakawoo, holding her arms out. "Goodbye, my truest, best sister."

Uli grasped Ipo's forearms, like how soldiers and warriors greeted each other. "Goodbye, my sweeter self."

"You better believe it," Ipo said, pulling back, still grinning. "Come along, *uuka*," she directed to Ephanie.

"Goodbye," the girl said, waving, seeming uncertain. Then she followed Ipo down the path, her own destiny awaiting her.

"We must be careful, stay hidden," Uli warned Lakawoo as they went back around the base of the island, gradually rising away from the coast and inward, toward the palace. Surely the king had guards looking for them. Even if they weren't, they were sure to be more vigilant because of the coming battle. Uli tried to disguise the path she forced through the jungle and make it impossible for any other to walk along it, but she couldn't hide the fact that they'd passed.

The day was hotter than usual under the trees, without any ocean breezes to cool the air. Annoying insects buzzed loudly in the sun, and gnats flew at Uli, stinging her eyes and choking her mouth. Loud *moomaki* birds cried in the trees. Uli remembered the cries of her children, or her sisters' children, naked and shoeless, dying in the jungle.

When they reached the first road, Uli bit back her scream. Didn't they understand how they hurt the earth with such a thing? Nothing could grow among these stones. And they hurt her feet.

"No," Lakawoo said as Uli raised her hands. "Ipo told me to remind you that you can't destroy the road. Not yet. We need to get to the palace first."

Uli pulled herself back. She knew better. They'd all agreed they needed to stay hidden.

Why was it so hard to concentrate that day? Her thoughts weren't as slow as they had been, but they weren't as nimble, either.

They crossed the road quickly, cutting up the hill toward the king's gardens. Flowers, bushes, and trees grew in straight, foreign lines. This wasn't how her people sculpted a garden. This was all from the damned witches. The king's gardens were too tame and safe; nothing from the jungle remained.

Roaring anger filled Uli's head, louder than any surf. Her feet slowed, sliding along the path instead of properly stepping. What was wrong with her?

"Do you feel it?" Uli asked Lakawoo as they drew closer to the palace.

"Yes," Lakawoo immediately replied. "It's like the binding spell has risen, so it's not just down in the rocks under the palace, but now, woven into the grass."

"Grass. Bah," Uli said, kicking at the green turf under her feet. Who had even *heard* of such a thing before the northern witches arrived? What was wrong with dirt and moss?

But Lakawoo was right. The binding spell spread from the ground, up into Uli's feet, seeping into her bones.

"How is the king doing this?" Uli asked. "Is he working with one of our sisters? Or does he have that much power on his own?" It unnerved her to think of a man with magic. That was reserved only for women.

"Is it him doing the work?" Lakawoo asked. "Or is the binding just responding to us being here?"

That made more sense—the binding didn't feel like it had thought behind it. It felt reactive, not directed.

It still was slowing Uli down further than she liked. And it made Lakawoo nervous. She twitched at every sound, and her right cheek developed a tick it hadn't had before.

Slowly, the women pushed on, into the next ring of public gardens. They rested behind a huge *mamapo'o* plant, hidden from the path. Uli's ears rang and sweat gathered under her breasts and slid easily down her back.

The king could *not* have such power. It had to be something else, from somewhere else. Were the northern witches helping him?

"I need to see what's going on under the earth," Uli told Lakawoo quietly.

"What should I do?" Lakawoo said. She shivered and her hands twitched. "The need—it's growing again."

Lakawoo's eyes had grown more bloodshot, the whites turning all red. She kept licking her lips, as if seeking that elusive sweet poppy taste.

"Stay here, as long as you're able," Uli said. "Then go down the hill. Do you hear me? Go down the hill." She paused, then lied to the girl. "You'll find your treat there. At the base of the hill. Down close to the ocean."

"Really?" Lakawoo asked, her eyes grown wide, her mouth, slack.

"Yes," Uli said. "Go down the hill. But stay here as long as you can."

Lakawoo nodded, but her body had already shifted away from Uli's.

There wasn't anything else Uli could do for the girl right now, except curse King Kawiti once again.

Uli closed her eyes, placed her palms flat against the ground, then shoved her awareness *down*, into the earth.

A soft tide greeted her. Instead of solid, steady earth, it was like pushing through a pile of feathers. The stones drifted instead of pressing back. It was worse than trying to climb a mountain of sand, never getting a foothold, always slipping and sliding.

Where was it coming from, though?

Up, Uli pushed. Through the waving layers, that made the ground more like surf. Up the hill. It had to be coming from the palace, but where?

Uli surfed back and forth through the earth, trailing her thoughtfulness behind her. She wasn't slowing down; no, just her body was affected by the spreading of the binding spell. Her own powers stayed strong.

Darkness settled over Uli's senses as she dove deeper into the hill. Instead of warm earth, now it felt as though the ground had fallen under a great shadow. It was like climbing to the top of the tallest mountain, where the air grew thin and cold.

The darkness formed a pattern. She traced a vein, then another, connected and woven together…

…like some sort of giant spider's web.

But what creature lay in the center of it? This wasn't the king's doing. No, this thing had taken the original binding spell of the king's and woven it into its web, casting its own magic.

Uli pushed herself into the center of the blackness. Cold struck her soul. Ice formed between her searching fingertips. The taste of metal filled the mouth of her body, so far away from her awareness-seeking magic, up on the ground.

But still Uli drove forward, into the morass of shadowy magic, until she found a line going *up*. Up from the darkness, up the hill, up into the palace rocks where the binding spell still lay, quiescent and powerful.

Up into the bottom rooms of the palace.

The ground around Uli shivered, scraping against her magical senses. Then it keened, wailing with sorrow. Tremors rippled through the earth and down, feeding the black hole.

It took Uli another few moments to determine what caused the earth to mourn so, why its cries fed the darkness.

Her stomach churning, Uli fled back to her body. She gasped, drawing in the warm air. She shivered uncontrollably, despite the heat of the day. Without looking around, Uli dropped to her side and rolled in the dirt, bringing more of her skin into contact with the cleansing earth, trying to dislodge any blackness that may have clung to her.

When Uli opened her eyes, she saw that she was alone. Of course, Lakawoo's own demons had proven too much for the girl.

But Uli couldn't take the time to find her now. She had to go seek Ipo and the girl—Ephanie.

They were walking into a trap.

Oka'u wasn't just a twisted bastard. He was some sort of dark creature—a demon spider—who fueled his darkness with the screams of his victims.

He wasn't a northern witch, but he wasn't a native of the Three Hands Full Islands, either.

Uli had never heard of his kind before. None of her sisters had ever dreamed of such a creature. It was a relief to know that none of her kind had helped King Kawiti.

However, Oka'u was so strong. He'd been aware of Uli's presence under the earth, she was certain. Tracking it, with that damn web of his growing under the entire island.

He'd be able to track Ipo and the girl as well, maybe all the southern witches.

Uli had to go warn Ipo and Ephanie away from the palace, before Oka'u captured them both in his web.

WERE THERE OTHER SISTERS HERE ON THIS ISLAND? ULI WASN'T sure. If there were, they were likely to have already been trapped and slowed by that creature's—Oka'u's—web.

Uli asked the goddess to direct her, like she had before. All Uli had were her faint memories, from the first time she'd come out of the jungle. How to steal clothes. How to bathe herself. She knew it wouldn't be enough to completely disguise her. But she would also move slowly and keep her eyes downcast, watching the earth. Maybe it would be enough to hide her power, at least in the village.

It wouldn't hurt that the web under the ground grew stronger as she walked, the weight of the mountain sifting back into her bones, slowing her body and her thoughts.

Uli promised herself that she would *never* end up in a hut again, filled with refuse, her children missing. But it was hard. The hut was comfort and an old, familiar home. As awful as that existence had been, she hadn't been aware most of the time. And if she went back, she knew she'd lose herself completely.

The girl had said she'd lose her thoughts again. Uli swore again that she'd kill herself first.

In her stolen clothes, with a stolen load of wood on her back, Uli sought the main road. Each step burned the soles of her feet. Her bones grew heavier, and her mind, slower. Other travelers to the marketplace from the palace cursed her and her speed. The road was narrow, to prevent a large army from walking along it, protecting the palace.

But it made for slow going among the merchants and laborers going to and from the palace to the market.

A young man cursed behind Uli. "Get a cart, grandmother," he spat.

Uli hunched in on herself, a thousand such insults flowing over her, thrown at her and her sisters over the years. She stubbornly kept the same pace though.

The young should learn to respect the old.

As the young man passed, he reached out to shove at her shoulder, maybe push her down.

Uli couldn't help herself. Her hand moved quickly, grasping his wrist and twisting. "You should always be kind to strangers," she hissed. "You never know who may show up at your door." Then she shoved him away and back.

Fearful, the young man hurried off.

Such a foolish boy. She'd not seek him, but maybe he'd learned some manners, before one of her sisters gave him a proper lesson, with a necklace of fire or feet that could never be free of the water.

A group of laborers passed Uli next, carrying a palanquin bearing a wealthy merchant. They trotted by, speeding past as many on the road as they could before waiting to pass again.

When had her people gained such haste? Why were they in such a hurry now?

It was the witches' influence, she knew. They spread like a second web, just as deadly as Oka'u's. How could she stop them? Or was it too late?

Finally, Uli reached the central marketplace. She stopped at the edge, off the road and out of the way of the busy people, casting her head in one direction, then the other, trying to get her bearings.

Where were the storytellers? Older women and men generally gathered near along the edges of the crowd, exchanging gossip. It was the best place to hear any news, particularly of the king and his kin.

It was also where Uli always went first when she came to a new market. She remembered delighting in the tales, though she had no coin or shells to share with the tellers.

Uli took another moment to dip her thoughts down below the well-trodden dirt. The web was much thinner here. Was it because it was around the mountain from the palace? Or was something else slowing its growth? Could the northern witches, who lived nearby, be any use?

With slow, lumbering steps, Uli made her way through the narrow, crooked lanes with stalls crowded in on either side, temporary huts or, sometimes, merely tables. Merchants in plain brown or tan vests haggled over songbirds, fish, fruit, and herbs. More than one weaver had beautiful cloth for sale, in patterns and colors Uli had never seen before. Stands sold fermented juice, as well as cooked and dried meats. Every third stall had an altar set up, to Hynla for wealth, or Ekuilli for health, or even Keereeka, for welcoming more guests and customers to their stall.

There was an urgency here, to all the sales being made. People were stocking up on supplies. A battle was coming. They prepared the best way they could.

At the far western end of the market sat the first of the witches' temples. Instead of colorful murals covering the walls, like her own people's temples, the walls had been woven in a clever pattern of brown and tan reeds, creating geometric shapes. Uli wasn't sure who it was dedicated to—black sashes hung down from the eaves on the porch. Maybe it was the fortuneteller's god. She hurried past. Could the witches feel her power?

Next to the temple, a large crowd had gathered to hear the storytellers. Uli pushed her way closer to the front to hear the speaker, but also to get a better look at the crowd, scanning for Ephanie and Ipo. She didn't see them, but the speaker was excellent and she quickly got caught up in the tale, one of her favorites, of the clever Hoopai outwitting not just the king, but the gods.

Had Ephanie and Ipo already come and gone? How could she find them? There was a group of elders standing opposite the temple, laughing at their own jokes. But Uli didn't see anyone she knew.

With great reluctance, Uli turned slowly away. She was going to have to look through the rest of the market again. She didn't know how else to find her sister, warn them both.

Uli stopped abruptly when she realized that just behind her stood another large woman in ill-fitting clothing, her hair matted and tangled.

Was this another sister? Had she found her way here on her own? Had she found herself?

Uli forced her eyes to the ground. They couldn't look at each other —that might warn the people around them that they were other than they seemed.

She had to talk to this woman. Maybe she could help find Ipo. She'd found Uli.

With shuffling feet, Uli pushed her way to the edges of the market. Without looking back, she knew the woman followed, unsteady in her own gait.

Taking an abrupt turn, Uli made her way up one of the side streets, where the huts were built too close to one another, touching. Just a bit further up the lane, there were some abandoned huts, the walls falling down and the roofs leaking. The yards in front of the huts were plain dirt with little growing, but maybe a pot-bird or two strutting across the property.

Another set of footsteps followed hers.

They reached the edge of the village, built up against the mountain. Refuse piles buzzed with flies. Gangs of screaming children ran out of the streets and into the encroaching jungle. When Uli reached the last of the houses, she turned around.

The woman's eyes burned into her, caught up in a fever Uli remembered all too well.

"Sister," the woman croaked. "It's been too long."

"Or not long enough," Uli automatically responded. She remembered fighting with this woman, and loving her, and falling into fights again.

"You followed the call," the woman said. "I didn't think you were bright enough."

"Brighter than you," Uli automatically replied. "Why would I follow your call?" she added, sneering.

What was her name? Uli tried to remember. Did she know her, now? Or only in the past, through her sisters and their sisters' memories?

"Only you would be stupid enough not to recognize the call of the goddess," the woman said.

"I followed no call," Uli said. "Not on this island."

"You're—you're not from this island?" the woman asked, her confidence faltering.

"No. I am Uli," she said.

"Pua," the woman responded, looking more closely at Uli now. "How did you get here?"

"Across the water beams, directed by two water shakers," Uli told her. "And now I must find two of my companions. Before that monster Oka'u gets them." And used their screams to snare more of her sisters.

Pua shivered. "Oka'u? He's worse than a snake. He's like black oil that slides out of our grasp. He isn't from our islands, but somewhere to the west."

"Have you fought him?" Uli asked. They would have to defeat him in order to tear the palace down.

Pua stared directly into Uli's eyes. "My sisters did," she said, her voice far away while her eyes burned. "You need to get him far from his web. He uses it to strengthen himself, heal any wounds."

"Thank you," Uli said sincerely. "When the time comes, I will remember your words. Now, I must find my other sisters. Will you help?"

"Someone has to help you," Pua said, with a sly grin. "You couldn't find the ocean even if you were standing on the beach."

"And you couldn't find the night when standing in the darkness," Uli threw back.

"Who are you looking for? Do you even remember?" Pua asked disdainfully.

Uli's back straightened at the sting. "Of course I remember. Ipo. She's a water shaker. Like you, yes?"

Pua nodded.

"And a white witch. One of the black robes." Uli didn't want to take the time to explain why they were working with the northern witches.

Pua only crooked one eyebrow up at that, but thankfully didn't ask any questions. "There are so few of us. Finding another southern witch in the market shouldn't be too difficult. Even for you. Come. This way," Pua said, turning and walking more quickly back toward the market.

Uli grinned, then forced her features to be blank again. Pua was a water shaker, and her sisters had fought Uli's sisters centuries ago. Why? No one remembered.

And they might fight again someday. It was their nature.

For now, though, they had a common enemy, and that was enough to draw them together. At least for a while.

As they neared the market, both Uli and Pua slowed their pace, their steps growing awkward and lumbering, their eyes downcast. At the first narrow street, Pua turned up, going north, while Uli went south. She figured they'd meet in the middle, hopefully with the two others in tow.

The day had grown hotter, and the people, less well mannered. Uli was shoved, her feet were stepped on, and once, a hand squeezed her butt through her skirt. Uli made herself turn slowly, but the offender had already slipped into the crowd.

Uli wandered from one stall to the next, through one narrow street to the next, searching for her companions. They had to be there. They were supposed to be there most of the morning, not going to the palace until much later that afternoon.

She refused to consider the worst: that the king's guards had already found them, taken them into custody.

Shouts sounded as Uli neared the center of the market. She pressed forward with the rest of the crowd.

Then stopped when the words resolved. "*Mahinapo! Mahinapo! Witch!*"

But the crowd wouldn't stay still, and pulled her forward.

The king's guard stood with swords drawn, surrounding Pua. She stood there, tall and proud and defiant. "Come closer and I'll spit on you," she warned.

Uli looked around quickly, but she didn't see anyone carrying buckets of water. There wasn't anything nearby for Pua to use.

"I'll come with you," Pua announced to the guards. "But I have done nothing wrong." She glared at the crowd, briefly catching Uli's eye and shaking her head. "Nothing at all. It's those damned mountain movers you want. Not me and *my* sisters."

Uli stepped back, letting the guards and Pua go, leaving waves of whispering gossip behind. Sorrow flooded over her, as surely as a jungle shower.

The girl had been right. Uli would always stand alone, in the end.

CHAPTER 10

The mynah bird only sounds as sweet as the true songbird.
 —Southern Islands proverb

EPHANIE LOOKED AT THE CLOTH IPO HANDED HER WITH horror. "This? You want me to change into this?" They were hidden behind an abandoned hut, the yard overrun with bushes and grass. Decay mingled with the scent of jungle earth, warm and wet. Flies buzzed loudly around them—Ephanie kept having to wave her hand to keep them from settling on her face, in her hair.

Ipo had stolen a length of cloth that she expected Ephanie to wrap around her like a native.

"What's wrong with it? Not good enough for you?" Ipo asked, standing with her fists clenched on her hips.

Ephanie sighed. "I can't hide my skin. I can't hide my height. None of the witches dress like this."

"I know," Ipo said with false patience. "But you need to hide you're a witch. This will help."

With distaste, Ephanie pulled a length of the cloth toward her. It was rough, though it was pretty enough, a rust color with a yellow cracked pattern running through it. She didn't want to wear it—it would make the others pity her.

Only a witch who never came into her powers would wear something like this. A witch who hadn't been taken back by her family. Ephanie had expected Ipo to at least find her something in purple, the color the witches recognized.

But that was exactly the sort of disguise that would fit Ephanie. Something to hide that she had come into her powers. Something to make people not look at her face, but shun her, pity her.

"All right," Ephanie said, giving in. She stripped out of her black robe easily. Ipo cocked an eyebrow at her nudity. "What? It was filthy." Ephanie also knew that other witches were concerned about being naked in front of others. However, Mama had always taught Ephanie not to be ashamed of her body, with or without its "leaves and flowers."

Homesickness slammed hard into Ephanie's stomach. She missed Mama, and her garden, and the quietness of the beach on her island, her favorite curved rock that sheltered her from the wind but that she could still look out from.

"Like this," Ipo said softly, showing Ephanie how to wrap the cloth around her, starting at her waist and circling up, across her chest and over her right shoulder.

"Why the right?" Ephanie asked. She'd seen women wear their cloth over both the left and the right.

"Shows you're single, eh?" Ipo said with a broad wink.

"That's not—" Ephanie sputtered.

"Yah, yah, I know," Ipo said. "But you can use it. Distract a guard or two."

Ephanie shuddered. She was a proper witch. Sometime, she'd mate. Not like her mother, who'd stayed with the same man, kept him there for love. The witches expected children, girls with power, not a family. Ephanie had been raised that the witches were the only family she needed.

But maybe not. Not with the scars she bore. Oka'u had been clever with his cuts, at least on her one arm, mimicking the first, so it looked as though she'd always used her own blood for her visions, like some madwoman.

Ipo drew a second stolen cloth around her own waist, over her chest and her right shoulder. "Never know who might be looking," she insisted. It was a dark green with a pattern of lighter green leaves on it.

After Ipo had dressed, she ran a hand through her short, gray-streaked hair, puling it back in the northern fashion. Then she hunched in on herself and her eyes lost their clarity.

"Ipo?" Ephanie asked, alarmed.

"Eh?" Ipo asked. "Oh darling girl. What sweets does my sweet want today?"

Ephanie shuddered. She recognized that tone, those words. Ipo used to talk that way, all the time, before the curse had been lifted.

"Ipo?" Ephanie asked again, needing to be reassured that the real woman still existed under the disguise.

"I'm still here, child," Ipo said, her eyes flashing with intelligence again. "But we both must play our part. You, a powerless witch child, and me, her simple nurse." Ipo shook her head, her features growing slack again. "Now us to market go, eh?" she asked in that singsong voice.

"To market," Ephanie said, drawing herself up, tall and proud (and thoughtless) as she'd always been.

"WE NEED MORE TARO," EPHANIE INSTRUCTED IPO. IT frightened her how easy it was to fall back into the role of directing the southern native. Had she always been so arrogant? The merchants listened to her as well, though she did notice that they weren't as kind as they had been when she'd worn her witch's habit.

The market was larger than the one Ephanie was used to at home, on Ailani Island. Instead of just half a dozen twisting paths through the square, there were three times that, and they stretched much further. The people all seemed to be in more of a hurry as well, though that might have been because they were trying to stock up before the coming battle.

"I want to hear a story," Ephanie announced after they'd finished their "shopping." They'd agreed that the old people who often sat near the storytellers would probably have the best, and most accurate, gossip in the village.

"Yes, *uuka*," Ipo said automatically.

Little one. That's what Ipo had always called her, despite Ephanie towering over her old nurse by a foot or more. Only now did Ephanie feel like the little one, with so much to learn.

They made their way to the north. Ephanie tried to hurry past the temple to Brikalla, then slowed. It was her guild, but they'd never know that. Instead, she frowned at the building as if it had wronged her.

Maybe it had. Her visions had never brought her any joy.

Now, in her role as a powerless girl, she could blame everyone but herself for her failure.

The storytellers held full court, with three of them together telling the tale of the young fisherman, the old priest, and the great fish, each speaking a role. Ephanie stood a while, caught up in the tale. They really were good, better than any she'd seen.

When Ipo nudged Ephanie's back, she turned with a sharp rebuke on her tongue. One look at Ipo's slack face and she swallowed down all her words.

Ipo was right. They weren't here just to listen to the tales. They needed to hear the news as well. If anyone would know about the king's heirs, it would be the old people in the village.

Slowly, Ephanie slipped through the crowd to where the elders gathered, laughing and telling their own stories. They talked in a flowing mix of both the northern and southern dialects. Ipo would be able to make sense of everything they said, even if Ephanie couldn't.

As they approached the edges of the crowd, Ephanie positioned herself so she could appear to be listening to the storytellers, while actually listening to the others.

Ipo leaned closer to Ephanie and whispered in her ear. "They're talking about the strange fish that they saw closer to shore last night— maybe from Niha's call? Or maybe disturbed from the depths of the sea." Ipo paused, and Ephanie heard them laughing, the women harder than the men.

She could only guess what kind of crude joke had been made.

At the first mention of King Makani, Ephanie turned around. "What did you just say about the king?" she asked.

A sly old woman replied. "Just that he better scatter his eggs. The witches are coming for him."

"My people would never do that," Ephanie said haughtily, drawing herself up tall. Then she realized what the old woman was talking about, and blushed when the old woman laughed and laughed at her. Still, she didn't back down. "What's so funny?" she asked, insisting that they deal with her, though she had a good idea of what they meant.

"Not just your kind have magic now, do they?" the old woman asked.

"Really?" Ephanie asked. She took a step closer. "What have you heard?" She figured playing dumb would be the best way to get information from this pair.

"The *Mahinapo*—the southern witches—have come back." An older man came forward. "The mountain movers and the water shakers."

"And the fire dancers," the woman added, shivering. "What I wouldn't give to meet one of them."

"What do you mean?" Ephanie asked. "Your people have magic?" She didn't mean for it to sound as condescending as it did, but she knew that it was a question they'd be expecting. She certainly would have asked such a question the previous week.

"Yes, we do," the old woman said, her own pride coating her voice. "We have our own magic. Stronger than yours."

"How could it be stronger?" Ephanie asked, though she'd already seen evidence of that.

"The mountain movers, that's really what they can do. Bring down an entire mountain on your head," the old man wheezed.

"Or raise one up, as a barrier between you and your enemies," the old woman added. "Like Tulana did, getting away from the tree demons."

"And what about the water shakers?" Ephanie asked, trying to keep them on track.

"They can drown entire villages," the old man said. "If they're working together, maybe an entire island."

"But they can also raise wells, where there weren't none," the old woman pointed out. "Call the fish when the village has been having troubles with their catch."

"It's the fire dancers, though, that are the worst," the man said.

Ephanie felt Ipo grow stiff behind her.

"They could stop a fire, too," the old woman said. "If it got too dry, and the jungle was burning. Take it into themselves."

"That's not what they mostly did, though, was it?" the old man sneered. "Mostly, they just destroyed our homes. Like the others."

"So what is the king going to do about it?" Ephanie asked, trying to draw them into the topics they needed to talk about.

"Seen the guards around?" the old woman asked, nodding to the corners of the market.

Ephanie nodded as if she had. There had never been any guards at the market on her island, so maybe any at all were significant, even if there were only a few.

"What else is the king doing?" Ephanie demanded. "What about his heirs?"

"Already sent some off," the old man proclaimed. "Scattering his chicks."

"Where?" Ephanie asked, trying to hide her delight. Maybe this would work, and she'd be able to have something useful to tell Uli.

"Who knows?" the old man said. "Though if I were him, I'd send them to the farthest island in the western region, like Hualani Island. Maybe even to your people's island, Mokolani," he added, winking.

Ephanie wasn't sure what the old man meant, but it was obviously an insult of some sort. She'd have to remember to ask someone later what the connection was between Mokolani Island and the witches.

"It won't be far enough," the old woman said, sounding worried. "And he hasn't sent them all away. More than half still remain here."

That was all useful. Ephanie didn't want to ask too many more questions, raise any suspicions. "But what about us?" she asked, too easily falling back into the role of a spoiled white woman. "How are we to be kept safe from these women?"

"Can't ever be safe from a woman," the old man said with a sigh. "That's just the nature them, eh?" he added, elbowing the old woman beside him.

"Oh, go on, you," she said, shaking her head. "Don't you worry, miss. The king will do what's best."

"Then maybe we should get going," Ephanie said, turning to Ipo. "Before *Mother* sends out the guard."

"Yes, miss," Ipo said simply.

"Thank you for speaking with me," Ephanie said formally to the old couple. "Both of you."

"Not many listen," the old man said.

"You take care," the old woman added.

Ephanie had only gone a few steps before an incredibly strong hand wrapped around her elbow. "And you take care of your *nurse*," the old woman hissed in Ephanie's ear. "She's too powerful and not simple enough. Someone in the crowd would point her out to the guard."

"Thank you, Mother," Ephanie said, throwing a worried glance over her shoulder at Ipo. She couldn't see the difference, but then again, she'd never supposed that her old nurse could be someone from legends.

Ephanie just had to make sure that Ipo got to fulfill her greatness.

"You can't go back with me," Ephanie hissed at Ipo. They sat in a grove of trees outside the village. They were closer to the ocean, here, the smell of salt and water swirling around them. Songbirds sang loudly above them, though even Ephanie could tell that there weren't as many birds here as in the true jungle. The heat of the afternoon still bore down on them. Ephanie would never tell Ipo that she liked the native outfit, though it was more comfortable than her robe.

Because they had a few hours to kill before going to the palace, Ephanie wanted to go back into the village, to the main temple of the witches. She might learn more news, find out what the witches had planned. "You need to wait here. You're too strong. That old woman recognized what you were. And so would others."

"You don't go back alone," Ipo said stubbornly. "You'd lose your way in a heartbeat."

"The village isn't that big," Ephanie pointed out.

"Would you leave the witches' temple on your own?" Ipo asked.

"Yes," Ephanie said slowly. She didn't think she would stay there. The other witches would never understand what she'd gone through. To them, she was a failed witch. At best, a betrayer of her people, aligned with women whose powers she didn't have a chance of understanding.

"Ah, *uuka*," Ipo said, her tone dripping with sarcasm. "The world too big and hard for you?"

"What do you mean?" Ephanie asked. Even kneeling down, she found her back stiffening.

"You're *soft*," Ipo said, her voice harsh, though she still had a twinkle in her eyes. "You want to go crawling back, hide behind your mother's skirts, instead of walking on your own two feet."

"You don't understand," Ephanie said bitterly. "I can't go back. My people are *ashamed* of me. They'll always be ashamed of me, will never trust me." The scars from her torture wouldn't erase the fact that she'd cut herself and enjoyed it.

Ipo sighed and shook her head. She pressed her lips together and looked away, before she finally looked back at Ephanie, her eyes still kind. "Your mother would take you back," Ipo said with certainty.

Ephanie nodded. "Yes. Mama said she would. But even she would be ashamed." Ephanie held out her arm. "I used my own blood for my vision. No one will ever trust me. I...I liked it. Too much."

"Do you trust yourself?" Ipo asked bluntly.

Ephanie sat very still. She didn't want to admit it, but the pain was so exquisite when she breathed out the word. "No."

"That's why I'm not leaving you alone," Ipo said matter-of-factly. She stood up and brushed off her knees. "Come on. Let's go."

"No," Ephanie said, refusing to rise.

"*Uuka,*" Ipo said. "I wasn't asking. You can't be trusted. You said so yourself. So you go with me. Until you can trust yourself."

Shaking her head, Ephanie still rose to her feet. "I'll never be able to trust myself," she whispered. The pain would always call to her, that clarity of time and thought when the knife sliced across her skin.

Ipo shrugged. "Maybe you'll always feel the need to use your own blood. But maybe you'll always be able to resist."

Ephanie had no response for that, though she doubted Ipo was right.

At some point, Ephanie would fail herself, and cut too deeply.

EPHANIE KEPT HER HEAD HIGH AS SHE WALKED UP TO THE PLAIN wooden gate that led to the temple grounds. Even as a powerless girl, she'd be expected to come and pray at the temple. Though she couldn't stay too long, or interact with any of the younger girls, because the witches always suspected that powerlessness was contagious.

It was late afternoon by this time: the communal rooms where the witches ate together would be empty.

The two temple guards, one on either side of the opening, didn't deign to look at her as she and Ipo walked through the gate.

What harm could a powerless witch do? Even they were more important than she was.

More guards waited just on the other side of the gate, though they lounged on benches there, either napping or playing knucklemen dice. They didn't stand, always ready, unlike the king's guards that Ephanie had seen. Their armor looked the same, brass chest plates, broad leather girdle, bare arms and legs. The only difference was that their armor was tagged with healer red instead of the royal yellow.

Ephanie paused for a moment to catch her breath. The complex here was so much larger than the one at home—and had so many more buildings! But it was set up the exact same way, with the temples to the north, directly ahead of her, the common eating areas and the kitchens to the east, classrooms to the west, and official temple rooms and sleeping quarters to the south.

Instead of huts with walls woven in geometric shapes, the temples were built out of real wood. Some even had columns painted white, not just stained with *tikatila* and left the natural, golden color of the wood. White stone roads cut across the pounded dirt.

Mother would have something to say about their landscaping. The flowers and bushes that grew between the paths weren't nearly as large or colorful as the ones she grew at their temple.

It didn't take Ephanie long to identify Hynla's temple—the god of luck. It made sense to her that a powerless girl would still pray at his temple, asking for her luck and her life to change.

Like the temple of Myatlu, the god of the underworld, Hynla's temple was painted in all the colors—the colors of the guilds, the apprentices, the acolytes, those who had retired and those in mourning. But instead of the colors drooping down, hanging from windless banners, spiraling toward the earth, Hynla's colors were painted on the walls and ceiling, reaching high and cheery.

There was always a chance, right?

Ephanie took a moment to let her eyes adjust to the dimness after the bright sunlight of the courtyard. The sanctuary was empty when they stepped in. Mats and colorful rugs lay piled up on the edges of the small, square room, used for when the priest or priestess felt moved to speak.

Cold stone made up the floor, uneven and gray. Ephanie missed the warm straw mats of the temple at home.

Up at the front of the room stood a simple altar, with a dark wooden carving of a god standing on one foot, his arms out and welcoming. Coins and shells littered the base of the statue, as well as the large purple *pikuu* flowers that smelled sweet.

After kneeling and bowing her head for a few moments, asking for Hynla's blessing on her unlikely allies, Ephanie turned to Ipo. "I'd expected more people here," she said softly. Maybe the witches were preparing for the upcoming battle.

Ipo nodded, whispering, "I remember this temple being more full, all the time, as well." She paused, then added, "Could always check the kitchens."

Ephanie sighed. Ipo was right, of course. There were sure to be communal tables where everyone in the temple gathered to eat. She uncomfortably scratched her arm. They might get more questions there than Ephanie wanted to answer.

Still, it was a good suggestion. She nodded and led the way out of the dark temple, into the bright light, and around the corner to the dining hall. She spied a group of acolytes in one corner, sipping sweet *pulaleena* juice and gossiping.

Maybe they'd talk with her.

At the threshold of the room, Ephanie turned to Ipo. "You can go out back," she said, waving her hand negligently toward the kitchen. "Just be ready to go when I call."

"Yes, *uuka*," Ipo said slowly.

It was just an act, but Ephanie still shivered deep inside at Ipo's slack jaw and blank eyes.

After picking up her own slightly sweetened juice, Ephanie sat down a few feet away from the other girls. They paid no attention to her, just kept chatting, their shrill voices disappearing up into the tall, woven roof. The long side of the hall opened out onto a courtyard, and the walls had been removed so breezes flowed through. It was a restful place, and Ephanie could easily wile away the rest of the afternoon here.

However, they still didn't know why the guards weren't out in more force, looking for the southern witches, or what Jahaka or the other northern witches were doing. It was possible that the guards were preparing for the upcoming battle, instead of out looking for them.

The group of acolytes left and a group of healers came in. They were concerned about a girl who'd been missing since the night of madness.

Ephanie shivered. She didn't want to think about being alone in the jungle, lost. Without Uli and Ipo, she never would have survived on her own.

Then a group of fortunetellers came in. Ephanie stiffened and kept her back to them so they wouldn't see her arms. According to them, Jahaka was meeting with many of the upper rank witches, probably to get some sort of understanding.

Ephanie almost laughed herself. If Jahaka would only consult *her*, she'd have a much better idea of the abilities of the southern witches. And their plans, at least of this small group of witches.

But the head of her temple wasn't about to stroll into the common dining room, recognize Ephanie, and insist she come and talk with her.

Then again, Ephanie could go and ask to see her.

If she did that, however, she'd never be free to kill Oka'u.

It was tempting, Ephanie admitted to herself. More tempting than she'd realized earlier, when she'd been talking with Ipo. To walk out of the dining room, go through the inner courtyard to the council rooms, announce her name, and ask to be taken to Jahaka herself.

But the southern witches had suffered, too, more than Ephanie had. She owed them for her rescue, and for how she'd treated Ipo all her life.

The sun soon slanted low through the windows. Ephanie had learned bad news—some of the witches were to be sent away with the heirs when they left.

Which meant the heirs who had gone were being protected, not just by their people.

Ephanie pushed aside the smooth wooden cup she used for her juice.

Time for her to go and meet the others. To walk into the palace.

To kill Oka'u.

EPHANIE LED IPO OUT OF THE TEMPLE GROUNDS, STILL PLAYING her part, her head high despite her status as a powerless girl. There were more guards at the gate, but they stood in groups, clumped on either side, not paying attention to anyone passing the threshold.

Still, Ephanie didn't breathe easier until both she and Ipo were into the regular street again, surrounded by people streaming into the market.

It was time for them to separate—for Ephanie to start along the palace road, while Ipo made her own way there.

Ephanie wished she had more information for Uli. If she were on her island, who would she go to? Would her old teacher know any of the gossip? Maybe, but Ephanie had never been that friendly with her, not like the other students had been. She would never have thought to go to Ipo or any of the southern natives, not even her mother's lover.

What was the use of being the one with a destiny if she needed other people all the time?

Ephanie laughed to herself and shook her head. She hadn't been able to do much on her own, except to make mistakes with everything she touched.

The stream of people going to the market ahead of Ephanie bunched up and slowed down. Though Ephanie stood a head taller than most of those in front of her, she couldn't see what was going on. Why had they all slowed? She had to get to the palace road, start making her way back.

Impatient, Ephanie pushed ahead of the group of people directly in front of her.

"Watch yourself, miss," an old man warned. He was shirtless and wore a net around his waist over his poor cloth. Obviously a fisherman.

Ephanie glanced back, then walked forward again.

Right into the group of the king's guard cutting up the middle of the path.

"Excuse me," Ephanie said, stepping back immediately, trying to get out of the way.

But the old man she'd passed pushed her back out in front of the guards.

Ephanie glared at him, then tried to sidestep the guards again.

The head guard caught her arm. "You should be more polite," he scolded.

"Yes, sir," Ephanie said, keeping her gaze down. Her heart beat loudly in her chest. She had to get away.

But Hynla, the god of luck, like always, had his face turned away from her.

"What are these?" the guard asked, turning Ephanie's arm over, looking at the scars running down her forearms.

"Just a foolish attempt to force my powers to come," Ephanie said, glad that they'd come up with a story earlier.

"Looks to me like Oka'u's work," said a second guard, looking over the shoulder of the first.

Ephanie couldn't help but stiffen and pull back. "Who?" she asked, but it was too late.

"Clever girl," the second guard said. "Hiding in plain sight. But not clever enough. Come with us."

"No!" Ephanie shouted. "I'm a witch from the northern peoples! You can't take me!" She hoped her shouts alerted the temple guards. "I was on my way to my temple!"

"Looks like you were just coming from there," the guard commented. He grabbed her other arm and wrapped that damned binding rope around her wrists.

It hurt just as much the second time.

"No!" Ephanie wailed. "You can't take me! Not again! I won't go!"

"You don't have much choice," the guard said. Suddenly more than+ a dozen guards surrounded Ephanie.

There were too many to fight, even for such a powerful witch as Ipo.

Shuddering, Ephanie let herself be dragged forward. Though she'd never had a vision of her death, she suspected she'd die in that dungeon under the palace, far away from daylight.

Or she'd succumb to her final temptation just to escape.

THE SMELL OF OKA'U'S ROOMS MADE EPHANIE TREMBLE uncontrollably—the deep rich copper of blood, mingled with the wet smell of earth and the salty taste of her tears. She'd stopped trying to get away from the guards after they'd punched her stomach hard enough she couldn't take a breath without pain.

Oka'u stood in the middle of the dark room, waiting to greet her. He was still the same filthy, tiny man, but his cheeks were fatter, as if he'd been supping at a rich table for the last few days. Torches flickered in the corners. Two tables filled the room: one holding Oka'u's instruments, his knives and ropes and burning wicks; the other, where his victim would be strapped down.

"No," Ephanie murmured. Her head dropped and she looked at the stained dirt floor. She couldn't draw a deep enough breath to be sick all over her feet, though she wanted to be.

As soon as Oka'u touched her, she was going to urinate on herself, shame herself even more. She just knew it.

"My dear, such a delight to see you again," Oka'u purred. "But I don't have time to see you today, not until later this evening. Duty calls. It will be so interesting comparing your reactions, though!"

That made Ephanie look up. Who else had Oka'u caught? Surely not one of the southern witches? They wouldn't let themselves be caught, would they?

"Oh, I'll let you find out for yourself," Oka'u purred. "But I'll leave you down here, this time. Closer to my work. So you'll be filled with anticipation. Like she was!"

With that, Oka'u strode out of the room. The remaining guards forced Ephanie into a pen built into the rock. It was much darker in there and stank of vomit, feces, and blood.

There were others here, shuffling in the dark.

"You're dressed like a powerless girl. But you're not," came a cracked voice.

Ephanie turned and blinked. Another witch, one of her kind, a healer dressed in red robes, stood there. How had Oka'u captured another northern witch?

Ephanie couldn't help it. She started to cry.

What little luck she'd had, had all run out, if he had more than one of her kind.

CHAPTER 11

Old winds blow the sharpest.
—*Northern proverb*

THE MORNING DAWNED BRIGHT AND CLEAR, AS ALWAYS. JAHAKA wished for the fall rains as strongly as any farmer. She longed for winds and rain and cold, anything to break up the monotony of the days. It was just another reason why the witches had to move back to the north. The weather here was always unnaturally nice.

Yet, Jahaka still called for the walls to be removed from the council chambers, so they could look out onto the fresh morning ocean, blue and sparkling below them. Gulls cried nearby. Colorful pink, red, and white hibiscus bloomed freely next to the sweet smelling star jasmine.

"Who has news?" Jahaka asked once all her counselors had assembled. The dozen of them looked at each other sleepily, their robes more bright than they were that morning. Even Vine, in her black habit, appeared to be dozing.

"Any news of the southern witches?" Jahaka prompted.

"No, none," Yarrow finally stirred herself to answer. "But that's not the odd thing."

Jahaka waited, impatient, for Yarrow to continue. "Well?" she eventually asked.

"The king's guard are still gathered in their barracks," Yarrow replied. "They aren't doing sweeping marches across the hills or along the coast. And they haven't asked for any additional guards to help in their searches."

"That is news," Jahaka said. She'd assigned three teams to help the king's guard when they came to ask, trying to anticipate the king's need.

Why hadn't they been used?

Jahaka added it to the growing list of things she would ask the king when they met later that evening.

"There's a girl missing," the head of the healers guild stated. "She disappeared the night of madness."

"Why has it taken so many days to be reported?" Jahaka asked, dismayed. It was very clumsy of the healer's guild to lose one of their own this way.

"We thought at first that she'd gone with a team to the far side of the island to provide help," the healer replied hotly.

"I'll send a message to the head of the local fleet to keep an eye out on the rocks, in case her body was dropped there," Jahaka said spitefully.

"Thank you, ma'am," the head of the healer's guild said before she sat back down with an obvious sigh of relief.

Why was everyone so tired that morning? Had something kept them all awake into the late hours?

Vine stood next. "The number of visions is dropping on every island, steadily decreasing since the night of madness. In fact, there haven't been any visions at all in the last day."

"What does that mean?" Yarrow asked before Jahaka could thank Vine for her report and shut her down.

"It means we're standing on the edge of a crisis," Vine said with obvious relish. "None can predict how the next few days will fall. Will the king win? Will his line survive? Or will some other force take the lead? No one can say."

"So we must prepare for every eventuality," Jahaka said smoothly.

"However, remember, no matter who wins, they'll still need our help and guidance."

The women of the council nodded in consent, though Vine didn't look certain.

The time was coming when Jahaka would no longer have to deal with Vine. In the meantime, Jahaka pointed at the old fortuneteller. "Why did it take you so long to report this decrease?"

Only then did Jahaka notice that her hand shook. A quick glance down revealed that the stigma of age spots now dotted the back of her pale skin.

Jahaka snatched her hand back. What was going on? Her body always just healed itself, automatically removed any signs of aging.

"It took time to gather the tales from the other islands," Vine said. She seemed resigned.

"Work with Illuna, the head of our messengers, to see if you can get your news more quickly," Jahaka said abruptly, instead of taking Vine to pieces, abandoning the start of her campaign to get rid of the prophetess. "If there's no more news, then we are adjourned," she added, standing.

The rest of the counsel struggled to their feet.

Something was going on. Something that had slowed down not only the brightest of the witches, but Jahaka as well.

She needed to find this latest threat. And eliminate it.

Jahaka raced back to her rooms. She threw the curtains over the doorway, hurling the sash that held them to the side onto her bed. What was going on? The balcony windows were open, and Jahaka strode over to them to get a better look at her arm.

Wrinkles. Age spots. Even her veins were more prominent.

A moment's quick prayer restored her skin to its youthful whiteness.

But why hadn't her body automatically repaired itself? What had failed? Why were all the witches so tired this morning? Jahaka closed her eyes and took a deep breath. She was strangely tired as well.

Had her body fought against that, instead of healing itself that morning?

Jahaka took another deep breath. Was there something tainting the air? Something she could warn the other healers about? But the air smelled sweet as always, filled with many flowers, and the tang of the sea underlying their fragrance. No, it was nothing so obvious as that.

Maybe the water? Jahaka dabbed her finger in the pitcher next to her wash basin. But it was pure and clean as always. More than one healer blessed their water supply regularly, insuring that it remained pure.

A knock disturbed Jahaka's investigation. "Come in!" she called, looking forward to tongue-lashing whomever it was who dared disturb her.

Yarrow came directly into the room. "My lady," she said, bowing her head. "There's been a disturbance."

"What do you mean?" Jahaka asked. Why hadn't Yarrow told her about this before, during the council?

"You may have noticed, this morning, all of the council seemed… not themselves." Yarrow hesitated.

"I noticed," Jahaka said. "It's not the air or the water," she added.

Yarrow breathed a sigh of relief. "No, it's the earth."

Jahaka drew herself up taller. "Is it the southern witches? Attacking us?"

"I don't know," Yarrow said. "But there's something in the earth that's affecting us. It's spreading like an oozing pond, deep under the ground."

"Can the growers stop it?" Jahaka asked. "Or at least divert it around us?" Why would the southern witches attack them? Jahaka had such plans for them!

Yarrow wrinkled up her nose, as if she'd just smelled something bad. "You remember that mixed girl? Daisy?"

"Yes," Jahaka said slowly.

"She's the one who alerted us to it. The other growers concurred, however," Yarrow hastened to add. "They're working on the problem." She hesitated again.

"What else?" Jahaka asked, bracing herself for the news.

"It's stronger in the east than in the west. The growers are leaving the compound now to take samples. But we think…we think it's coming from the east."

The east? There wasn't that much directly east—the land fell away, and the island curved around, and…

"The king," Jahaka breathed out. "It's coming from the palace."

"We don't know for certain," Yarrow said quickly. "That's just speculation, for now."

"No, it's coming from the king," Jahaka said firmly. Intuition came over her, like it had at her mother's funeral, at other times, when she *knew* what had happened.

It was a blessing from the goddess.

"This binding already existed, under the palace. It was why the king wasn't afraid of the southern witches, despite the way they move the earth. He knew they couldn't tear down the palace. It was *bound*. And now that binding is spreading."

"We've never seen anything like this before," Yarrow said. "Not in any of our myths or even in the southern island tales."

"Only healers visit the king from now on," Jahaka declared. "Everyone else is too vulnerable. Make our temple safe," she growled. "Make this land holy and sacrosanct. We need to show the king that he does not rule *here*."

"Yes, my lady," Yarrow said with a grim smile. "And the heirs?" she asked.

"The heirs of the king?" Jahaka said, standing even taller. "We will accompany them everywhere they go. Healers who know the water. Who know all illnesses. The king won't turn us down."

"Of course, my lady," Yarrow said, bowing her head.

They understood each other.

When the time came, all the heirs would fall ill, and no one would be able to cure them. If the healer wasn't able to perform those duties, there would be prophetesses who would need royal blood for a fortune.

The heirs wouldn't survive for long.

～

JAHAKA TOOK HER TIME GOING TO SEE ROBYN THAT AFTERNOON. Though the old storyteller had said it was urgent, Jahaka wanted to make sure she knew her place. There might be a time when Jahaka would need to release the old storyteller, maybe send her to train others on a far island.

Robyn sat alone in the room, kneeling under the mural of Brikalla sending dreams to her people following the terrible wave that took Alokai Temple. Her eyes looked like dark, smudged smoke, despite the lighter gray robe she wore. Sweet incense flirted with the smell of chalk.

"I'm honored you came to see me, my lady," Robyn said, bowing her head low, touching her forehead to the floor.

"It was my pleasure," Jahaka replied, seating herself comfortably beside her old teacher. "What news do you have?"

Robyn continued to address the room, not turning to speak directly to Jahaka. "I found something in one of the oldest stories," she said. "The verb had been badly translated until recently." She paused, taking a loud deep breath, wheezing. "Originally, we thought that the word used was *fold*. It has the same root. It's actually frequently used as a synonym. But it was nonsense, so we never included the story in our regular tale cycle." She struggled with another breath.

"Are you all right?" Jahaka asked, concerned. Though she knew she might have to let Robyn go, she didn't want to do so soon.

"I am fine, my lady. There's just been—trouble today. With many of us."

"I know," Jahaka said. She wasn't about to tell the storyteller what they'd learned. "We're taking care of it," she declared.

Robyn looked sharply at Jahaka for the first time. She studied her silently for a moment, her dark eyes as hard as the obsidian knife the fortunetellers carried. "Good," she pronounced eventually. Then she looked forward again and continued her tale.

"As I said, we mistranslated the term. It isn't *fold*, as in 'fold together.' It's *bind*. But again, they're used interchangeably in many ways."

"What is the tale?" Jahaka asked when Robyn merely wheezed for a bit.

"After Hinanuli was thrown down the mountain, and the islands were lost to ash and waves, King Kawiti performed a *binding* ceremony. Not a folding ceremony. We had thought it had to do with the folding of the king's feathered cloak. But instead, it might have been to bind the people together."

"Ah," Jahaka said. That made sense. This was exactly the sort of thing that she'd been hoping Robyn would find. "Is there anything else?"

"It's said that the king couldn't perform this ceremony alone, that he needed his closest advisor with him. A man described as being slight, named Tak'o. Otherwise the binding was impossible." Robyn turned to look back at Jahaka again. "I will continue to look through our oldest writings, to see if there are any other mistranslations, and to re-vision all the myths in light of what we know now."

"Thank you," Jahaka said sincerely. "Your research is invaluable." And it was.

King Makani couldn't do the binding by himself, any more than his ancestor could. He needed his closest advisor.

Which meant that snake Oka'u. Who was also small of stature, shorter than most.

Jahaka had never trusted him.

Somehow, he must be helping the king perform the binding, just has his ancestor had. But how? And was he behind the spreading lassitude of the witches?

Jahaka was going to have very, very long talk with King Makani that evening.

"MY LADY!" ONE OF THE TEMPLE GUARDS CAME RUNNING UP TO Jahaka as she crossed the courtyard back to the main temple.

"Yes?" Jahaka asked, alarmed. What had happened that a guard was panicked? The afternoon had grown much warmer, the blue sky whiting out in the heat. Jahaka didn't know if the growers had managed to reverse the spread of that damned thing oozing under the earth, but the heat didn't help with her own exhaustion.

"My lady, the king…the king's guard…they've taken one of our own." The guard looked steadily off into the distance, as if afraid to meet Jahaka's eye.

"What do you mean?" Jahaka asked. It wasn't that girl that had been reported missing that morning, was it?

"Outside of the temple, half a street away, the king's guard picked up a young woman. Yesterday. She was dressed like a powerless witch, but she claimed that she was actually a northern witch, on her way here to the temple."

"They took her anyway?" Jahaka asked. How dare they? The king was completely mistaken if he thought he could get away with this sort of thing.

"She had cuts, ma'am. Down her arms," the guards said quietly.

Jahaka froze.

In all the madness, she'd forgotten that there was a second witch missing as well. The little fortuneteller, Ephanie.

Had she escaped from the southern witches and been on her way back to the temple? What a treasure trove of information she must have! "Miatlu plague us!" Jahaka cursed.

The guard flinched.

"What else?" Jahaka demanded of the man. There had to be something else, something more beyond the king's guard taking the girl.

"Some of the guard think she did come here, to the temple," the guard said, standing perfectly straight. "She prayed at Hynla's temple."

This fortuneteller, disguised, had come to the temple? Just to pray? Or for some other reason?

Was there a traitor among her kind? Was the girl actually working for the southern witches?

It didn't matter. The king did not get to keep any of Jahaka's people imprisoned.

It was time to pay King Makani a visit.

~

By the time the cool of the evening blew its soft winds

over the temple compound, the growers pronounced success. The strange oozing pool had been diverted, and now curled along the temple compound wall.

It was significantly stronger the closer to the palace the growers tested.

Jahaka chose to walk with two minor acolytes, both healers who, though young, had strong powers. They would be able to keep up with her, she judged. Though Vine wanted to go as well, Jahaka didn't want to have to deal with the old woman if she fainted from exhaustion once they got to the palace.

If Jahaka could have had her way, she would have had Aleekona as her guard. But he wasn't officially sponsored by the temple, and she couldn't call him.

She still supposed he was there, tracking her, just out of sight in the darkness of the streets.

The evening grew quiet, even the chorus of cicadas and buzzing flies calmed, maybe by the binding spell. No one was in the streets, and even the few guards who waited at the intersections seemed more like statues than men. They passed along the road to the palace in eerie silence, as if no one wanted to break the spell.

Many torches lit the front of the palace, more than Jahaka had remembered from before. All three stories of the stone palace were lit, torches planted near every window. But despite the lights, darkness crouched just off the path, outside the circle of light.

What had the king invited into his palace?

The cold of the stone floors pressed against Jahaka's feet. Instead of it being a soothing feeling, cooling them after the walk to the palace, they bit her skin with the cold of ice. More torches lit the hallways and rooms, but darkness licked the edges of every flame.

King Makani waited for Jahaka in the second throne room. The seat for the throne was carved out of pure white stone, while pillars of rock encircled with glossy green leaves and bright red flowers rose from it.

Oka'u waited beside the king. He looked as though he'd been stung by many bees, his cheeks swollen and his eyes red. Even his arms were puffy. Two guards waited at the door, a discreet distance away, able to deny hearing anything of value, but also close enough to reach the king.

They had no idea of the power of the healers. Jahaka comforted herself with the knowledge that it would take only a touch and the smallest of prayers to drain away the life of the king.

He'd never know what had struck him so low.

Jahaka politely waited through the slow greetings, asking after the king's heirs and health without any show of impatience. She needed to be gracious, without even a hint that anything was wrong.

King Makani needed to be lulled.

Oka'u studied Jahaka and her companions. Jahaka didn't deign to look back, not until it was close to the end of the greetings. "And how is your closest advisor this evening?" she asked politely.

"I am very well," Oka'u said. "As strong as a bull whale."

Jahaka doubted that. He looked swollen, but not with muscles—more like a mosquito who'd supped too much blood.

"First, I wanted to offer you our assistance," Jahaka said, now that the pleasantries were over. "I have teams of my strongest healers prepared, ready to accompany your heirs wherever they may be going."

"Thank you, your offer is most generous," King Makani said. "But it's really of no need. My heirs have all gone, left under cover of night, disguised." The king chuckled. "I don't even know where they've all scattered to."

Jahaka stifled her disappointment. The witches would just have to find the heirs another way. There were temples on all the larger islands, and on many of the smaller ones. She'd just have to get word to all of them to look for a rich merchant or lord who'd just moved to the island.

She knew the king and his heirs would never be able to fake poverty, or act as anything other than royalty.

"I'm very pleased that your line and reign are safe, and so well protected," Jahaka said. She was pretty sure she sounded sincere. "However, I must bring up some bad news. There are two witches missing from our ranks."

"Two?" the king asked, seeming surprised. "Whatever happened?"

"There a young healer who went missing the night of the madness.

We've been searching for her, but we haven't found her. Then there's the young prophetess."

"The southern witches have her," the king said dismissively.

"Possibly," Jahaka said, nodding wisely. "I'm curious, though, why you haven't had more guards out looking for them."

"We've been searching other ways," the king said.

"What other ways?" Jahaka asked, keeping her tone sweet. "And how may we help?" Was that what that oozing blackness under the earth was supposed to do? It just appeared to sap the strength and vitality out of everyone who walked on it.

It was stronger here, but since Jahaka was aware of it, she could fight it.

"Traditional ways," Oka'u said. "Since the madness, the king is aware of every rock on the island. He knows when every songbird falls. He is naming the winds, and setting every bush and tree to tremble at his passing."

Jahaka inwardly shivered. Was King Makani building his legend to become a god?

"Then tell me, O Great King," Jahaka said, keeping reverence in her voice. "Why did your guards snatch up the prophetess as she was leaving our compound?"

"What do you mean? What happened?" the king asked, glancing at Oka'u.

The king didn't know. Were the guards reporting to Oka'u now?

"As a young witch was leaving our temple, palace guards snatched her up, in the middle of the market," Jahaka said with relish.

"She was dressed as a powerless girl," Oka'u replied smoothly. "How were the guards to know?"

"They were looking for her," Jahaka accused. "So they knew she was one of us."

"All they saw were the cuts down her arms," Oka'u replied.

"Which marked her as a fortuneteller," Jahaka countered.

"No, as one of mine," Oka'u said smugly.

It took Jahaka a moment to understand what Oka'u meant. "You've been torturing one of my witches? One of my people?" she accused him.

"Of course not," the king assured Jahaka quickly. "We've only collected troublemakers. Those driven mad, and unable to control themselves. Like the men you hold in your pen. We don't have any who are falsely accused."

They were lying. The pair of them.

"I would like to see the pens, to make sure. If she was dressed as a powerless girl, it would have been an innocent mistake for your guards to take her," Jahaka said smoothly.

Oka'u and the king looked at each other. "It isn't a place for a delicate lady," the king said after a moment.

"Then it's good that there aren't any here," Jahaka said, stepping forward. "Shall we?"

"If you insist," King Makani said as he rose from his throne. "Just remember, these are dangerous people."

"I'm sure that your guards can take care of them," Jahaka replied sweetly. "Unless you think I should bring my own, as well?"

"Wonderful!" Oka'u said. "Though they should be instructed to get you out of the palace if anything occurs."

"What do you think might occur?" Jahaka asked as they walked from the room.

King Makani sighed. "The southern witches."

THE PENS OUTSIDE THE PALACE HAD RECENTLY BEEN REBUILT since the attack of the southern witches. The fence circling the area had wide poles every few feet, sunk deep into the earth. Instead of rope or net, solid boards were woven between the poles, cleverly interlocking. Guards had been placed as often as the poles, standing warily, armed with unusually tall pikes, perhaps to attack a foe from a distance.

However, despite that, the pens still stank of feces, vomit, and blood. Raised lines in the earth, like a large burrowing mole had made tunnels under the ground, still marred the flat surface. Some were more than two feet tall. Pens had been moved around the earthworks.

The pens themselves were rough boards, notched together, maybe three feet high. A prisoner couldn't stand, but would have to crawl to enter. None of them were long enough for someone to lie down fully either.

Of course, each pen held multiple people.

Jahaka's stomach churned but she made certain her face never reflected what she felt. She would probably have to burn her robes when she returned to the keep; they'd never smell fresh again. People moaned piteously, or cried.

"At some point, you'll have to visit where we're keeping your men," Jahaka told the king. "To see how we're keeping the people affected by the madness." They were all linked by ropes, and kept outside. But at least they could stand and walk, they had shade they could go sit in during the heat of the day, and they had a decent latrine.

The guards rousted the prisoners from the pens, one by one. Jahaka shivered inwardly at the state of their wounds. Long strips had been peeled from their flesh. Oka'u's work, she was certain.

He was a monster in more ways than one.

Most of the prisoners had dull expression. Was it the torture? Or were they more affected by the king's binding, since they were right here, laying on the earth, on top of it?

One of the women, a larger one, caught Jahaka's eye. "Witch! You, witch."

Jahaka broke away from the group and walked closer to the old woman. "Yes?" she asked. The woman was squat, with solid legs and arms. She had short hair—much shorter than the natives usually wore it. Her grin showed missing teeth, while freckles danced across her almost flat nose.

"Girl gone," the woman said simply.

"There was another witch? Here?" Jahaka asked, ashamed at how shrill her voice got.

The woman nodded. "Then the *Mahinapo* save her. Not me," she added sadly.

"She's lying," Oka'u said smoothly as he slid next to Jahaka.

The woman glared and bared her teeth at him. "*Naheelaka*," she hissed. "*Katipoa*."

Spider. If Jahaka remembered correctly, it was a particularly nasty species, tiny and black, which spun poisonous webs.

"I will get the truth from this woman," Oka'u assured Jahaka.

"Why don't you let my people take her?" Jahaka asked. "We have…very effective ways of getting at the truth."

Jahaka didn't doubt the woman spoke the truth. However, if she left the woman here, the woman wouldn't survive the interrogation. She knew it with the certainty of the sun rising each morning.

"How about we do a transfer of prisoners tomorrow?" Oka'u proposed. "One of ours for one of yours?"

The woman wouldn't survive until the next day, Jahaka knew. "Certainly. We'll just take her along now, and send you a prisoner when we get back to the compound."

"No," King Makani said. "She stays until morning. And we'll have the truth." Then he turned away, leaving the pens.

"I'm sorry," Jahaka told the old woman after Oka'u had also slid past her.

The old woman shrugged. "Hurt and hurt and hurt," she said. Then she gave her wild grin. "At least I hurt him first."

Jahaka did shiver then. The woman was dangerous, unrepentant.

Maybe it was best that she be put down, like a wild dog.

Jahaka hurried past the rest of the prisoners, certain that she wouldn't find Ephanie. They'd stashed her somewhere else.

She was equally certain, though, that the old woman wouldn't be the only one feeling the bite of Oka'u's knife that night.

Jahaka pressed her lips together and held back her scream of frustration when she found a guard waiting for her outside her rooms. All she wanted to do was strip off her robes, bathe herself in cool water, and sink into a dreamless sleep.

"Yes?" Jahaka asked the guard. "How may I help this evening?"

The guard—young, and an obvious mix of witch and southern, with dusty skin and blue-green eyes—shifted from one foot to the other. "There's a messenger, my lady. Waiting for you."

"Can't it wait until morning?" Jahaka asked, peevish. She took a step forward, about to push by the guard, when he suddenly shifted. He grew stiff and tall, and blocked her progress.

"No, my lady. You *must* go and hear this messenger." The guard didn't look directly at Jahaka, but instead stared stonily off into the distance.

Jahaka bit her tongue and didn't tear into the young man. He was just doing his duty.

The messenger who'd insisted on speaking to her now, though… If his message wasn't truly earth shattering, she'd skin him alive. Then she shivered. No, she wouldn't skin him. Not actually. Not like how Oka'u was probably doing with his prisoners, maybe right now.

Jahaka shivered and slipped along the hall, going quickly down the back staircase, through the acolyte's wing, and to the council rooms by the back route.

None could track her progress that way.

A strange man stood in the council room, his back bent, his arms folded behind him. He stood so still Jahaka wondered if he was ill.

"My lady," the man said as he turned around.

Jahaka was impressed that he'd heard her—she'd entered as quietly as possible so she'd have a chance to study him first.

"Yes?" Jahaka asked, sweeping by the man and marching to the chair of judgment at the front of the room.

Dark shadows flickered outside the torches that lit the center aisle. But it was a soft night, not hungry, not like the darkness at the palace.

The man in front of Jahaka was old, older than she'd expected. The hair on his head was still black and long, but it might have been dyed, as his chest hairs glinted with silver in the torchlight. Wrinkles lined his face and his hands looked rough and chapped. He wore only a short black vest over his brown pantaloons and straw sandals.

"My lady, I am Wehil, from Bakalani," he said proudly.

Jahaka sat up stiffly, suddenly wary. She'd heard his name before, probably from Enekai, since he was from the same island.

"I regret that I bear sad tidings," Wehil continued. "Enekai is dead. Killed in an attack by his brother."

"Of course," Jahaka said, fighting to stay calm, suddenly

remembering. "You were his oldest teacher. He'd mentioned you." Enekai had trusted Wehil, the older man had taught him how to grapple and fight.

"He requested that if anything ever happened to him, I go to you, so that you would hear the word directly from me," Wehil added.

"Was it a large attack?" Jahaka asked. Enekai had assured her his fortress was better protected than the king's, even.

"No, ma'am." Wehil sighed. "It was at a dinner. In front of family!" He took a deep breath and controlled himself. "There wasn't anything any of us could do."

"I see," Jahaka said. "Thank you, Wehil," she added. "Anything you need, you have merely to ask."

"Thank you, ma'am," Wehil said, bowing his head and leaving.

Jahaka sat alone in the council room, on her judgment throne, wondering when the gods had judged her so harshly.

CHAPTER 12

Only the sharpest knife leaves a single cut.
—*Northern proverb*

ULI WAS SURPRISED THAT THE CAVE WAS EMPTY BY THE TIME SHE got back. Where had everyone gone? The water shakers were supposed to be waiting for her here. Why hadn't Lakawoo returned? The cave stank of fish from their earlier meal. Water dripped at the back, a lonely, echoing sound. The sun never warmed this far under the earth, and Uli longed for the beach.

But she couldn't go out, couldn't risk getting caught. There weren't many patrols, but there had been a few, and after Pua had been picked up, Uli had worked harder at staying hidden. She looked mournfully at Ipo's firepit, but she had no talent with fire.

Uli knew from her sisters' dreams that there was fire buried deep under the earth. It took effort to reach it, and would destroy most of the island if she drew it up. However, she had the strength pull it up, she knew, should the need ever arise.

So Uli sat alone, humming her sisters' songs to herself, rocking back and forth, biding her time as the tide went out.

Ipo came back first, alone. The sky was just starting to darken, and the smell of the ocean had receded with the tide. "They took her," she said as she cast a ball of fire onto the twigs Uli had gathered. "Ephanie. I couldn't protect her. There were too many of them." Ipo turned a stony face to Uli, but Uli still felt her sister's anguish.

"The king's guard?" Uli guessed.

At Ipo's sharp nod, Uli admitted, "I found another sister. They took her as well."

"We need to go save them," Ipo said, her voice full of determination.

"We can't," Uli said. "Not yet." Not until she could figure out how to block the king's binding.

Ipo turned her fierce glare on Uli. "The girl won't survive. And we said we would meet at the palace, later this evening. To destroy the heirs still hiding there. Or have your wits already turned slow, and you've *forgotten?*" She spat the last word, like the curse it was.

"I don't know if any of us can survive at the palace," Uli shot back. "There's a web, deep under the earth. It turns all of us *slow* and worse, *soft.*" She paused and sighed. "It's spreading the king's binding across the whole island. And it's powered by those who are tortured." It still made her sick to her stomach to think of it.

At least it wasn't from the northern witches, she was sure of it.

"Then we must go and get our sisters now," Ipo argued. "So they can't be used."

"It's too powerful," Uli insisted, shivering. She didn't know how to get through that web with her mind intact. The hut she'd woken up in still haunted her, along with Ephanie's vision.

Nila and Hinan came in together. "The guards got Lakawoo," Nila announced.

"No," Uli wailed. She'd really hoped the girl had just been lost, that they could find her.

"We must go save her," Hinan said.

"She won't go," Ipo said, her arms crossed over her chest, pointing at Uli with her chin.

"You must," Nila said. "You're the strongest of us all."

"But the binding that the king is using is stronger than all of us," Uli said. "I can't fight it. And neither can any of you."

"We have to do something," Ipo said after a moment, her body wound tightly, her arms holding her in.

"We pray," Uli said firmly. "And we plan. We will get them back," she assured the other witches.

"Before they're dead?" Ipo asked after Uli had turned away.

Uli had no answer to that.

DREAMS OF BEING CHAINED TO HER HUT BY A ROPE OF LIVING fire haunted Uli through the night. She couldn't figure out how to untie the burning rope without burning her hands to a crisp. But she couldn't escape: even when she stretched out the rope as far as it would go, the hut followed her, haunting her like a hungry ghost.

The morning brought a clear dawn, but no clear thoughts. Uli sat like a lump on one of the outer boulders of the cave, looking out over the sea.

She didn't see how she could save anyone. Even the long, involved arguments with the others far into the night hadn't brought any ideas.

The binding was too strong. Uli couldn't dig deep enough to break it. And she couldn't stop the spread of the web.

It would reach the beach soon. The island would be unwalkable. The very earth would have turned against Uli. But what could she do? Her sisters were here.

The memory of the fire returned.

There was fire Uli could direct. Fire from deep under the earth.

She wouldn't call that, though. Not unless they left her with no choice.

In the meantime, she would walk with her sisters, up the twisting path, behind the palace, to see how close they could get.

Uli made them a new path through the bush, pushing aside plants and shrubs, then closing off the path behind them, twisting trees and redirecting roots by changing the earth around them. The earth smelled fresh, moist, and black as Uli plunged through it.

But even that clean scent couldn't keep her head straight.

She found touching the rocks helped, the bones of the earth. She kept her mind there.

They had only gotten a third of the way there before Hinan paused, bent over, panting. She clutched at her seaweed necklace, at the net wrapped around her hips.

When Nila came up to help, Hinan growled at her. Her eyes had grown black, just the barest whites showing. Her hands had lost their humanness and turned clawlike.

"Take her back down the hill," Uli instructed. "To the cave. Away from the binding." The web was strong there, but it was buried deeper underground. It was Uli's fault that it had risen at all.

Hinan batted away Nila's hand the first time she offered it.

"Hinan!" Nila rebuked her. "It's just me," she added, pleading.

Hinan shook herself, her hair waving like anglers underwater. "Ssss," she hissed. She held her head away, and her body stiff, but she still took Nila's hand and docilely followed along.

Ipo glared at Uli. "Don't expect me to go peacefully," she warned.

"Never expected you to have a brain in your head," Uli threw back.

"At least I won't be digging in the dirt," Ipo predicted.

"No, you'll go *soft*," Uli replied.

"I'll be drawn to the kitchen," Ipo added softly. "Where the fire is caged."

"I lived at the foot of the mountain," Uli told her. "I touched strong stones every day."

"How far up, before we lose ourselves?" Ipo asked.

"The web trickles down this way," Uli replied after a moment of searching. "So maybe we'd get halfway to the palace, maybe most of the way."

"We have to save our sisters," Ipo insisted. She stubbornly turned and began walking again.

Uli cleared the path, walking behind her. The rocks kept her sane, but she knew it would only be a matter of time before her mind dribbled away and all she had left was her hut and the faintest of her sister's dreams.

Ipo stopped and brought forth a tiny flame in her palm. They walked until it went out, close enough that they could see the palace in the distance. Then Ipo shook her head and took a step backwards. "No closer," she warned. "Not for me."

Uli nodded. Her own power here had diminished as well. She could probably go a bit further, however, maybe all the way into the palace.

"I want to burn that place to the ground," Ipo softly growled.

"We'll find another way," Uli assured her, though all the way back to the cove, the earth whispered in her blood, *liar.*

~

ULI SLEPT THROUGH THE HEAT OF THE DAY IN THE COLD CAVE. She remembered napping this way in her hut. She kept her hands spread out on the rocks around her, holding her in place, keeping her there. When she got up, none of her other sisters were waiting for her.

Was she already alone?

Ipo came rushing in before Uli could call out. "Come. Quickly."

Uli followed Ipo easily out of the cave, climbing over the rocks without slipping or cutting her hands, unlike her sisters, then up. Nila stood on a ledge just over where they rested. Uli looked around nervously. They were too exposed here, dark against the yellow limestone rock. Hinan rested at Nila's feet, providing her a solid force to lean against, as Nila leaned out over the edge of the rock, looking further south.

"Look," Nila said, pointing. "There, on the point."

"It's a pirate," Uli said dismissively. This side of the island wasn't very well patrolled. Proper fishermen came and left through the easy— and well-taxed—piers on the north side of the island.

"Not just that," Nila hissed. "Look at his cargo."

Trunks, boxes, poles of green bananas, trays of flowers…and then went on another box, tied with a yellow ribbon.

"Only some of the king's heirs had already left the island," Ipo said. "What if that's another one, on his way?"

"Then maybe we have something to bargain with, for our sister's life," Uli replied, relieved. Finally, they might be able to do something.

"Should we swamp the boat?" Nila asked, leaning back. She reached down a hand and helped Hinan rise to her feet.

"No, they would just get another one. And it would raise their suspicions. We need to get closer," Uli told them. She wanted to encase the prince in rock, let him see how it felt to be caged, unable to break free.

"How?" Ipo asked, looking at the sheer cliff. "If you make us a path, we'll be noticed."

"I'll go alone," Uli said. She could climb this rock—it was her friend.

"It's better if we swamp the boat, first," Nila said darkly.

"Just be sure to get him," Hinan added.

"I won't fail you," Uli promised.

Though there was still a voice in her head that wondered if she still lied.

ULI COATED HER BLACK SKIN IN THE CHALK OF THE CLIFFS, trying to blend in better and not be seen so easily. She even matted her hair with mud. The protective coating felt good, cool against her skin. It wasn't anything like when she'd carried the weight of the mountain inside her bones: this was different, armor outside, instead of stones inside.

Besides, carrying the mountain for all her life had made her strong.

Uli clambered easily up the slope, punching finger holes in the soft limestone when there were none. She didn't give herself a walking route, no, she clung like a vine to the cliff face, shooting rapidly across the boulders.

Waves crashed beneath Uli, her water sisters calling to her. Did they want her to succeed? Or were they hunting for her blood? She was never sure.

They were water. She was earth. They would never have an easy alliance.

Uli's muscles trembled as the sun continued to climb toward the west. But she didn't pause. She reached hand over hand, digging in toe holes, not looking down (though she knew the rock would catch her before the waves).

The hill dipped into a final cove before it sloped out again, so Uli couldn't see the boat. She poked her head around before she crested the point, looking for it.

It still rest in the harbor, lower now, with all the goods an heir to the king might need.

What if it was just a supply ship? And not something that would carry one of the king's heirs?

If that was the case, she'd just destroy the boat, fling rocks at it from the cliffs. It wouldn't give her and her sisters the advantage they needed, but it would still hurt the king.

Uli continued to climb across the rocks, one shaky handhold at a time. Her toes cramped, and she pressed them out against the cool stone. Only a little further. Then she could start either with her revenge or with a plan.

As the sun dipped lower, Uli finally saw the passenger for the ship.

He was short, shorter than Uli expected. But his chin was raised haughtily and he didn't deign to even nod at the workers loading his ship for him.

Uli clambered down the cliff. She needed to get on solid ground in order to get to him. The rock was unforgiving, not giving her an easy path. She was tempted to make one, but she couldn't risk being seen.

By the time Uli's feet landed on the solid earth again, the last of the prince's boxes were being loaded onto the ship. He was overseeing their loading personally, Uli realized. What was in this precious cargo?

The last box had planks along the edges, and was carried by four stout workers on two poles over their shoulders. Their muscles bunched under the weight. But they carried it onto the ship and deposited it in the center of the deck.

The prince turned to the merchants gathered there, obviously saying goodbye.

Good. Uli could get to him, raise up rocks to defeat him. She just needed to get a little closer, away from the hill.

The top of the last box was pried off. A breeze from the water carried a sickly, overly sweet scent.

Uli paused in her dodge from rock to rock. That scent. It was familiar.

A large woman rose up from the box, swaying.

Uli suddenly remembered the scent, not because she knew it personally, but from her sisters.

It was Lakawoo. She was being held prisoner, taken with the prince to wherever he was going. Though Uli couldn't see them, she knew how bloodshot Lakawoo's eyes must be, could tell the younger witched smacked her lips together, again and again, seeking the last of the sweet poppy remains.

Uli had to stop him. She drew herself up, ready to dart out from behind the rocks, race across the beach, when one of the king's guards casually came up from behind Lakawoo and place his black blade against her throat.

The witch barely notice. She laughed and moved her body suggestively. The guard moved slightly away, but kept his knife firmly at her neck.

Lakawoo wasn't just being held prisoner. She was collateral. She was there to see that the prince got out of this harbor safely. She'd probably be on display when they made landfall, guaranteeing no witch would attack then either.

Uli swallowed down her bile. She could take the prince—he was still on land. Drive a spike of rock up through his heart, or lock him away so solidly that none would ever be able to rescue him.

But she couldn't do so at the cost of Lakawoo's life, who was already on the water. The rocks were buried under too much sand and debris for Uli to be able to bring them up quickly enough to kill the guards.

Lakawoo laughed again, the sound echoed over the water, sending chills down Uli's spine.

Her sister was no longer herself.

Uli turned away from the beach, away from the prince and her chance of using the prince as a bargaining chip with the king.

Lakawoo had found her way out of the poppy dance before. She'd do so again.

And the chorus of *liar* danced through Uli's very bones.

~

ULI COULDN'T LOOK ANY OF HER SISTERS IN THE EYE AS SHE told them the news. Ipo turned her back on Uli, facing the wall at the back of the cave, and refused to turn around.

Nila and Hinan shared one of those long looks, then announced, "We must go."

"To where?" Uli asked. They weren't going to be stupid and try to take the palace by themselves, were they? Hadn't she already shown them that morning that they didn't stand a chance?

Water shakers could be so stupid. No wonder her sisters always defeated them.

Nila and Hinan looked at each other, nodded, then answered. "To Rakakeelani, in the south," Nila said. "All of our sisters are joining together there."

"Why would you gather on that hunk of rock?" Uli asked, perplexed. There was nothing there, just a handful of huts, not even a proper village.

Again the two looked at each other, then Hinan replied. "We gather together. In strength. For the attack."

"Attack?" Uli asked. "What are you going to attack there? Did one of the king's heir go to hide there?" It would be clever, she had to admit. No one would ever go searching for someone with royal blood in such a place.

"No," Nila said. "To attack Hilani. The king and this island."

"What do you mean?" Uli asked, drawing back, shivering. The water shakers were going to attack here? How? Why?

"Can you bring down the palace?" Nila asked.

"I can't, not by myself," Uli admitted. "But maybe if I could gather some of my sisters…" She didn't think there were any more on the big island. They may have all gone to Ailani, where she'd first raised the mountain.

However, Uli wasn't strong enough to tear down the palace on her own. Not with that spider there, powering his web, binding the stones until they were stronger than the mountain.

"If the king is dead by *Inkahai,* the morning after the final day of

Keereekayah, we will hold back the wave," Hinan promised. "Otherwise, we will drown the island."

Uli looked at them, horrified. "You'll kill all your sisters here!" she protested. "And all the people here as well!" It was why she held back: she could never kill her sisters. Not like that.

"And we'll free all of our other sisters on all the other islands," Nila countered.

"Not until you kill every one the king's heirs," Uli said. Just killing the king wasn't good enough. It would greatly weaken the binding spell, yes, but it wouldn't be enough.

"We'll get them as well, one village at a time," Hinan said.

"And what if an heir is living far inland? Will you drown another entire island? Kill everyone else?" Uli asked bitterly. No wonder the villagers hated the *Mahinapo*.

The water shakers would kill Lakawoo, and any other of their sisters being held against their will.

"Our sisters will all be free," Nila insisted.

"Do you only dream the sweet dreams?" Uli asked. "Do you not remember the curses and fights?" The villagers sometimes hunted the witches, drove them away when they could. Some claimed the witches had no use beyond war and destruction. Uli had seen her sisters driven from their homes, unwilling to fight the fishermen surrounding them.

Hinan shook her head. "It's only when we band together that we are strong."

"No, you're wrong," Uli said. "In the end, each must be strong enough to stand alone."

She wasn't one of these modern witches, changed by the years, dependent on each other.

She would fight alone, as the little northern witch had said.

THE MORNING DAWNED CLEAR AGAIN, GRAY CLOUDS ONLY VISIBLE in the far distance. Though Ipo had kept the fire going all night, Uli still felt chilled to her soul. Nila and Hinan had left as soon as the light struck the water, skating away to Rakakeelani to meet the rest of their sisters.

To aid in the destruction of the main island; not just the king, but everyone here.

Uli had to get to the palace. The rocks pressing against her thighs and shins brought no comfort or clear thoughts, just a steadfast presence. They held her soul comfortably, as slow moving as the mountain.

"I know you think we must fight alone," Ipo said, coming up from behind Uli. "And you might be right. Or maybe the old ways aren't the only ways, not anymore."

"What do you mean?" Uli asked, drawing herself out of the rock. The spider's web hadn't reached here, might not for a while. This place was too much of itself, just cliffs and rocks, nothing green or growing to break up the rock and make it easier for the web to pass underneath.

"There are other witches here," Ipo said.

Uli shook her head. "No. I haven't been able to find any of our sisters."

"I don't mean them," Ipo said. "The northern witches."

Uli turned to look at Ipo. "What do you mean?" she asked, her heart rising uncomfortably in her chest, drawing her up out of the ground.

"They have power," Ipo insisted.

"Pffft," Uli said. Those skinny white women couldn't brace themselves against a solid wave. They were like the winds they were named after, easily blown down and away.

"They do," Ipo said. "We need to go see them. They can help."

"How?" Uli said. "Can they dig under the palace like my sisters? Or light the guards on fire, like yours?"

"They can drain the life out of a man with a touch," Ipo said. "Their healers can both cure and kill. They can also salt the very earth, poison it so that nothing every grows there again."

"They're too friendly with the king to turn against him," Uli said. "They'll turn us over to the king's guard and collect their reward with a smile."

"The king has at least one of their kind in his prison," Ipo argued. "They'll at least listen to us."

"They won't help," Uli said, shaking her head.

"Then we fight our way out," Ipo said with a smile, fire suddenly outlining her arms. "We aren't without power, either."

"I'll go with you," Uli said, slowly rising. "To the witches' compound. But they will turn against us."

"Not everyone will turn against you," Ipo said softly. "You might not end up fighting alone."

"Bah, you're right," Uli said, trying to be jovial. "It was a northern witch who told me that. Why should I believe her? They don't have that much power. I choose my own way."

Or the way the goddess laid before her, which was often the same.

THE SPIDER'S WEB HAD SPREAD FURTHER DOWN THE HILL. ULI directed their steps around it, trying to avoid it as long as she could, leading Ipo through the denser parts of the jungle where the earth would rise easily under Uli's touch.

But it would only help so much. The power of the web sapped their strength. They panted like two old women as they steadily climbed, sweating in the early morning air.

They planned on going around the bottom of the hill and approaching the witches' compound from the west, instead of going up the mountain and down into the village first.

However, there was no path, just the one Uli could raise.

And soon, Uli could no longer force her way through the dense trees.

"We'll have to go back," Uli said, stopping.

Ipo leaned against a palm tree, panting. Bushes had torn her arms and thighs, leaving bloody trails. Ipo had long since abandoned the net she wore around her hips when it became too entangled. "No," she said, shaking her head. "Forward. We can force our way through."

"No one forces paths through the jungle," Uli snapped at her. Only her sisters had that power.

"Then find a path," Ipo pleaded with her. "Use your clever eyes. Find a way."

But my eyes were never clever, Uli wanted to complain.

She still did as Ipo asked, sought the less overgrown parts where the vines weren't strung so tightly between the trees, where they could walk without tearing their legs apart, where they could breathe without the clouds of gnats, stinging flies, and mosquitoes.

It took them hours instead of minutes to cross even a small patch of the jungle. But at least the trees didn't fight them. It was a normal jungle, with normal growth.

By the time sunbeams kissed the horizon, they were through the worst of it.

Fields were easier to cross. They stole clothes and washed as best they could before they found the road.

Uli kept her whimpers to herself. These rocks were foreign to her. She swore they deliberately cut her feet. She wanted to blast them to pieces, but she couldn't.

That was only her sister's dreams, of the earth moving beneath her palms. Or a passing dream of her own, so many moons ago.

Ipo put her arm across Uli's shoulder. Though Uli was already sweating, she still leaned into her sister's heat. "So warm," she murmured as she kept walking, kept putting one foot in front of the other. They had to reach…somewhere.

"Shhh," Ipo said. "Soon."

Uli nodded and let herself be led. It was wrong, to take these steps. To travel this way. To not walk among tree and rock and bush.

But the goddess had put this path in her way, and she must walk along it.

Darkness gathered across the sky. Ipo tried to hurry them, to get Uli to walk faster. "We need to be inside by dark," Ipo muttered.

Why? Uli was not afraid of the dark, or the creatures who lay in wait there. They wouldn't bother her.

"But the guards might," Ipo assured her.

Had Uli spoken out loud? She didn't remember.

Ipo turned them, and turned them again.

Then there was a gate. And guards.

Uli drew back, but Ipo held her steady. "Please. We must see the head mistress. Now."

Finally the guard stepped back and they stepped across the threshold.

Immediately, Uli's feet cooled. The rocks no longer bit into her soles. She shrugged Ipo's arm from around her shoulder, then glanced back in awe at the gate.

Somehow, the witches had stopped the spread of the spider's web. Their ground was clear of it.

Uli took a deep breath and shook her head. Maybe these witches did have some power. Maybe she could learn from them.

THIS WAS THE HEAD OF THE WITCHES? ULI SHOOK HER HEAD. Jahaka was pale, skinny, and had no power. She ruled through *cunning*.

She was soft.

"We know the king has taken your prophetess," Ipo explained to Jahaka. "The guards took her from me."

"Why didn't you fight them?" Jahaka asked.

Uli wanted to slap the bored expression from the witch's face. How dare she question Ipo?

But Ipo answered easily enough. "There were too many of them, mistress," she said quietly.

"I see," Jahaka said, openly sneering.

Uli suppressed her snort when Ipo raised fire and set it dancing all across her own shoulders. "I would have had to burn down the entire village," she said mildly.

At least the head witch no longer looked bored.

"I see," Jahaka repeated, this time with much more interest. Then she turned to look at Uli. "And you? What can you do?"

Uli bared her teeth at Jahaka. "Just this," she snarled, driving her fingers into the earth and plowing through it, toppling the stones that lay on top of it, leaving furrows of freshly turned earth between where she stood and the head witch sat.

Let her try to fix those. Uli hardened the earth with a passing thought.

"Did you bring any of the—what were they called—water shakers?" Jahaka asked.

Uli glanced at Ipo. She felt like Nila, suddenly, always looking to Hinan before speaking. She shook herself and replied without Ipo.

"They've all left Hilani. They're on their way to Rakakeelani."

"Why ever for?" Jahaka said, puzzled.

"To lead the attack," Ipo said quietly. "They will drown this island rather than see the king and his line continue. We only have until dawn two days hence before they kill everyone."

"We have to stop them," Jahaka said. She paused, then asked, "Why did you come? Just to bring this news?"

"We are here to help fight," Uli said. "We must free our sisters—and yours—from the king's prisons." She didn't bother telling this soft woman that she planned on killing the king. She might be too squeamish.

"My people could stop the wave," Jahaka said softly, looking out into the distance.

"How?" Ipo asked.

At least she sounded as doubtful as Uli.

"By working together." Jahaka stood. "I will call my sisters together. We will fight." She swept from the room, leaving Uli and Ipo alone.

"*She's* going to fight," Uli pointed out to Ipo.

"She meant to fight with us, to bring us along, too," Ipo said, defending the high priestess.

"No, she didn't," Uli said. "She thinks nothing of us. Of our powers. Of our people."

"She can't fight without us," Ipo said stubbornly.

"She intends to. How will you convince her of your worth?" Uli asked. "You can't."

"You think they're just as worthless," Ipo pointed out.

"But I'm right," Uli insisted.

"No," Ipo said. She shook her head. "I'm staying. I'm fighting with them."

"They won't have you," Uli told her.

"They'll have no choice," Ipo said determinedly.

"They won't have me," Uli said, backing away slowly.

"So this is how it ends?" Ipo asked, her tone as bitter as uncooked kale. "Sister against sister?"

"I'm not against you," Uli said, shaking her head. "I just can't fight with you. Not with *them.*"

"Then fight alone, sister," Ipo said. "And fight well."

"You, too," Uli told Ipo before she slipped out of the room and out into the night.

She took several deep breaths, preparing herself for the biting stones of the road, before throwing herself through the threshold and down the path, back toward the ocean.

Maybe she'd be able to think once she arrived there.

CHAPTER 13

When people are friendly, even water tastes sweet.
—*Southern Islands proverb*

EPHANIE STRUGGLED THROUGH THE BLOOD. IT WAS SHE COULD smell, all she could taste at the back of her throat, drowning out even her own tears and screams. She pushed her way through the sticky red river, diving down past the sweet call of her own pain and toward the looming darkness.

If only she could get there! She could escape, maybe not forever, but for a brief respite, out of pain and into the darkness.

But just before Ephanie reached the haven of unconsciousness, Oka'u pulled her back.

He always pulled her back.

Ephanie screamed again, this time in frustration. Her mind bled around the edges and her power seeped away.

The next time she would be weaker, and weaker still.

Whatever Oka'u was after, deep under her skin, he'd find it and tear it away and there would be nothing left of her.

The pain went on, wave after wave, caressing every nerve, forcing her to puke out her guts, pee down her leg, mewl and beg without thought.

Anything to make it end.

But Oka'u was a master, playing her body for more and more. Release was denied again, and Ephanie struggled to breathe.

"See, my dear?" Oka'u said, tenderly stroking her sweating temple. "Only I control when you stay and when you go."

Ephanie shivered, trying to draw away, but she was held too tightly to Oka'u's table by the damned bindings of the king that dug into her skin and hurt as much as everything else.

Again, Ephanie struggled to shake her head. No. He didn't.

She still believed in her goddess. In Brikalla.

Her goddess would take her away from all of this. Soon. Without his leave. It was the best way she knew to defy him.

Just to have another vision, and be out of his control for a while. No matter what he bound her with, she'd be able to break free then.

And take her own life, in service to the goddess.

Ephanie prayed through broken lips every waking hour to her goddess, more earnestly than she'd even prayed as a child for her powers to come.

But a vision never came.

EPHANIE AWOKE LAYING IN THE BACK OF THE CELL. DAWN, THE other northern witch, hovered over her.

"Just lie there," Dawn instructed when Ephanie tried to sit up. "You lost so much blood."

Ephanie lay in the dark and just breathed. Pain wracked her; Oka'u had stripped skin not just off her arms, but the back of her hands as well. She flexed her fingers and gagged, the pain hitting her like a blow to the stomach.

At least the bastard had left, and all she heard was quiet weeping, not another woman screaming.

"I can help—" Dawn started.

"No." Ephanie cut her off quickly. "Save your strength. Help the others. I can heal myself." Though her skin closed slower now than it had, her blood still congealed rapidly.

"Little witch," came a deep, accented voice. "You're awake."

Ephanie struggled again to sit up. This time a warm arm wrapped around her shoulder and helped, so Ephanie could lean against the rough rock wall. "Ipo?" she asked, though she knew that couldn't be who it was: none of the southern witches would allow themselves to be captured.

"No, no. Not Ipo. Pua," the woman stated.

Slowly Ephanie made out the woman who squatted in front of her, large and dark, with short, matted hair. She wore an ill-fitting top, but her bare arms were clear of cuts.

Oka'u hadn't gotten to her yet.

"Black robe, yes?" Pua asked.

Ephanie nodded. "Yes, I wear the black robes."

Pua looked over her shoulders, making sure no one else was close. "You know Ipo?" She dropped her voice down to a whisper. "Uli?"

"Yes," Ephanie hissed. She pushed herself up and regretted the movement instantly. "You have word?" she asked.

Pua shook her head. "They look for you."

"They will come," Ephanie said firmly.

Pua continued to shake her head. "No. Too strong. Damn spider." She sucked in her breath and swallowed. "Hard to stay here, focused," she complained.

Ephanie reached out to touch Pua's arm. Her own skin screamed at the movement, the pain lightning sharp along her nerves. She still bit her lip and did it anyway, touching the warm skin. "Stay," Ephanie said.

"You can't help," Pua said, laughing and shaking her head. "The other one can. She gives me strength. I give her strength. We are sisters."

A clanking noise in the outer room made Ephanie stiffen, despite her wounds.

Oka'u had returned.

"You watch," Pua said as she turned and took Dawn's hands.

If there had been more light, Ephanie wondered if she would have seen Dawn pale, as if she'd been drained of all her blood, while Pua grew darker and larger.

"You watch," Pua hissed again as she dropped Dawn's hands.

Dawn crumpled to the ground, passed out.

Ephanie cried out as she tugged Dawn closer to the wall, out of the way of the others, her newly healed skin tearing. Once the healer was safely out of the way, Ephanie crawled to the edge of the cell, gaging every time she stopped to wipe away the tears. There was a crack in the planks about midway up, and if she kneeled, she could see the torture room.

Pua was already strapped to the table, with Oka'u crooning over her.

Bile filled Ephanie's mouth but she made herself watch and bear witness.

Rolling syllables flowed from Pua's mouth. Ephanie didn't know what she said, but she recognized the pleading tone in her voice. She'd heard it often enough.

Before Oka'u started, he performed the same ritual he always did. First, he bowed to the four corners of the room, as if asking the gods to bless his dark sacrament. Then he tipped his head back, raised his arms by his sides and waved them, as if he were trying to fly. He usually let off an undulating cry that lifted all the hairs on the back of Ephanie's neck. He finished by bringing his hands up over his hand, then lowering them, kneeling down toward the ground, *pushing*, as if to open a double door.

After closing his eyes and apparently praying, Oka'u rose. He seemed skinnier after he performed his ritual. He didn't stagger or waver, but was he as strong as normal? Or did the ritual take away some of his power?

Oka'u stood next to Pua, talking to her softly in her language, as if trying to calm her, running his fingers across her hair.

Ephanie shuddered for Pua, as she was too tightly bound to do much but lie there and suffer.

Pua's voice took on a higher, begging note as Oka'u picked up his favorite black blade and set it against her skin.

"Shhh, shhh," Oka'u told the now weeping woman.

Then he sliced a long cut down her forearm.

Pua shrieked loud and long. Her blood poured out freely, much faster than Ephanie had ever seen.

After just a second cut, Oka'u paused. He also seemed surprised by the amount of blood freely flowing from Pua's arm.

Pua never stopped her shrieking cries, not even as Oka'u turned to his table to pick up a clean rag to bind the wound.

Ephanie held back her gasp, though she knew no one would hear it over the noise Pua made.

A living rope of blood rose behind Oka'u like a snake. It undulated closer to him, reared back, then struck.

Oka'u's gasp could be heard as Pua's cries turned into a chanting prayer. The blood rope wrapped around Oka'u's throat and choked him, hard.

Ephanie cheered fiercely. *Let him die!*

Before the blood rope could finish the job, guards came rushing into the room. One tried to pull at the rope, but it flowed out of his hands like water.

Another saw clear to the matter, though, and struck Pua in the head with his club.

With a hissing sigh, the magic seeped out of the blood and it spattered to the ground. In a cracked voice, Oka'u stopped the guard from striking Pua again. He said something in her language, then repeated it so Ephanie could hear.

"I have other plans for her."

Chills raced down Ephanie's back and she fell back into the cell.

If the strongest of them couldn't escape, what chance did she have?

EPHANIE TOLD DAWN WHAT HAPPENED WHEN SHE CAME TO. "What did you do?" Ephanie asked after Dawn had finished weeping.

"Pua was a *Mahinapo*—a water shaker," Dawn explained. "We knew what Oka'u would do to her. How he would bleed her, like he bleeds all of us. Feeding it into that dark spell of his, under the table."

"Oka'u has magic, too?" Ephanie whispered. A man? How could they ever fight him?

"Yes. He's not from the southern islands. Pua called him a spider." Dawn shook her head. "She called me sister," she added as tears started to flow again. "Said our magic was the same. I work with the blood, she works with water."

"Really?" Ephanie asked. How could that be? The southern witches were so much stronger than her northern brethren.

Then again, a healer could kill as well as cure.

"I gave her my power, as much as I could," Dawn confessed. "Not just healing, but beyond. Everything."

Ephanie slowly nodded. That made sense. It was like the time she'd killed the prince for her vision; there was too much power, and her visions continued.

The goddess wasn't through punishing her yet.

"He'll kill you once he figures out what you've done," Ephanie told Dawn.

"No, he keeps me alive so I'll help the others. He'll think it was the fault of his web or that she was too strong or something," Dawn assured her.

"I wish there were some way you could help my power," Ephanie confessed. "Not that a vision is going to help us here," she added bitterly.

"Don't say that," Dawn said. "You just need to find the depths of your power," she added. "Pua said that we were all sisters, the mountain movers and the growers, the water shakers and the healers, and the fire dancers with the fortunetellers."

"Really?" Ephanie breathed out. Could she make the fire dance, like Ipo and Lakawoo? Or was it just the fire from her goddess that ran through her skin?

The clanking sound that meant that Oka'u had returned, and was about to start torturing his next victim, cut off her thoughts.

Or would Ephanie live long enough to find out?

～

Ephanie sat up, panting in the corner. There were at least half a dozen other women in the cell right now, but she didn't let any of them approach her. She bit down the bile that rose again and again with Dawn's screams.

That bastard was going to kill her.

When the broken voice finally stopped crying, Ephanie was surprised they opened the gate again and dragged Dawn inside.

Oka'u hadn't just cut her. No, he'd broken her fingers, dislocating all the joints.

Only the most powerful healer could cure Dawn's hands, and no one that powerful was in this pit.

"Help?" One of the other women in the pit came forward and asked Ephanie. She held out her hands and beckoned for the others to come over. Together, they lifted Dawn up and carried her toward one of the corners.

The first woman sat with Dawn's head in her lap, while another stroked her arms gently.

Ephanie watched closely, but Dawn's fingers didn't miraculously heal.

Still, they comforted her like she was one of their own.

Sisters.

Ephanie pushed down on her fear, tried to control her trembling and the screams already rising in her throat the next time she was tied to the table. Instead, she forced herself to pay attention to what Oka'u said, the movements he made.

Was he related to a mountain mover? Was his power the earth?

She didn't recognize the gods he called to, but she was now certain that he prayed, just as she did, to perform his magic. Whatever this torture was, it wasn't just about pain. It was doing something else, something for his gods.

Something Ephanie had to stop.

Bitter laughter erupted from Ephanie when Oka'u came to stand next to her. She didn't know why. She still tried to cringe and felt violated by his touch.

She relished the surprise in his eyes. "Your gods will turn against you," she said in a raspy tone.

It wasn't a prophecy. She knew that. But the words still felt as though they came from somewhere beyond her. "And you will burn like Hinanuli, in the pit of the mountain."

"Yours are the unimportant gods, weak," Oka'u hissed at Ephanie. "They haven't the power or strength to stop my magic, the magic of my people, the magic of my god."

"But our gods are many, our people many. Yours are few," Ephanie said, her voice still ringing truth from the air.

"I am still mightier," Oka'u assured Ephanie as his blade kissed her arm. "Who is in control of whom?"

Ephanie couldn't answer that as the pain welled up and carried her away in its exquisite embrace, until it grew too much, as always.

But she'd found a key. Now she just had to survive to pass it along.

"HE'S ALONE," EPHANIE SAID AS SOON AS SHE COULD SIT UP. IT was night, she was sure of it. The humid air tasted different in the night, and the cries of the prisoners in the other pens seemed louder.

"We're all alone, here," Dawn said. She sat in the corner, her ruined hands cradled in her lap.

"No, we're not," Ephanie insisted. She forced herself to stand and walk over to Dawn. The other women sitting with her still hummed. They formed a semicircle around the girl, some squatting, some lying down. They wouldn't stop the guards from taking her the next time they came in, but they did seem to be trying to provide some kind of shelter for her.

"Sisters," Ephanie said. "*Teeka*," she added in the southerner's tongue. She painfully sat down, her own arms aching. The skin wouldn't heal properly anymore; it wrinkled like an ancient woman's skin, bubbled up with pain and grief.

The other women nodded. "*Teeka*," they repeated.

"We can help each other. Stand together and fight that bastard," Ephanie told Dawn.

"None of us have the power to fight him," Dawn said brokenly.

"Not alone, no. But together we do." Ephanie insisted. "You gave your power to Pua, so she could fight. But it wasn't enough, because it was just you two. It must be all of us, together."

"Witches don't work together," Dawn replied.

"Not since Alokai Temple," Ephanie admitted.

"Alokai?" one of the women asked—Ika.

"Great wave," Ephanie started. She started making hand gestures to help illustrate the story, but stopped when the pain washed over her. "Destroyed temple. Witches move here."

"Yes, yes. Great wave. Like here," Ika said. "Witches stand together to stop."

"Yes," Ephanie said. She turned back to Dawn. "We need to work together to stop him. Or he'll kill us, one by one."

"I can't give you my strength like I could Pua," Dawn pointed out.

"Not the same way, no. But maybe there's another way," Ephanie said. "It wouldn't do any good to give me your strength before he takes me out of here. He'll just drain it away. I need it afterward, when the bastard is done."

Dawn dropped her head to her chest. "There's the old tale of Shoal, the greatest healer. She could heal by just whispering a prayer, and have it be carried on the wind." She raised her head and stared at Ephanie. "I'm not that strong."

"You won't know if you don't try," Ephanie told her. "But you won't be by yourself. Ika, here, will help. And Moa, and Laki, and Ekunu, and Noilu, and—"

"Yes, help. Pray," Ika said. "*Teeka.* Together."

"All right," Dawn said. She sighed. "I'll try it. Next time you're…"

"Yes. Next time," Ephanie said. It had to work. Because there wouldn't be too many times after next time.

~

IN THE BRIEF MOMENTS WHEN EPHANIE COULD THINK, SHE

wondered just how badly she'd touched that nerve of Oka'u's. The torture seemed to go on and on this time, longer than usual.

Or maybe he was trying to make sure that she had nothing left—no tears, no screams, and no more blood—before he freed her.

But Ephanie fought her way back from the darkness. He didn't get to kill her. That was the privilege of her goddess, or at her own hand.

Not his.

When Ephanie awoke, her hands and arms felt like limp rope, no bones left. But the room was brighter than she expected. She blinked her eyes open. The ceiling was much farther away.

And so was the cell.

She was still on the table, not tied. Oka'u puttered beside her, rinsing his blade clean of her blood.

Warmth flowed through Ephanie's bones. She wasn't healing—Dawn and her sisters weren't that strong. But she was awake, and she had more strength than she normally did after one of her sessions with Oka'u.

And she was growing stronger every moment.

Damn it, though, why weren't her arms cooperating yet? She need to move, needed to stand up and kill that bastard. She just had to get her legs moving.

Blessed mother, what was wrong with her? Ephanie struggled to move, cursing her weakness without making a sound. She flexed her toes, curled them, then drew them up.

Finally. Ephanie pushed her head forward, making herself sit up. The room swayed dangerously. But Ephanie tucked her legs under herself, more gracefully than she'd expected, then swung them off the edge of the table.

The clever channels cut into the hard packed dirt, designed to channel the blood away, cut into the soles of Ephanie's bare feet. But she stood up straight now. Fire filled her veins. Ephanie had the power now to walk, to dance, to run.

This wasn't the healing, no. This wasn't Dawn or any of her sisters.

This was from Brikalla. Ephanie's prayers were being answered.

This was a vision.

Greedily, Ephanie reached for the nearest knife. Pain licked her bones. The smell of blood called to her.

She *needed* life. Blood. Something. Now.

Ephanie refused to turn the knife against her own skin, though it cried out for the kiss of the blade.

His would have to do.

"I know you're there," Oka'u said without turning around.

That silky voice drained away Ephanie's courage. Her shoulders drooped. The hand holding the knife fell to her side. She swayed like a boat in the wind.

"I was hoping this day would come," Oka'u said, turning now. His face shone brightly with all the power he'd drained away from Ephanie, sticky with sweat, and bloated. "When your puny goddess would dare to challenge my mighty God."

Ephanie struggled to raise her knife again. He would *not* get the best of her. She would turn it on herself, first.

The vision clawing at the back of Ephanie's brain diminished.

How was Oka'u doing that? He shouldn't be able to do that.

"We were once like you," Oka'u continued in that smooth voice. He drew closer to Ephanie.

Ephanie shuddered as he touched her gently, pushing the hair back from her forehead and tucking it behind her ear. The touch of a lover.

She should kill him now.

"But our gods lessened as they multiplied, fornicating in the woods like common men. The great Mikaleenu saw their error. So he learned the secret to absorbing them. Sought them, one by one, taking them into himself, until he was the greatest god of them all."

Ephanie couldn't stop shivering as Oka'u circled around her. She was holding a knife, damn it! There was a vision there, in her brain, somewhere. She should be able to use it.

"So while you may only call the fire dancers sister, I can call all of them *teeka*. I have the power to use the blood, like you, but I can push it far under the earth. I can drain away your life, or give it, with just my voice."

"But you are still all alone," Ephanie murmured. He'd pushed more power at her, bragging, with his words. She struggled harder, was rewarded by the blade turning away from her thigh.

Oka'u was holding her steady with his voice, but it cost him.

He was not invincible.

"There are few who are like you. Apprentice in all the powers, master of none," Ephanie sneered. "No matter how great your god, you're still human. And you can never do all your god does."

"Hush," Oka'u said. "My patience wears thin."

"Too bad," Ephanie said, turning to face Oka'u, her strength welling up from her pain. "You killed my sisters," her voice boomed, like it did when she was giving a prophesy. "You thrive on suffering. Not for the purity of vision, but for your own selfish delight. You are an abomination. You will die."

Ephanie sighed and deflated. She wasn't as tired as when she'd given a full prophesy, but the effects were similar.

Dawn's spell was wearing thin. Ephanie was fading. She struggled to stand upright, but instead, swayed.

Oka'u looked surprised. He held himself in place.

When Ephanie didn't move or say anything more after a few moments, Oka'u shook his head and laughed. "That's it? That's all you're going to say?" He took a deep breath. The darkness in the corners of the room streamed toward him. "Die."

CHAPTER 14

A prayer can either kill or cure.
—*Northern proverb*

JAHAKA WOKE TIRED THE NEXT MORNING. HAD THE BARRIER failed? Was that damn magician's web now under their compound?

When Jahaka sat up, she realized it was nothing more than regular fatigue. She hadn't slept well. Though she didn't remember her dreams, her legs were as tired as though she'd been running all night.

But she'd never caught what she'd been chasing, that much she knew.

Jahaka looked out the window toward the open water. Of course, the day dawned clear, though there was a touch of fog out at the horizon. Jahaka stayed where she was instead of getting up and starting her morning prayers.

What was she to do?

The king had sent his heirs off without her witches. They were scattered, and probably all traveling incognito. She'd sent off messages to as many of the far-flung islands as she could, but there might be too many heirs who slipped out of her fingers.

Too many who could come back and claim the throne.

Not like Jahaka had a replacement for the king anymore. Not with Enekai dead.

The sorrow drenched her again like a cold wave.

The king was positioning himself to become the southern island people's next god. That revolted Jahaka. Though they didn't have the same gods, it still wasn't right for him to be deluding his people that way.

He had to die. Him and all his heirs. But how? Jahaka couldn't risk herself, couldn't get her own hands dirty. He still held her people as well.

Jahaka considered sending for Vine, to see if any of her fortunetellers had a vision of how they might make it right.

But they were poised on the tip of the knife. Jahaka felt it in the air. Everything was uncertain, despite the clear dawn.

The ships were still coming. If they didn't contain Enekai's army, then whose? And how could she find out?

They'd be there in just four days, at the end of *Keereekayah*. Jahaka had brought healers to the island in preparation, but had acquiesced, and sent some of the more talented growers and fortunetellers away, all the while shaking her head, believing those women should have had stronger faith.

Now, Jahaka wished she'd sent everyone away, as far from Hilani Island as she could get them.

Slowly, Jahaka rose out of her bed. She was tired, yes. Her body wasn't failing her, not yet, not for a few years, but she could count the months, now.

That didn't mean Jahaka was about to give up.

Jahaka walked nude to the balcony, stretching her hands up far above her head, then sweeping down to touch the floor with her palms.

She was still the high priestess for all the northern witches, a force to be reckoned with.

Let them all beware.

~

"THE GUARDS REPORTED THAT ANOTHER INCIDENT TOOK PLACE in the market, the day before yesterday," Yarrow started off the council meeting with.

Jahaka sat on her judgment throne, still considering and discarding appropriate actions. Yarrow's announcement made Jahaka sit upright. "What do you mean?" she asked. She was glad that she hadn't allowed any public viewing today; the council had too many serious things to consider.

"Earlier yesterday, the king's guard also removed an elder woman that they called a southern witch from the market," Yarrow reported.

"Really?" Jahaka said. "Interesting. I hadn't known the king's men were actually looking for them."

"The reports are varied, I'm afraid. But it seems they just ran across this woman. She said she knew nothing, hadn't been involved the night of the raid," Yarrow said. She looked pale this morning as well.

"I would have thought the southern witches were more clever than that, to be just caught in the market," Vine commented.

Jahaka nodded. Unless they had another motive, to get one of theirs into the palace. "What happened?" she asked.

"Something happened to the woman—maybe she was shoved? Another report says that someone tried to steal from her. Instead of reacting like a slow-witted fool, she turned and cursed the person. Fluidly. The guards happened to be nearby and witnessed it. They knew that she was only pretending to be stupid." Yarrow paused. "Evidently, many of those who were considered slow were actually cursed witches."

"Interesting," Jahaka said. "Has the king sent guards to gather up any of these other women?" She suspected she already knew the answer, but asked anyway.

"Not as far as we can tell," Yarrow replied. "The king's guard stays near the palace, guarding the king."

A true god wouldn't need such protection. But Jahaka kept such thoughts to herself. "Anything else?"

"Do we have any other news from the west?" Vine asked. "Any word on a fleet gathering there?"

"None," Jahaka replied. "And it makes no sense to send any messengers—they won't return in time."

The mood of the council grew even more sober. The battle would be upon them soon.

Oak gave a report of the healers, their supplies, and how ready they were for treating the wounded. Vine reported no more visions from any of her seers, though many had uncomfortable dreams.

Hadn't they all? Jahaka ordered the guards doubled through the marketplace. If another southern witch came through, they should know about it first, and snatch her up before the king did.

She also ordered another sweep around the island. Just because the king wasn't actively looking for the other witches didn't mean she couldn't.

"WHAT DO YOU MEAN, YOU THINK YOU SAW A PRINCE LEAVING the island?" Jahaka fumed at the guard reporting to her. They were in her private chambers, as the head of the guard had felt the news important enough to disturb Jahaka's sleep. She paced her room with a robe barely belted on.

The guard shifted nervously from one foot to the other, eyes downcast.

Jahaka sneered at him. Too much of a coward to take a look.

"There was a ship leaving one of the coves on the southern side of the island. Late, just as the sun was setting. Yellow ribbons marked more than one of the boxes on board. And the young man on board." The guard paused, sighed, and then looked up, directly into Jahaka's face. "It had to be a prince. Prince Muoi. I'm sure of it."

"How can you be so certain?" Jahaka asked. She let doubt drip from her words, but just to learn why the guard was so sure.

"I've met him before, my lady," the guard said. His gaze shifted from her face to the black, open curtains beyond her. "Our unit trained with the king's guard for a while."

Jahaka weighed the emotion in the guard's carefully chosen words.

He obviously didn't think much of this princeling. "Do you know what island Prince Muoi was heading to?"

"No, my lady. But we sent a boat out after it, directly. Once it lands, they'll report back," the guard said with grim satisfaction.

"How many units have trained with the king's guard?" Jahaka asked. She usually didn't bother with those sorts of details. Usually, Jahaka let Yarrow—high priestess of the healer's guild—deal with it.

"Only a dozen, ma'am," the guard said. He glanced at her, then looked away again. "Some think it's a waste."

From his tone, Jahaka could tell he didn't. "And why is that?"

"All guards train with a highly regarded healer. Maybe two," the guard reported. "Why do they need to learn other tactics?"

"Why indeed," Jahaka mused. It was why Aleekona was so valuable to her: he'd trained with both as well. "Your name?"

"Linden, ma'am," he replied stoutly.

"Expect to hear from me or one of my agents, soon," Jahaka said. She'd have one of Aleekona's men contact this Linden, see if he could be recruited to her private army.

He was obviously wasted at the temple. Besides, that way she could keep a better eye on him.

"Thank you. You may leave now," Jahaka said. She turned back to the dark ocean outside her window, noting the changed air once the guard had left.

At one time, she might have invited him to stay. Reward him, and herself, for a job well done.

But this Linden seemed too shy, at least for now.

Should Jahaka add more sweeps around the island? There wouldn't be many more heirs leaving, she was certain. Probably most of them had gone by now.

Plus, now that they knew where one was, they'd be able to find the others. Carefully watching the correspondence, the ships coming and going—she'd find them all.

Regardless if Jahaka didn't currently have a replacement for the king, she was still going to leave him heirless.

～

AFTER THE COUNCIL MEETING THE NEXT MORNING, JAHAKA walked through the temple compound, heading toward the south end, behind the common quarters, where the prisoners were kept. They'd converted one of the gardens to a holding pen.

It wasn't very fancy: the fence on the one side was merely rope strung between posts. The far side was the wall of the temple compound, which was taller than a man standing on the shoulders of another man. Just beyond it was the jungle. The growers kept the tree branches well back, making it difficult for anyone to get in or out of the compound from there.

Guards stood every few feet along the fence, looking bored. The prisoners weren't in pens, like in the king's yard. Instead, they were tied to poles, three or four of them together, bound by neck, one wrist, and one ankle. They could stand, stretch, even walk a few paces. But there wasn't very far any of them could go. The ropes were living vines, created by the growers. Anytime they tried to get too far, the vines around their necks tightened, though never enough to kill a man.

The prisoners were taken to a latrine at the far edge of the camp every morning and evening. They were given water barrels, and could sluice themselves clean once a day. Plus, all of them could reach the shade of the wall when the sun grew too hot.

But Jahaka had better use for this space, now.

The head of the guard—Marrow, maybe?—came trotting up to meet Jahaka as she approached the gate of the camp. "My lady," he called. He wore the usual outfit of fitted-brass breast plate, leather girdle, though he also had leather bracers on his arms and around his shins.

Jahaka paused, waiting for him to catch up.

"Come to see our prisoners?" Marrow asked, obviously puzzled.

"After seeing the king's pens the other day, I wanted to see our own," Jahaka replied smoothly.

"Yarrow insisted on these conditions," Marrow replied worried. "So the prisoners can walk and move around. They even can lay down at night. We give them blankets," he hurriedly added.

"Yes, yes, we treat them much better than the king does," Jahaka said dismissively. She looked pointedly at the rope barring her entrance.

"You wish to go in there?" Marrow asked, incredulous.

"I can already smell them from here," Jahaka said. "I know they're not all in good shape."

Marrow opened the gate. "It isn't because we didn't give them an opportunity to bathe themselves," he said. "Some of them are, well, violent."

Jahaka could make out the ones he meant. They were separated from the others, each on their own line, where they couldn't do any harm to anyone else. They looked mild enough, like that woman Jahaka had met. But she didn't doubt that they would, as she had said, "Hurt and hurt and hurt."

"They seem calmer near the wall," Marrow told Jahaka as she strode toward the most dangerous of the men.

That make sense. Possibly the damn spell that tired out her witches also would tire them out.

None of the men would meet her eye. Most looked away, or spat, or made a warding sign with their arms crossed over their eyes, to turn away any evil or bad magic.

Jahaka walked all the way through the enclosure. Some of the prisoners still looked dazed, as if they couldn't believe they were there. Others glared at her, baring their teeth.

She counted as she passed—thirty some in all. "Our transport ships for the guard take twenty in each, don't they?" she asked as she passed out of the camp and back into the rest of the compound.

"Yes, my lady," Marrow replied, obviously relieved that they were outside the enclosure.

"Arrange for two of them this evening. Transport these men to the far side of the island, and release them there," Jahaka commanded before nodding and stalking away.

"My—my lady? Are you certain?" Marrow asked, rushing to get in front of Jahaka.

"I'm not used to having my orders questioned," Jahaka replied. "But yes. Release them. All of them. The king needs a sign of good faith from us," she lied. "They are all his people. Natives."

Let him deal with the consequences as well.

"SLOW DOWN," JAHAKA INSTRUCTED THE GUARD WHO STOOD before her, panting. "Who is here?"

"Two women, my lady. Southern natives. Who insist on seeing you immediately," the guard replied, still breathless.

Could it be? Had a pair of southern witches finally decided to seek out their northern sisters?

Jahaka had them taken to the council rooms, where she could sit on the seat of judgment.

Maybe all her plans hadn't crumbled to nothing.

The two women shocked Jahaka: they seemed barely tame, let alone civilized. At least the one, Ipo, had her hair shorn and addressed Jahaka as "Mistress" or "Ma'am" or even "My lady."

The other—this Uli—was barely human. She had hard eyes of stone and contempt for all she saw.

They admitted to losing the girl, Ephanie, to the king's guards.

"But why didn't you stop them?" Jahaka asked Ipo.

The flare of flame that stretched across the woman's shoulders and arms startled Jahaka. She'd never seen such a thing before.

She had to bite her lips together so she didn't declare, *blasphemer!*

"And what do you do?" Jahaka managed to ask Uli.

Furrows raised under the smooth stones, as if great claws scratched across the ground from underneath.

It was going to be hell getting the hall's floor flat again.

That the water shakers were going to attack Hilani with a huge wave struck a chord in Jahaka. She barely listened after that as an image formed in her mind.

Like Alokai Temple. They were going to drown. Unless Jahaka led all the witches to defend the island.

Should she? Was it worth saving the king?

Yes. It would put him in her debt. And no matter what he claimed, it would be the witches of the north who saved the people, not him.

She would be able to kill his plans of godhood after showing how strong she and the other witches were. She would be able to stop this wave.

When the southern witches questioned how, Jahaka told them, "By working together. I will call my sisters together. We will fight." She swept from the room, leaving Uli and Ipo alone.

Yarrow waited in the hallway outside the room. "Gather all the witches together," Jahaka said to her. "We need to make a stand on the south side of the island. We'll have a chance to right our history."

"How?" Yarrow asked. "What?"

"We will defeat the wave this time," Jahaka assured Yarrow. "There will be no weak link. We will all work together."

"Witches don't work together," Yarrow answered automatically.

"We do now," Jahaka said firmly. She turned to go back into the room where Uli and Ipo waited, but paused and didn't cross the threshold when she heard the two witches arguing.

Jahaka didn't understand everything they said to each other. But she caught the general gist of it—Uli thought they should fight alone, while Ipo thought they should join with the witches.

When the large woman burst from the room, she moved with a speed Jahaka hadn't thought was possible. But Jahaka didn't call out to her, didn't instruct the guards to stop her. Just let her go, out into the night, away from the safety of the temple.

Jahaka slipped back into the hall where Ipo remained. The southern witch stared out the window at the dark ocean. Small curls of flames still danced across her back.

"I'm sorry your friend couldn't stay," Jahaka said. And she was. Though Uli would have been a liability, Jahaka still had wanted to study her, to learn more about her power; see how it could be used, tamed, and directed.

Ipo gave a soft laugh, echoing through the quiet night. "Your priestess gave her a vision, once."

"Really?" Jahaka asked, coming to stand beside Ipo, despite how she smelled and the danger of her flaming skin, determined not to show any fear.

"Ephanie. Yes. Nila called the fish for her to kill, so that she could curse Uli, predict that in the end, she'd fight alone, no sisters standing beside her." Ipo turned to look up at Jahaka. "It's probably best that she didn't stay. She doesn't speak your language as well as I do, doesn't know your ways."

"Where are you from?" Jahaka had to ask.

"Ailani. I fed Ephanie, when she was a child," Ipo admitted. "When I was bound with the king's curse. Before Ephanie set me free."

"The killing of the prince," Jahaka breathed out. That one accident had set all of this in motion? She shook her head, wondering at the machinations of the gods.

"Yes," Ipo said. "But your people wasted the blood. So Uli collected it and used it to free the rest of my sisters."

Jahaka shivered. Now she doubly regretted not stopping the southern witch before she left. "Where will Uli go?"

"I don't know. The web, pushed by that spider Oka'u, drains us all of thought and reason," Ipo said.

"Ah," Jahaka said primly. They didn't need to know that the northern witches were also affected. Let them believe they were immune. "Should we look for her?"

Ipo gave Jahaka a strange, grim smile. "No. She will fight alone. And win."

"Who will she fight?" Jahaka asked.

But Ipo never answered her.

A SMALL SONGBIRD SAT ON THE RAILING OF JAHAKA'S PORCH when she finally retired to her rooms. There was so much to organize, so many of her council to convince to go and meet this wave. She'd have to talk with them all in the morning.

The sight of the songbird made Jahaka sigh. It was her signal that Aleekona wanted to see her that night.

He'd sent the small red bird only twice before. It was a rare bird, easy to train, but difficult to raise in captivity. No matter how large of an enclosed space the birds had to fly around in, they seldom survived to adulthood.

Should she go? He might understand if she didn't. It was so close to the night of the battle. The guards had been instructed not to allow any of the priestesses out after dark. The village wasn't as safe, either from the southern island natives or the king's guard.

But Hynla had been smiling on Jahaka all afternoon, inspiring her to release all the prisoners, finding that princeling and his hidden island, as well as bringing the southern island witches to her. Surely his favor hadn't passed yet.

Maybe she could even take Aleekona back to bed for a night, to reward them both.

They might both be dead in a few days' time. They should celebrate life that night.

It didn't take much to convince Marrow to escort Jahaka out of the temple gate, for him to hurry down the streets with her. It took more concentration than Jahaka cared for to keep her steps nimble, her attention focused.

That damn Oka'u's spell was growing stronger. And probably powered by her own people's blood as well.

Ephanie. They'd rescue her as part of the price of saving the king and the island from the wave.

Just wait until King Makani saw the power of her people.

Jahaka didn't pass anyone on the streets that night. All the huts were dark, curtains hanging over the doors and windows. She didn't hear the sound of chanting or prayers, either. Just the far off sound of the waves and the cycling cry of the cicadas.

There would be celebrating in the street once her people saved them.

"Stay here," Jahaka instructed Marrow when they reached an intersection close to Aleekona's house.

Marrow stared stonily at her. "You're joking, my lady."

"I can see to my own business," Jahaka told him coldly.

"Normally, my lady, yes, yes you could. Not tonight. Not in times like this. I will not leave you, and would die before I lost you," Marrow told her harshly. "You may walk alone, but I will be right behind you. You cannot stop me."

"I could," Jahaka pointed out. It wouldn't take much to drain him enough to sleep.

But she needed his good will. She needed him to escort her back. She wasn't stupid—there were dangers in the night, hidden guards and assassins.

Marrow stood stiffly before Jahaka without meeting her eye.

"Very well," Jahaka said, giving in ungraciously. "But you will never, ever, remember this place. If I ever find out that you or your guard have visited it again, I will drain years from your life, years that you'll never gain back, until you're old and hunched over and in constant pain. Then keep you that way for decades."

"Yes ma'am," Marrow said, still without looking up at her.

It wasn't an idle threat: there were healers who could do such work.

Jahaka didn't have the power, but maybe she'd be inspired.

Aleekona's hut was the same as it always had been, as dark inside as out. Jahaka knew better than to step too far from the door, letting her eyes adjust, willing herself to see in the darkness.

More than one set of lungs breathed across the room.

Jahaka's heart leapt into her throat. Had she been betrayed? Should she have brought Marrow even closer? If she called for him, would he be able to reach her in time?

Then Jahaka straightened her spine. She wouldn't call, not unless her need was desperate. Let these foolish men try to take her.

"I know you're there, both of you," Jahaka said softly. "So you might as well come into the light."

"See? I told you she would know," came a warm, chuckling voice.

She knew that voice. But from where?

A lamp suddenly flared to life. The two figures Jahaka expected were illuminated.

But they weren't the two figures she expected.

Instead of Aleekona and some surprise guest, across the table stood Wehil, the guard who'd reported Enekai's death to her.

And Enekai stood beside him, very much alive.

CHAPTER 15

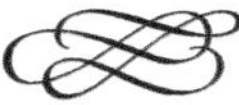

A name is merely a vase that the girl fills until it overflows into a woman.

—Northern proverb

THE SHARP ROCKS OF THE ROAD CUT INTO ULI'S FEET. SHE wanted to flee the road, this abomination cut into the land, to blast it back to proper earth, but Hinanuli had set this path before her. Uli's sisters sang beside her as she ran, a passing shadow through the night, around the guards before they even felt her approach, past her people hiding in their huts.

Down, Uli ran. It was against her nature to run downhill. She always needed to climb, higher into the mountain, but her feet took her down.

Down and down, the zigzagging path. Sharp leaves cut at her legs when she strayed too far from the center of the road. Stars wheeled above her, made bold by just Ty, the red moon, sharing the sky that night. The crickets chirped lowly, but they were hushed by the sound of the waves striking the shore down below.

Why was she going down? The mountain was behind her. Uli

slowed, not remembering, forgetting even why she ran. She had to run. She was supposed to. But to where?

Stumbling, Uli left the hard path, sinking her feet into the cool sand. Flies bit her ankles, distracting her. She needed to get to the water. Yes, that's where her sisters had gone. Into the water? No. Across.

Uli lunged forward, walking straight into the surf. The cold water shocked her breath, leaving her gasping as a wave slapped high against her thighs.

Now she remembered. Uli looked back over her shoulder at the lights far above the water. The northern witches. Their temple. Ipo had stayed there. Uli had left to be alone in the world again.

She couldn't go back. That bitch Jahaka just wanted to *use* Uli, for her own plans and schemes. She might have some power, but she didn't have the heart of her true sister, of Ephanie.

Uli could only go forward. She lumbered through the waves, heading back around the coast. The rocks no longer cut her feet, but rose up to support her, to brace her against the constant waves.

It was too far to walk all the way around the coast that night, back to their cave. Uli wasn't sure she wanted to go back there and be all alone. So after getting out of sight of the fishermen's boats, along the sheer cliffs where no one came, Uli pushed inland again, burrowing into the rock, carving herself out a new cave, one that would fit only her.

Crawling up the rocks like a crab, Uli pulled herself over the lip of the cave. It was perfect for her, the rocks soft and covered in chalk, the smell of the jungle nearby. Outside, she heard the waves lapping at the shore. She let them rock her to sleep, ignoring that she had no fire, no sisters to dream with, nothing to keep her warm that night except bare stone.

It was enough.

～

SCREECHING GULLS WOKE ULI IN THE MORNING. SHE remembered where she was the instant she opened her eyes. The cave wasn't tall enough for her to stand, but it didn't need to be. It suited her just fine. Pale pink shells mottled the brown walls in patterns as complex as the stars. The sun rose behind her, just kissing the shore, promising warmth that day.

If only Uli wasn't alone. If her sisters, other mountain movers, were there with her, they might stand a chance against Oka'u. But if her sisters had heard her call, they had all gone to Ailani, where she'd raised the mountain.

More gulls cried. They fought over a fish high in the air, one diving from far above, trying to snatch it from the other.

Uli called out them, cawing. Maybe they would hear her, and bring breakfast to her as well.

But the greedy gull with the fish wheeled away, taking his prize with him.

Hungry, Uli climbed down the front of the cliff face. Little fish swam among the shoals, and small crabs clambered over the rocks. It didn't take long for Uli to scoop out what she needed. She rested in the calm water, leaning against a rock. The tide was going out. The waves were calm. Uli drifted, thinking of her sisters. Nila and Hinan would be with their sisters by now, on Rakakeelani, preparing for war.

Would the northern witches be able to stop the wave? They hadn't before. But this time, they had Ipo. If they used her well, everyone would live.

Uli wouldn't drown. She'd raise up the rocks, higher than the wave, when it came. Whoever came with her would live as well.

Uli paused. Could she raise up another mountain? Call her sisters here? They wouldn't arrive in time—they couldn't walk across the water on the beams.

But maybe, maybe, they could come and help. She could warn them, at least, of the coming wave.

Uli looked around. She'd have to move further up the coast, away from the fishermen. It took time to raise a mountain, and she'd be visible from the water.

But once she did, any of her sisters still here on the big island would know.

And they'd come looking for her.

~

ULI CLAMBERED OVER THE ROCK, SIDESTEPPING FROM ONE boulder to the next, around the tip of the point. No illicit ships lay moored off the shore that morning. The tide continued to go out, leaving a strip of wet, sandy beach below. Uli thought about climbing down and walking where she could, but the rock gave her strength and comfort, despite how her muscles shook.

Gulls cried over the water, cheering Uli along. The wind blew gently, carrying the scent of deep open water, then switching and bringing the heady scent of the jungle stretching far above the cliff face.

It took Uli longer than she expected to reach the private cove where she'd first created a cave for herself and her sisters. She told herself not to, but she clambered over the rocks and into the cave. It still smelled of smoke from Ipo's fires, the fish from Ephanie's foretelling, and the musky scent of her other sisters.

Where was Lakawoo? Had she freed herself again? Uli would have to find her. Was Ephanie still alive, buried deep under the palace? Ipo would make sure she didn't drown. And Pua? Had she been drugged, and then used as a shield, like Lakawoo?

Uli turned her back on the cave and marched out to the small beach. The tide had turned and was coming back in, but Uli raised a sandbar as she walked, out away from the cliff.

Any fishermen or boats coming around the edge of the island would see her. Uli didn't care. She was ready now.

Uli stomped her feet as she circled, chanting the old prayers again, as she had when she and Ipo had raised the first mountain.

Oenonu, green goddess,
Make way for the mountain.
It grows taller than the plank tree
Wider than a waterfall.
Bones of the earth—rise!
Oh mountain,
Make yourself known.

Come kiss the sky
And set the stars
Dancing above your head.

Rumbling earth greeted Uli's chant. The vibrations tickled her toes. Grinning, Uli continued her march and her chant.

But the earth didn't rise. Boulders didn't pile up out of the sand.

Determined, Uli started again. She stomped harder, pushing her power into the earth. Rocks lay dormant beneath her, she could feel them.

They should have awakened at her touch.

However, the rocks still slept, uncaring, unknowing.

Uli dug deeper, jostling sand and stone. She *pulled* as hard as she could, bringing the baked rocks up to the surface, expecting more to follow.

Sluggishly, a few stones rolled up, then a few more. The pile they built was only a little taller than Uli.

Then the trickle of rocks slowed.

This was no mountain. It was a cairn for marking someone's passing. Fishermen built them on beaches when they'd lost a man at sea.

Uli pulled again and again, trying to bring the rocks up. She howled in frustration, tipping her head back as she clawed at the earth. She poured everything she had into the ground, that familiar home, the only place that had ever been a comfort, expecting a river of rocks to erupt, answering her call.

But only a few more stones climbed up out of the bowels of the earth.

Defeated, Uli sank back on her heels, bowed her head, and wept.

She'd waited too long. Even the stones had turned against her. The spider's web was everywhere.

As Ephanie had predicted, Uli was truly alone.

And Hinanuli demanded more from her.

With one last push, Uli emptied her very self into the rocks. She stripped herself bare, pushing all the strength of the mountain, her sisters and their dreams, even her very *name* into the unforgiving stones.

Until there was nothing left of the great southern witch Uli, and only Mahina remained.

~

THE COLLECTION OF ROCKS IN FRONT OF MAHINA REMINDED her of the stones in her jungle, right near her hut. She reached out and touched her thumb to one, smearing the chalk across the pad of it, like she always did.

These stones were special, just like hers. Sacred to the goddess.

But what was Mahina doing here, on the beach? Had she come down for fish? Or maybe for a man? She didn't remember. Her hands hurt as if she'd been weaving ropes all day long.

With a sigh, Mahina heaved herself to her feet. She wore an odd skirt. Had she been in the village? Mahina turned to face the solid cliff face, looking up toward the jungle. There must be a way up.

Hinanuli would show her when she started climbing.

Mahina took two steps away from the tall tower of rocks, then turned and went back.

The stones hissed at her. They wanted to come with her. She needed to carry them close to her skin.

Mahina reached down and picked up two of the sharp rocks, the white and yellow limestone pricking her palm. Their slight weight comforted her. She knew she must take them with her, in the name of the goddess. And show them to others, too.

A strange pouch that Mahina didn't remember hung from a belt she also didn't recall. She slipped the rocks into it and started back up the path, going back to the jungle.

Back to her hut.

~

THE JUNGLE WAS DIFFERENT. HOW LONG HAD MAHINA been away?

The trees were the same, and the snakes, and the bright *mamapo'o* berries. But the wind didn't blow from the right direction, and she couldn't find her waterfall.

Or her hut.

Mahina marched around the clearing where she was *sure* her hut should be. It looked like the right spot. There was a tree to lean a woven wall against. And a slope where she could toss the bones of fish and the skin of fruit, until it filled or she started tossing them in the corner of her hut again.

But her hut was not there.

Mahina walked all around the clearing again. Maybe she'd gotten confused. Was it her sister's dream that she was having again? Where was the base of the mountain, and her stream of clear water? Her traps? Her vines?

The stones she'd picked up at the beach and put into the strange pouch slapped against her thigh as she walked. Finally Mahina squatted down and held the bag in her hands, crooning.

Where was her hut? It had to be somewhere.

The answer came from the rocks she held in her hands.

Someone had stolen it.

Mahina gasped. She'd been so confused since the goddess had called her. There had been so much madness since the night of the moon, when Ty had risen and called to her.

Maybe that was when someone took her hut.

Tell the king, the stones whispered to Mahina.

The king? Mahina blinked. Flies beside her buzzed, and cloud of gnats swarmed just ahead.

She *should* tell the king. Someone had stolen her hut. During the madness. He should get it back for her.

Mahina heaved herself to her feet, dropping her bag so it swung on her belt again, slapping against her thighs as she stomped off.

Off to see the king.

And maybe show him her stones.

CHAPTER 16

A bundle of sticks cannot be broken.
—*Southern Islands proverb*

LIGHT EBBED AWAY FROM EPHANIE, AS IF THE FLICKERING torches were being snuffed one by one. The pain that had been receding welled up again, every cut on her arms alive and on fire. The sweet scent of her own blood filled her mouth with *want* and *need*.

The vision scratching at the back of Ephanie's brain dug in its claws, demanding to be let out.

Oh, *pain*. It rolled over Ephanie, sweetly stroking her arms and tugging at her hair like a lover. Such an exquisite release. All she had to do was turn the knife, just a little, and let it kiss her skin sweetly.

No. Ephanie pushed the knife away. She would not take her own blood, no matter how tempting the song was. It was not the time. It was not *her* time.

The darkness spread, wrapping around Ephanie like wet rope. She struggled to free herself, to lift her arms away from her sides. Sketched out on the floor, glimmering in the dim light, a web strung of black despair and screams lay all around her. She only had to move her feet a little, push to one side, to find a space between the strands.

With that single step, Ephanie took a deeper breath. As long as she stayed clear of the web, she'd have more strength. She turned to face Oka'u and brought the knife up.

"Die," Oka'u repeated, this time spreading his fingers and directing the spell at Ephanie.

Ephanie reeled back. Despair overwhelmed her, and her darkest thoughts overwhelmed her: she'd never be able to prove her worth, never be trusted by the other witches, never be able to sleep clear of nightmares for the rest of her life, never be able to fully *see* what the goddess wanted for her, where her destiny lay.

But Ephanie could see now. She had a vision, and it *must* be fulfilled. Her sisters continued to chant behind her, lending her their strength and reminding her that she was many.

Oka'u was alone.

"No," Ephanie finally said, pushing forward, as if against a storm wind. The need for his life trebled and Ephanie took another step forward. "Not me. Not this time."

Sweat trickled down Oka'u's forehead, along his temples, and dripped off his chin. "You will stay still," he demanded. He kept his hands in front of him, pushing, pulsing with power.

Ephanie laughed. He had no control of her. Not anymore. The goddess ruled her now.

Need filled Ephanie. The need for life. For blood. For him.

Too late, Oka'u realized that he couldn't contain her. Before he could turn and run, or even call out for the guard, Ephanie pounced on him. She held him to her, one arm wrapped around his chest, his head barely reaching her chest.

The knife kissed Oka'u's skin, flowing across his neck, sliding across it as easily as a stick across sand.

Ephanie brought her cupped hand up to catch the blood.

For a moment, Ephanie struggled to merely hold the blood, not to bring it to her lips to taste it.

But that was Oka'u's wish, not her own.

Ephanie made a second cut, deeper. She had enough blood now. The vision wanted her to throw it.

However, Ephanie used the knife one last time. She turned the blade and thrust, driving it into Oka'u's heart, pressing his warm body hard against her own.

Ephanie dropped Oka'u's body as the vision took hold of her. She nearly cried out when he hit the floor: torturer, lover, brother, damnation, god.

But she couldn't mourn him now. Instead, eagerly, she flung the blood across the floor. The clever channels didn't carry it away. It shimmered in the darkness, calling her attention.

Ephanie saw the witches, all standing in a line. Their wore robes of every color, more colors than witches should. This wasn't on the main island. No, this was someplace where the world was stone and tame, filled with white pillars and no jungle.

This was Alokai. This was where they burned witches.

The wave came, towering, from the west. A single witch broke the line. Ephanie gasped. She'd killed thousands, demanding their sacrifice to fulfill her vision of the witches traveling to the southern islands.

Then a second vision came, another wave. Another witch who could break the line, this time in the future.

Jahaka. Not taking the hand of Ipo.

The vision demanded Ephanie give Jahaka a choice: to fully join with her sisters, or to not be there at all.

Ephanie had to stop the wave. She, and all her sisters.

EPHANIE EXPECTED TO BE EXHAUSTED AFTER HER VISION. SHE'D never heard of anyone having a vision of the past before. However, she felt stronger, better, than when the vision had started.

The torture room still filled her with dread, the dim torches, the constant stench of sweat, vomit, blood, and tears, the way the channels cut her feet and carried away blood.

However, the black web no longer stretched across the floor. It had died with Oka'u.

Ephanie quickly freed the other prisoners. As she suspected, all those who Oka'u kept closest to him were women. There were three pens, with half a dozen women in each.

"Thank you," "*Mahaleeno*," came the whispered replies as Ephanie opened each gate. These women came out with tear-stained faces and fierce determination.

Dawn walked out, tall and proud, cradling her broken hands in front of her. Ika and the other women walked with her.

"We heard the prayer," one of the women from the other pens said. "We prayed as well."

"Thank you," Ephanie told them. "I couldn't have done it without all of you."

Ika walked over to where Oka'u's body lay. She toed him, rocking his dead body with her foot, then spat in his face before turning away. The others followed, spitting and cursing him, stepping on hands and feet. Ephanie admired their restraint. She still wanted to tear him limb from limb.

Finally, Ephanie turned away from the honest desecration of Oka'u's body and went to the door. No guards stood on the other side.

Ika came to stand beside her. "There. At end," she whispered, pointing toward the end of the hall. "They didn't like screams. But they stayed." She spat at her feet.

Ephanie didn't know whether to feel sorry for the guards or glad that the other women she was with were so fierce.

"We need to get out of the palace, and to the south beach," Ephanie told Ika. "We need to stop the coming wave."

Ika looked at her, then called for Moa, who spoke the witches language better than most.

"Water shakers?" Moa asked after Ika had shared Ephanie's news in their singsong language..

"Yes," Ephanie said slowly. The wave didn't come from nature, but from some magic.

"Can you stop this wave from swallowing Hilani?" Moa asked.

"Yes," Ephanie said firmly. "That was my vision, what I used the blood for. I must get there." She hated the whine that crept into her voice—she'd heard it too often when she'd been on Oka'u's table.

"I will get you there," Moa said fiercely.

The women gathered together at the door to the torture hall, and at Moa's signal, burst out and into the hall, swarming the guards.

The men didn't stand a chance.

"This way," Moa said,. "Follow me." She lead them quickly out of the lower levels and into the daylight.

Ephanie gasped in the clear air. Nothing had ever smelled so sweet as the tangy air. She turned her face toward the sun. She'd thought she'd never feel it again.

All the women stopped and stood still for a moment, breathing and feeling. Tears pricked Ephanie's eyes.

But she couldn't stop for long. Her vision drove her. The time was soon.

They had to stop the wave from drowning the island. She couldn't fail this time.

EPHANIE HAD NEVER FELT MORE POWERFUL, OR MORE HUMBLED. The dozen women who accompanied her would not brook any opposition. They weren't trained fighters, and some of them were still hurt from their time under Oka'u's knife. However, none could match their determination.

At least three groups of guards ran from them rather than fight.

It didn't take long for Moa to lead them to the southern beach. There, a large group of witches had already gathered, with more joining, and a large boat full of women just sailing into the harbor.

Ephanie felt as though everyone turned to look at her when she stepped onto the beach. Her clothes were torn and bloodstained, her hair fell in filthy strings, and her arms carried long scars, the skin barely healed. The other women were in just as bad shape: bruised, dirty, and bloody. Dawn still carried her broken hands in front her.

However, Ephanie didn't care. They'd come through Miatlu's third hell to get there. How they looked didn't matter.

"Where's Jahaka?" Ephanie demanded as she marched across the sand. "I must speak with her."

The old priestess, the one who was the head of the fortunetellers here on the island—Vine, Ephanie remembered, reaching for her name—came forward. "You've seen," the old woman said. Her black robes sucked up light on the bright, sunlit beach.

Ephanie had to blink her eyes and turn away. Anything dark reminded her too much of *him*.

"Yes," Ephanie replied after a moment. "I must see Jahaka. Please."

"This way," Vine said, threading her way through the crowd.

Ephanie had never seen so many witches in one place, not even the start of the celebration of *Keereekayah*. There were more than a hundred women here, all arranging themselves in lines.

"A single line," Ephanie muttered. "It has to be a single line. Or else we'll be lost."

Vine glanced over her shoulder at Ephanie and said, "We know. They'll straighten out. You weren't the only one to see the wave."

"Did others see it break?" Ephanie asked bitterly. She wasn't supposed to speak of her vision to any but whom it involved, but all these women would die if Jahaka didn't make the right choice.

Now Vine stopped and peered at Ephanie. "No," she said coldly.

Ephanie glared back. She didn't fear this woman. And her sisters still stood behind her.

"I must see Jahaka," Ephanie repeated. They were running out of time.

Vine sharply nodded and walked more quickly. The other witches moved to the side for her. Was it because of the blackness of her robe? Or because of Ephanie and the others who followed her? Ephanie couldn't guess.

Finally, they came to the center of the group. Jahaka stood in the traditional red of the healers, not wearing the yellow vest that had become common on the islands, or the orange-yellow robes of official office. She directed the others with urgency, her movements precise.

Jahaka was a formidable leader. Ephanie could see that. People listened to her with respect.

But she stood alone. Ephanie could see that, too.

Ipo waited to one side, just watching. She wore a red skirt with cracked red lines running through it, and merely a vest, black, the color of the fortunetellers. Around her waist hung a brown twill net. She noticed Ephanie before Jahaka and gave a great hooting cry.

Jahaka started and looked around as Ipo surged forward.

"*Uuka!*" Ipo said. She stood back from Ephanie, looking her up and down. "You look like you've been dragged through the river and over the mountain, then through hell and back."

For a moment, Ephanie paused, stung. Then she remembered Ipo telling her about the *leeleen*, after Ephanie had been so shocked by how Uli and Ipo had insulted each other just before they'd gone to the village.

"And what have you been doing?" Ephanie demanded. "Baking fish and peeling fruit with your soft hands?"

Ipo threw her head back and laughed and laughed. "It's good to see you, *teeka*," she said.

Ephanie stood taller. It was the first time Ipo had called her *sister* and not *little one*.

Ipo nodded to the women who still waited behind Ephanie. "*San teeka?*" she asked.

"Yes," Ephanie replied. "My sisters."

Finally, someone who understood. Ephanie had shared so much with these women. She wished there was a term that meant closer than a sister. But *teeka* would have to do.

However, the vision still had to be fulfilled.

"Priestess," Ephanie said, her voice changing. She felt her back stiffening. "You have a choice before you. You must take the hand of those beside you and fully be part of them or you must leave the line. If you stay and don't commit, you will break the line and the world will drown. Not just this island, but all the others will fall."

Ephanie swayed as the words left. She would have fallen, but Moa came and threw an arm around her waist.

Jahaka paled. "I will commit," she said sternly.

Ipo looked doubtfully at Jahaka. "Will you?" she asked, holding out her hand.

Lines of witches started to form around them. Another hooting cry came, only one that rang out loud and long.

Ephanie turned. In the distance, on the horizon, she could see the water rising.

The wave was coming.

Moa held out her hand to Jahaka as well. "Join, *uuka*," she said.

Jahaka looked disdainfully at Moa. "You don't have magic. You're not a *Mahinapo*. A witch."

"I love this island, this land, this life," Moa said fiercely. "I have shed more blood than *you* to give it freedom. I will see the land of my heart live. Will you?"

"You need their courage and strength in order to defeat this wave," Ephanie said, still feeling the power of the vision coursing through her, her voice still rough with the word of the goddess. "They are as much a part of this—maybe more—than you are."

Ephanie reached out and grasped Moa's other hand. "We have no time, priestess. Decide."

CHAPTER 17

A twisted path is safe from both gods and demons.
—*Southern Islands proverb*

Jahaka couldn't catch her breath. Enekai, alive? Here? How had that happened? Where was Aleekona? Was he part of this as well? The night outside the hut grew still.

The two idiots stood on the far side of the table, grinning at Jahaka, as if this were some kind of *Keereekayah* surprise.

These men. They knew nothing of guile or surprise. Or, clearly, how to get the resources they needed without giving away too much in return.

"I'm pleased to see you, my lord," Jahaka said, forcing herself to smile. "I take it that your 'death' was a plan to get your brother, Taunoa, to pledge his army?"

That was the only thing that made sense. With Enekai out of the way, the people from the western region would have no choice but to follow Taunoa. The nice little battle would draw them all together, unite them into a solid force.

Jahaka admired Taunoa for usurping Enekai's plans so neatly.

Unless Enekai was really such an idiot that he gained absolutely nothing from the ruse.

"You see, Wehil?" Enekai said proudly. "I told you that she would figure it out."

"Very clever, my lord," Jahaka said as she walked around the table. *The fools.* "And how is your miraculous resurrection going to be announced?" She just had to get within touching range of him.

Possibly both of them.

"Well, my dear," Enekai said, drawing Jahaka's hands into his own. "I had thought, after we had won the battle, that we could spread the word around that you had cured me."

Jahaka paused. That would increase her status, certainly.

But she wasn't looking for godhood, not like the king.

And since she was certain no one was to know about Enekai's lie until after the battle, if he were killed there, well, it wouldn't be much of a loss to his brother.

"How clever," Jahaka murmured.

Why didn't the fool see that such a lie would mean his people would never trust him again? That he'd just given his brother all the power?

Jahaka placed her hand over Enekai's heart and *pushed.* "I'm so glad you're alive," she murmured.

But he wouldn't be for long.

Jahaka *pushed* with her power again, tearing small ruptures in the veins and arteries of Enekai's heart.

The next time his heart pounded strongly, one would break, and he'd die and be forgotten, his body dropped into the ocean with all the other casualties of the upcoming battle.

The battle that Jahaka was now determined to win for the current king. "I'm assuming the battle plan is the same?" she asked sweetly.

"We will have additional ships, Taunoa's, that will make landfall to the east," Enekai said.

Should she believe him? Or was he lying, trying to get her to split her guards? He was certainly a better liar than she'd thought.

"So be sure to keep your people away from that side of the island," Wehil said seriously.

"Thank you," Jahaka said. "I will make sure we're well deployed." Then she took a step back from her former lover. "But I must return to the temple," she said. "I'm glad you told me before the battle," she said honestly. She glanced at Wehil.

Aleekona could take him later, if he survived.

Enekai hesitated.

Jahaka knew Enekai wanted to ask her to stay for the night. However, she couldn't take the chance that he'd die in her bed.

"Good night," Jahaka said, walking back around the table. "I will see you after the battle, when you victoriously come to shore. The people will sing your arrival."

"Good night," Enekai said. His eyes brimmed with all the things he wanted to say to her.

He'd had such potential, but had turned into such a fool. Giving away everything.

Jahaka slipped back out into the cooling night and marched back to the temple, Marrow falling into silent step behind her.

A touch of regret slid into Jahaka's heart as she crossed through the quiet village. If only Enekai had followed the original plan. Maybe they could have done more. Swept his armies from Hilani Island to the mainland.

Jahaka would find another way to move the witches from these cursed islands and back where they belonged, before their pure blood became any more muddled.

"WE NEED TO SPLIT OUR FORCES," JAHAKA ANNOUNCED AS SHE strode into the council chamber that morning. The sun had barely crested the horizon, its long red beams stretching like fingers made of blood across the water. Despite all the walls being in place and enclosing the room, the sound of witches issuing orders and preparing filtered in. Sweet incense burning on every altar scented the air, overlaying the smell of fear.

All the council women looked grim. Ipo stood among them, worry creasing her forehead. Jahaka wished she could send the southern witch away—just use her knowledge. Ipo wore a clean skirt, black with a pattern of crackling red lines running through it, a black vest without a shirt underneath, and what looked like a fisherman's net around her waist. She stood beside Vine, the pair of them sucking away all the light in the room.

"We need to put four groups on the east side," Jahaka added. Not her personal guard—no. Jahaka no longer trusted Aleekona. His loyalties could obviously be bought.

Maybe, after the battle, Jahaka would start over again, this time with Linden the guard leading.

"Why?" Oak asked. "I thought we needed to keep our focus tight."

"I have new intelligence," Jahaka told the group. "There are more ships coming from the east."

Vine stepped forward. "We need them in the south," she said. "The wave is going to be greater than we thought."

"Did one of the priestesses have a vision?" Jahaka demanded.

"Two, actually," Vine said. "We need to gather as many of the witches together as we can there. It will take all of us to defeat the wall of water coming."

"Two units?" Jahaka suggested, happy for some guidance from the goddess, finally.

Hesitatingly, Vine nodded. "There's been no visions of the other attack, not since the first one with Ephanie," she added.

"We will defeat it," Jahaka insisted. "We must." They couldn't allow the island to be drowned, particularly not by the southern witches.

The king must see how valuable Jahaka and her witches were. He would have to admit their power.

And they had to defeat the attack as well.

"The wave will be coming soon," Ipo said.

Jahaka shivered. Ipo's accent struck her as foreign and wrong, particularly in her judgment room. "Get as many as you can to the southern side," Jahaka told Oak.

"We've already started loading boats," Yarrow reported. She seemed puzzled. Had she figured out that Jahaka had wanted them to lose?

They had to help the king win, now.

"We should go," Ipo said urgently.

Jahaka almost dug in her heels and said, "No." But she wasn't stupid. If Ipo thought the wave would arrive soon, Jahaka wasn't going sabotage their chances.

Ipo followed the council out to the boats as if she was guaranteed a spot. Vine strode beside her. Ipo kept looking around, as if watching for someone. Were there more of the *Mahinapo*, the southern witches on the way?

But no other southern witch showed up.

It didn't take long to sail around the island. Jahaka was gratified to see how many of her people were already there, spread across the white sand. She strode to the middle of the group, already issuing orders about forming multiple lines that would join into a single one when it was time.

Jahaka found that she breathed easier on the sand than she thought she would. Was the damn spell weaker here? Did it only affect the village and the palace?

She looked up only when Ipo gave a great cry. Was the wave coming already?

Ephanie and a group of southern island women strode across the beach. The girl looked dreadful, sick and pale, her black hair hanging in strings, her clothes still marking her as a powerless girl, though the way she walked belied that. The women walking behind her—all southern natives—weren't in any better shape.

Had they been released from the king's prison? Or had they escaped?

When Ipo insulted Ephanie, Jahaka almost surged forward. How dare this native address one of her priestesses this way?

Jahaka couldn't believe it when Ephanie insulted Ipo back, and the woman just laughed.

Teeka? Sister? Why would Ipo now call Ephanie sister? The southern islanders always just called the northern witches *uuka*, little one. What had changed?

Jahaka now saw the way the skin on Ephanie's arms bubbled. The other women bore the same marks. Was that from being tortured? It looked uncomfortable. The healers would have to take care of them, though it was against tradition to remove any scars that a fortuneteller inflicted on herself.

Yarrow had already approached the group, taking aside the single other northern witch. Despite the filth covering her, Jahaka still recognized the robe of a healer. The girl's hands folded in front of her like claws, hurt and broken.

Was this the girl who had been missing?

Jahaka couldn't believe the pronouncement laid on her by the girl. How dare she, or even the goddess Brikalla, question her commitment? She would take these native's hands. She would save Hilani. This was her destiny.

AFTER EPHANIE HAD ISSUED HER STINGING CHALLENGE, THE words of the goddess echoing strangely across the beach, Jahaka reached out and grasped Ipo's hand, then the hand of this other strange southerner.

Power rocketed through Jahaka, binding her talent to those around her. Jahaka tasted the strength of their force—earthy and harsh—more solid than any temple walls. It coursed through her, setting her blood to sing.

But Jahaka no longer felt completely alone and isolated. Joining with these women, mingling their powers together, would leave them connected.

Always.

Jahaka wrenched her eyes open. The wave approached, dark and hungry, a solid wall of water. Shimmering in the bright daylight rose a transparent purple barrier. The wave roared, louder than anything Jahaka had ever heard before. Magic rose to greet it, cackling like a great bonfire.

They would defeat it. They had to.

Jahaka's powers intertwined with those around her, wrapping like vines around the trees in the jungle, connecting them all together.

Those vines would be unbreakable soon. Jahaka would always feel these women, always be aware of their presence. She'd never be completely alone in her own head, with her own thoughts.

It was worse than how their pure northern blood had mixed, been polluted.

She'd never feel alone again.

Witches weren't supposed to work together. Now, Jahaka understood why. Once they did, they'd lose something of themselves.

With a wretched cry, Jahaka pulled away from the others. She couldn't stay in that line, couldn't become part of that greater whole.

Ipo growled at her, like angry fire, reaching for the other strange southerner. They grasped each other's hands quickly, and the line held.

The wave struck the magical wall with a crash louder than any thunder. Jahaka shivered where she stood, swaying with the force of energy. The wave pushed, trying to break through, hungry to drown them all, to take their lives, as if it had a fortune to tell.

The wall stood.

More water surged up. The witches swayed with the force, as if blown by a strong wind. They pushed back, lightning splaying through the wall, so bright Jahaka had to look away.

A final, third wave struck, but it wasn't as high as the first two. Stinking seaweed, fish, even rocks and small logs carried in the water hit the wall with force. This time the witches didn't sway, just held tight, and the water drained away, leaving its debris behind.

The witches stayed joined together. Their power was much weaker than when they'd first joined. But they hummed with an energy that Jahaka had never felt before.

These women were changed. Forever.

They'd all have to be left behind when the witches moved back to the mainland. They were impure, muddled, worse than any of the powerless girls.

Maybe they'd have to be killed, first.

Jahaka started making her plans.

CHAPTER 18

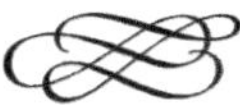

A true river rises with a song, its name carried only in notes.
—*Southern Islands proverb*

Mahina didn't like the men she saw. They weren't good men. She stayed on the edge of the jungle, looking out into the village, where all the huts were too close together and she couldn't breathe. There were too many men. And they were fighting. In the streets. Trampling the few gardens the people had. And dying.

Blood. Too much blood. No one could use all the blood being spilled, so it lay wasted on the ground.

The goddess would be angry, later.

Mahina didn't see how she could get to the king's road, to walk from the village to the palace. The fighting was fiercest there. The men with the blue chest pieces surged like waves against the others, the ones in red and yellow, who held the road. Great tree trunks blocked the way as well.

How long would they survive? They fought bravely, but they were dying.

And more men in blue kept coming, like ocean waves.

Mahina needed to get down that road. The king was at the other end. Maybe she could go through the jungle…but that would take too long.

The road needed to break. The stones hurt Mahina's feet. She didn't remember why the rocks hurt her feet, or if they hurt her children's feet, or maybe her sisters'. But the road was wrong. It needed to be broken up.

A sudden sigh pushed through the air, like the booming quiet that came after the thunder had passed.

Mahina stood upright. She hadn't realized how tired she'd been before. She wasn't tired now. The road still hurt her, yes, but not like it had.

Something big had changed. She could hear her sisters calling to her now. There weren't many on the island, most had left. And her children had left as well, without their shoes.

Mahina didn't know how to break the road. Her sisters knew. If they could *push*, right there, raise up the center, just a bit…

With a thunderous roar, the road buckled. The blue men and the yellow men and the red men all scattered. A crest rose down the center of the road, the stones spilling to either side. The logs rolled away.

Mahina was pleased, thankful to her sister.

The men in red and yellow kept running, their lines broken. The men in blue chased after them, spilling all their blood and washing them away.

Mahina followed all of them, the earth warm and welcoming between her broad toes. Many men yelled at her. Some even ran up to her with their knives. But Mahina didn't let them stop her. She either ran away from them, or sometimes pushed them down. She had to go see the king. He would know about her hut, how to find who had taken it.

The palace had smoke coming out of some of the windows. Mahina shook her head. Bad cooks. Careless. It was why she didn't cook in her hut.

She needed to find her hut.

No guards stood at the door. It had been broken. The wall, which was stone, had been attacked. Mahina shivered. Why would someone attack a door? There was always another window to go through.

More blood pooled on the stone floor. Bodies, too. Mahina grew uneasy. Why were so many dead? Was there a plague? Or was it just the fighting? Some of the deaths didn't seem natural, the faces pale and drained, or their limbs dried down to just bones.

This wasn't her sisters' work. This was some demon.

Mahina heard guards walking behind her. She didn't want anyone else to yell at her, so she went through the first door she saw, barreling into it.

The door didn't want to open for her. Maybe that was because the outline around it was so skinny. Mahina pushed again, finally making the door open for her.

Maybe this was why someone had fought the doors before.

The room was small and airless. Just a single man stood there, wearing a broad yellow vest with many feathers tied to his hair.

"How did you get in here?" he demanded. "No one could come through that door. It was sealed with stone."

Mahina shrugged. "I didn't want to see the guards," she complained. "I came to see the king."

"Why do you want to see the king?" the man asked.

Maybe he knew the king. "My hut was stolen," Mahina complained. "During the time of madness. The king will know where it is. How I can get it back."

The man laughed. It wasn't a happy sound. "You want me to find your hut? You stupid woman."

Mahina turned, surprised. "You're the king? Why are you here?"

"The palace is under attack," the king said. "In case you hadn't noticed. My guard put me here to protect me. No one should have been able to get through that door."

Mahina shrugged. "Who stole my hut?" she demanded, advancing on the king. "Where did they put it?"

"How should I know?" the king asked.

Mahina reached into her pouch and showed the king her nice stones, the ones she'd picked up at the beach, the ones that whispered to her. "The stones said you knew. That you would be able to help me. You have to help me! Where is my hut?"

"Bah!" the king said. He slapped Mahina's hand to the side, sending the rocks skittering across the floor. "Your stones told you? Your stones? You're worse than the *meha-meha*, listening to the fish in the stream and starving to death!"

Mahina went scrambling after her stones. The king shouldn't have done that, shouldn't have made her drop them. Her stones were important.

In her haste, Mahina stepped on the first stone. The sharp edge drove into the sole of her foot.

A wave of light followed, cascading through the woman, lifting the edges of her darkness.

Power filled the woman. Clarity, as well.

"You should have listened to my stones," the woman said. She walked over to where the other stone lay, then deliberately ground it into the floor, using her other foot.

Another wave passed up, from the sole of her foot to the tips of her hair, flooding her with purpose. With magic.

And her true name.

The great southern witch Uli knew herself again.

She drew herself up and glared at the king. "I know why the door opened to me," she said silkily as she slid forward. "Because Hinanuli knew that your time was done."

"What?" the king said, backing away.

Uli spread her right hand over the floor, fingers wide, then raised it.

The rocks followed, two spires made of stones tumbling upward. They reached out for the king, wrapping around his wrists like a vine.

"You thought you could escape?" Uli purred as she stalked around her victim.

"You. You're one of the mountain movers." The king struggled to free himself, but the rock was as unforgiving as the curse King Kawiti had laid down so many decades before. "How did you escape the binding?"

"Through the blood of your son," Uli crooned. "The northern

witches wasted it. She let it seep into the soil. Just like the blood of your guards is being wasted now, in your stone hallways."

"You won't get away with this," the king threatened.

"How are they going to stop me?" Uli demanded. "Your guards have been routed. The palace is falling. The witches won't save you. And your pet sorcerer, Oka'u, is gone, isn't he?" Uli remembered the dream of her sister, the white wave passing along the road as the web deep underground shriveled and died.

The king pulled on the stone holding him, but he couldn't break free. "You have to let me go. Taunoa, the leader of the western men, won't be any easier on the *Mahinapo*."

"Bah," Uli said. "He will deal with us. He'll have to." She drew closer, just so she could look the king in the eye. "He isn't of your bloodline. He can't stop us."

"You'll tear the islands apart, just like you did in the past," the king predicted. "You'll fight and get out of control again. You nearly killed all of us last time."

"My sisters won't do that, this time," Uli said, though she knew she lied. The water shakers had already proven that they didn't care, that they'd kill everyone to get their way.

"Yes, they will." The king sighed. "I'm glad I won't be here to see it. To see our people drown in ash and washed away by unnatural waves."

"They won't!" Uli proclaimed. "This time will be different." But she felt the magic in the air, knew the wave was already coming.

The witches would stop it. Or they wouldn't, and Uli would be dead.

Better the king die now.

With a twist of her hand, Uli drove a stone spike through the king's heart. He gasped and shuddered, then wilted against the stone holding him up.

As his blood dripped onto the ground, Uli felt another wave roll back. This time, it was the king's binding.

She could tear the palace down, now, if she chose.

But Uli stood alone, as Ephanie had predicted. She stood without any sisters, here in this closed-off room, the stone meant to be a prison.

Uli would always be alone.

Maybe it was better that way. Maybe she should never get close to any of her sisters. Because they would always fight each other, taking the *leeleen* too far.

Uli remembered that now, how her sisters had always thrown one insult too many, and they'd fought and fought and fought, trying to tear the three handfuls apart.

Shrugging, Uli left the way she'd come, her footsteps shuffling across the floor. All would see her as a slow, mad woman, still carrying the weight of the mountain in her blood.

Uli would get out of the palace alive, away from the battle, leave Hilani and find another island, another mountain, that was just hers.

And damn any who came too near to a rocky death.

ABOUT THE AUTHOR

Leah Cutter writes page-turning fiction in exotic locations, such as a magical New Orleans, the ancient Orient, Hungary, the Oregon coast, rural Kentucky, Seattle, Minneapolis, and many others.

She writes literary, fantasy, mystery, science fiction, and horror fiction. Her short fiction has been published in magazines like *Alfred Hitchcock's Mystery Magazine* and *Talebones*, anthologies like Fiction River, and on the web. Her long fiction has been published both by New York publishers as well as small presses.

Find Leah's books here.

Follow her blog at www.LeahCutter.com.

Reviews

It's true. Reviews help me sell more books. If you've enjoyed this story, please consider leaving a review of it on your favorite site.

Come someplace new…

Are you a traveler? Do you enjoy exploring strange new worlds, new cultures, new people?

Journey into the various lands envisioned by Leah Cutter.

Sign up for my newsletter and I'll start you on your travels with a free copy of my book, *The Island Sampler*.

I will never spam you or use your email for nefarious purposes. You can also unsubscribe at any time.

http://www.LeahCutter.com/newsletter/

ABOUT KNOTTED ROAD PRESS

Knotted Road Press fiction specializes in dynamic writing set in mysterious, exotic locations.

Knotted Road Press non-fiction publishes autobiographies, business books, cookbooks, and how-to books with unique voices.

Knotted Road Press creates DRM-free ebooks as well as high-quality print books for readers around the world.

With authors in a variety of genres including literary, poetry, mystery, fantasy, and science fiction, Knotted Road Press has something for everyone.

Knotted Road Press
www.KnottedRoadPress.com